I0741196

Scattered Seasons

Book Two of the Season Avatars

Sandra Ulbrich Almazan

Copyright © 2015 by **Sandra Ulbrich Almazan**
Book Cover Design by Maria Zannini of Book Cover Diva

All rights reserved. No part of this publication may be reproduced, distributed or transmitted in any form or by any means, without prior written permission.

Sandra Ulbrich Almazan/Solar Unicorn Publishing
www.sandraulbrichalmazan.com/solarunicornpublishing.com

Publisher's Note: This is a work of fiction. Names, characters, places, and incidents are a product of the author's imagination. Any resemblance to actual people, living or dead, or to businesses, companies, events, institutions, or locales is completely coincidental.

Book Layout © 2014 BookDesignTemplates.com

Scattered Seasons/ Sandra Ulbrich Almazan. -- 2nd ed.
ISBN 978-0-9838903-9-3

A CURSE AND A QUEST...

Gwen extended her hand, palm up. "I have something similar embedded in my hand, and it won't come out. Since it cut me, I can't access my memories of healing. I'm lucky to remember parts of the One Oak's history."

The Ava Fall stilled. "You were cursed by a shard too? Where did it happen?"

"On my family's estate, northwest of here, near Lake Verdan."

"That's a long way away to find another piece of pottery just like the one we found here. It can't be a coincidence."

"Where could they have come from?" Gwen asked. "And who would target Avatars?"

"I have no idea. But if the shards are as old as they look, they could be from someone's pottery collection, like the one in the Winter Wing."

Gwen raised her eyebrows. "Pottery? Who collected that? I don't think anyone did. None of the Wins seemed interested in that sort of thing."

The Ava Fall smiled wanly. "No, no one is. It was a test. Ugh." She rubbed her forehead. "Are you sure you can't heal? Margaret would have flushed this wine's effects from me in a heartbeat."

Gwen raised her injured hand. "Maybe after I figure out how to treat myself first. I was hoping the Ava Spring could help me. But now what do I do?"

The Ava Fall reached for a sandwich and devoured half of it before replying, "Without Margaret, our Season is done. We can't link and send our magic out to protect Challen, and you can't link with us. You have to find the rest of your quartet and take over."

DEDICATION

This book introduces my "Fem Four," so it seems fitting to dedicate this one to the Fab Four themselves. Twenty years ago, I became a fan of the Beatles after watching the *Anthology* on TV. Thanks to John Lennon, Paul McCartney, George Harrison, and Ringo Starr for their four-fold synergy that inspired me to create the Season Avatars. The four of you have made more love and light in this world than you could ever take.

CONTENTS

The Shard 9
Leaving 17
Aunt Gabri 25
To the One Oak 35
Three Season Avatars 46
Spring's Study 58
Bull Rock 72
Jenna 83
Lady of the Waters 96
Wistica 111
The Water Clock 120
Kron Evenhanded 129
The Hall of Records 137
Kron's Story 147
The Ball 163
The Avatar of War 170
Suspicions 175
A Missing Shard 184
Rainbow River 190
Kay 204
Tradetown 213
The Former Fallswoman 221
Traveling with Kron 228
Spring Meets Time 245
Afterword 253
The Season Avatars 255
Other Works By the Author 258
About the Author 259

CHAPTER ONE

The Shard

Lady Gwendolyn lo Havil fixed a smile in place as her head throbbed. She wished she could blame it on her future mother-in-law, or at least her pink-and-green striped wallpaper and clashing drapes. Gwen hadn't felt this much physical pain since she was twelve springs old and her healing magic had blossomed. What could be causing this? The stress of the wedding planning, or something related to her Avatar magic?

"Gwendolyn, dear? Are you paying attention?" The false sweetness in Lady Shellinda's tone wouldn't have flavored her weak tea. "I was asking if you and William wanted my second-best plates for the wedding luncheon."

If she meant the ones imported from Fip, with the country's war eagle in the center of every dish, then no. Gwen could never forgive Fip for the war that had brought Challen into its empire. It had taken place several hundred years ago, but she still remembered that life, and all the injured people she'd treated, more clearly than she liked.

Gwen drained the last of her hot chocolate, wishing the cup wasn't so dainty, and rose. "I think I need some fresh air, Lady Shellinda." William's mother complained flowers made her sneeze. Gwen had postponed trying to heal her affliction and was now secretly glad she'd done so. Maybe she could steal a few moments to be alone, cure her headache, and figure out what had caused it.

"Well, if you insist. But I wouldn't advise staying out there too long. There's still much to be done before the wedding next moon."

And if I don't hurry back, she'll choose something horrid for the lunch menu.

Gwen lifted her skirt hem off the floor as she left the parlor and slipped into the garden. Bright sunshine made her squint and her head pound even harder. Row after row of tulips marched in front of her like a squadron showing her the path she was meant to travel. Her late mother had established a maze in their garden and changed the path through it every year. Gwen wished she was there now, someplace where she could hide instead of being exposed to watchers from the house. She forced herself to glide casually through the flowers. Although she took deep breaths, they didn't calm her. Something stirred at the edge of her magical senses. Something that didn't belong in Challen.

What is it? Is it close by, or do the reigning Season Avatars feel it too?

Gwen might be a Season Avatar for the Goddess of Spring, First of the Four Gods and Goddesses of Challen, but by herself, her magic was limited to healing. Linking with the other three Avatars—one each for the God of Summer, Goddess of Fall, and God of Winter—would allow her to share thoughts with the other Avatars, pool their magic, and spread it throughout the country. Although only one quartet of Avatars served at a time, Gwen and the other Avatars of her birth year would replace the current Avatars soon.

I wish that would happen before this marriage, as unlikely as that is. As her father and aunt were fond of pointing out, she was eighteen, old enough to be married and start a family. They didn't understand she felt more ready to be an Avatar than a wife. She remembered magic from her previous lives as an Avatar. She also retained some personal memories, such as being married to the Summer Avatar more often than not. William was a sometimes childhood friend, sometimes childhood tormentor, but he hadn't been born on a solstice or equinox, so he wasn't an Avatar. Plus he wanted her to start having children, and she wasn't ready for childbirth, not after the way her mother died.

Gwen rubbed her head. This wasn't the time to be fretting over the wedding or children she hadn't conceived. She had to learn what was giving her a magical headache. Was it a Chaos Season, when all of the seasons appeared at once and the Avatars had to return everything to normal? It had never given her a headache before. The flowers around her were still untouched, but the air felt cooler, bringing up goose bumps on her arms.

Gwen rubbed her skin to warm up as she surveyed the garden. A brown form lying in the path several yards away caught her eye. As she approached it, it resolved into a human figure. One of the gardeners, judging by his clothes and the trowel by his side. He wasn't moving, and the flowers around him were brown and wilted in the middle of a snow patch.

A mini Chaos Season. Maybe this is why my head hurts. What happened to the gardener?

She stripped off her gloves, then knelt by the prone man. He was still breathing, but a gash on his forehead streamed blood into the soil. Perhaps he'd been hit by a hailstone. If so, it must have already melted. She pressed her hand against the cut, sealing it. Once that was done, she focused her magic inward, checking for more serious damage. The injury didn't seem serious compared to others she'd healed during her several lifetimes as Spring Avatar, but she would still recommend to the butler—Lady Shellinda would consider herself too far above her servant to be concerned about him—that the gardener be given a day or two to rest. Since this was a head injury, someone should watch him for any unusual symptoms so she could heal him again if necessary.

Not that it would be necessary, with all of her experience from previous lives.

Gwen used a withered leaf to wipe some of the blood off of her hands before she stained her silk gown. As she stared at the soil, she noticed a pottery shard next to one of the frostbitten tulips. She pressed her lips together when she noticed a rust-colored edge on the shard. Maybe it had assaulted the gardener. It was lighter in color than the dirt, and it had marks on it that she had never seen before. Where had it come from?

She picked up the shard to look at it more closely. The air was still, eerily still. She was careful not to touch the edges, but it turned in her hand as if it was alive. She let it go, but it clung to her.

By All Four... "Get away from me!" She shook her hand, but the shard bit into her palm. Gwen reached for it, then thought better of touching it with her bare skin. She covered her free hand with part of her skirt, then tried wrenching the shard free. The gardener stirred beside her, and Gwen wondered if she would need him to help her pull the piece of pottery away. Then it snapped. Her palm burned for a moment before her magic made the pain disappear.

She stared at the shard. A corner was missing—a corner shaped like the bulge in her skin. She'd healed so quickly there was no scar to show where she'd been wounded. The piece of shard didn't hurt, but By The Four, it didn't belong there.

Gwen drew a line over the bump, willing her skin to split. But for once, her healing magic refused to obey her. Pressure built in her head. If she wasn't already squatting, she might have fallen over. Was the pottery shard poisoned? She hadn't detected anything unusual when she'd healed the gardener. Still, something was interfering with her magic.

Have I ever come across anything like this before? Gwen searched her memories from previous lives. No, nothing had ever gotten stuck under her skin—or anyone else's—and refused to come out. However, the farther back she went, the more familiar the pottery shard seemed. She'd always considered her oldest memories the least trustworthy and least complete, so even this information didn't help her.

Goddess of Spring, what do I do now?

A trail of cold reached past her wrist and up her arm.

"Freeze it!" Never had swearing felt more appropriate. Gwen grasped her affected arm with her other hand and pressed down, trying to block the cold. For a moment, it seemed to work, but then the cold shot past her elbow, then to her shoulder.

"What happened?" Finally, the gardener opened his eyes. "My flowers! My precious tulips!" He blinked as he gaped at her. "Lady lo Havil? What are you doing out here?"

Cold squeezed her throat closed. She gestured toward the house, even though no one there would be able to help her either.

Then the cold numbed her head, halting her pain—and everything else.

* * *

Gwendolyn lo Havil, you're needed at the One Oak, a woman's voice told her. The voice seemed to come from far away, and it sounded familiar. Gwen knew it wasn't her mother's voice, but perhaps it was someone else she loved. *They figured out a way around Our protective barrier. Winter was faster than the Time Twosome, but they will pay for what they have done to My daughters. It's your season now, so you must take care of them.* The voice became even fainter, a whisper of a whisper. *Memory…time…hidden…Kron….*

"Gwendolyn!" Her father's voice drowned out the woman's words. "Wake up, child. You're never ill, and you're not the fainting sort." He sounded annoyed, as if she'd done it to inconvenience him.

She opened her eyes and immediately recognized Lady Shellinda's parlor. Someone had placed her on a loveseat, and a maid waited nearby with smelling salts, several cloths, and a cup of tea. A hot drink sounded wonderful after the cold, but she forced herself to remain prone for a few more heartbeats before sitting up and accepting the tea. Moving slowly after an injury seemed wise, but she couldn't say why.

"What happened?" her father asked. He paced back and forth, leaving footprints on the thick rug.

What exactly had happened out there? Gwen carefully made a fist. Pain brought back her memories of the incident. "There was a man...hurt...I had to help him."

Her father sighed. "Yes, one of the gardeners found you. He remembered getting hit in the head with something, but he doesn't know what happened between that and when he woke up." His voice became stern. "I certainly hope there wasn't anything … improper about the situation."

"By the Four!" Lady Shellinda fanned herself. "And with only a moon before the wedding, too."

"What?" The tea spilled onto Gwen's skirt. "All I wanted to do was help him! That's my duty as a Spring Avatar!"

Lady Shellinda and her father exchanged worried glances. By the Four, why couldn't they be more accepting of her role as Avatar? Yes, she wouldn't be able to inherit her father's estate when he returned to the God of Winter, but William would manage it for her children. That was the main reason for this marriage. Gwen's father worried the Fip monarch would distrust the lo Havil house for having produced an Avatar. That implied ties closer to the native Challen gods than to the Fip God of War. But the king knew how important the Season Avatars were to Challen. Without them, Challen would be subject to countless Chaos Seasons, each of them capable of killing or hurting people or damaging property. Why couldn't her family be proud of her instead of wishing she was like everyone else of their class?

"Chaos Season," Gwen said, suddenly remembering. "There was a Chaos Season. I'm afraid your garden was affected, Lady Shellinda. Did it go outside the garden? Was anyone hurt?"

"Another Chaos Season? That's the third time this moon! Why can't the Season Avatars manage their magic properly so we don't have to suffer through this?" She strode to the window. "I hope it doesn't take them long to undo the damage. The gazebo is the perfect spot for the ceremony."

Gwen repressed a sigh. The Season Avatars had to take care of any injured people first, then crops and animals, before they could get around to flower gardens.

"Speaking of the ceremony," Gwen's father said, "where is the groom?"

"He went hunting in the woods early this morning. He was supposed to join us for lunch." Lady Shellinda frowned. "Did Chaos Season extend into the woods?"

Gwen could only shrug. She hadn't gone that far, and she couldn't sense the extent of Chaos Season on her own.

"Maybe we should search for him," Gwen's father said. "With your permission, Lady Shellinda, I'll round up some of your stable-hands and look for William."

Lady Shellinda crossed to the window. "Thank you, Lord Gerad, but that won't be necessary. I see the riders now. There's William's favorite mare...." She put her hands to her mouth. "But one of his friends is leading her. William's tied to the saddle."

Gwen passed her tea cup to the maid and raced out of the room before anyone could stop her. Dizziness made her first few steps wobbly, but it passed quickly. She made her way to the entrance closest to the stable. The butler had anticipated her by summoning two manservants to assist the hunting party when they entered the house.

William's companions helped him stagger inside. He was covered in a blanket, and from what Gwen could see of his clothing, it looked askew. William's valet would have never let him leave the house looking like that. His boots left water behind with each step. His lips were blue, and he looked around the room as if he'd never seen it before.

"What happened?" she asked.

"Chaos Season, what else?" one of William's cousins replied. "We spotted a stag with antlers as long as you are. I suppose that should have tipped us off that Chaos was active, but we were too excited by the idea of bagging that trophy. We all took off after him, and he led us a merry chase—"

"The long way around, no doubt," Gwen said. "What happened to William? Something with winter?"

"Aye. Snow came down so thick I couldn't see my hand in front of my face. We were separated. I and the others retreated, but William got caught in the heart of it. By the time we realized he was missing, we had to dig him out of a snowdrift with our bare hands. Of course, once we found him, all the snow melted away."

"My poor child!" Lady Shellinda drifted into the room, arms open wide. She stopped well away from her dripping son. "What is it, Gwendolyn? Snow sickness? Can you heal him?"

Gwen opened her mouth to assure her future mother-in-law that yes, of course she could do this. She'd done it more times than she could remember. But when she searched for her memories of healing, she couldn't find them.

CHAPTER TWO

Leaving

Gwen's hand throbbed as she stared at her betrothed. She knew she ought to be able to heal him, despite having helped someone else a short while ago. Her healing magic was still coiled inside of her, waiting for her to guide it. But her knowledge had been blocked.

"Goddess of Spring, aid me." The prayer wasn't just to buy her time with her human audience, but a genuine appeal. "Help me heal William."

No direct response from the Goddess. The Four seldom intervened directly these days, even for the Avatars who were charged to carry out Their will. What should Gwen do? Should she go ahead and try to heal William, even if she couldn't remember how? She stared at his too-pale face and found her answer. She had to do something. If she couldn't pass by a servant without helping him, how could she turn away from the man she would marry?

I hope I don't make a mistake. I'd never forgive myself if I end up hurting him. She took a deep breath. "I'd like everyone to leave the room while I work, please." She couldn't afford the distraction.

Lady Shellinda let out a gasp. "How improper!"

"Unacceptable," Gwen's father said. "Not until the wedding."

"By All Four, does he look like he can compromise my virtue?" Gwen shook her head. "Or do you think the Goddess of Fall wouldn't protect me if I called upon Her?"

No one knew how accurate pictures of the Four were, but the Goddess of Fall was shown as a young girl on the verge of womanhood. Her Avatars were always female as well, and no matter what season a woman was born into, she could pray to Fall if she felt threatened by a man. Invariably, the Goddess would send some sort of animal to attack the man if necessary. That said, Gwen knew of no such attacks within her current lifetime. Fall's reputation was so well known even foreigners like the Fips were very polite to the women of Challen. Any protests by the older generation were purely ceremonial, something Gwen didn't need to worry about when she had a patient.

"But what will people say if they find out?"

"Would you rather the groom be too ill for the wedding, Lady Shellinda?"

Lady Shellinda glared at Gwen, but she pressed her mouth into a firm line and marched out of the room.

Gwen's father waited for the servants to leave too, then lowered his voice. "I don't think Lady Shellinda appreciates the idea of a strong-willed daughter-in-law, Gwen, even if your healing duties will keep you away from the estate most of the time."

Gwen shrugged. "She always knew I'm meant to be the next Spring Avatar. Did she think the Goddess would give that task to someone weak? I have to lead three other Avatars every time Chaos Season strikes somewhere in Challen." *But can I do that if I don't remember how to heal? What if I can't remember how to link with the others?*

"Even so, be careful." He pressed his hand briefly on her shoulder. "Go and heal William, then."

He left the room, but his footsteps halted quickly. Gwen suspected he lingered nearby to chaperone. Annoying, but not as big of a problem as her blocked memory. She hesitated for a moment, then advanced toward William. She knew she needed to touch him, so she took his hand in hers. It was cold and stiff, almost like a corpse's. It unnerved her to think soon he would caress her with this hand. She poured heat into his skin, then realized her mistake. Too much warmth would cause as much damage as too little, and she'd overdone it. Spots of blood bloomed under his skin. She released him and blinked hard, holding in her frustration. Freeze it, why didn't she remember how to restore someone with snowsickness? She had hundreds of years of experience in her head—if only she could recall them.

Is there any way I could cure myself? Gwen could ease her own aches and pains, but she'd never tried to self-heal anything more serious. She'd never had to. But she closed her eyes, placed both hands on her forehead, and pushed.

Dots of lights danced in her vision, but nothing else.

Gwen massaged her temples, trying to coax her memories back. For a heartbeat, she could *feel* the answer, as if it wanted to come to her. Then, it slipped away.

With a sigh, she returned her attention to William. Even without her help, he'd regained some warmth and color. Only his hand looked discolored from her touch. Some Spring Avatar she was.

She took her hand in his again. "I'm sorry I can't do more for you, William," she whispered. "Be well. Be well." Could she restore him by will alone?

His eyes opened slowly, and he peered around the room before fixing his gaze on her. "Gwen? Gwenny? Can I kiss you yet?"

He must be feeling better if that was his first concern. Or was this part of his snowsickness? She wasn't sure. "Not yet, William. The wedding is next moon." She put on a smile for him. "How do you feel?"

He leered at her. "You could make me feel much better."

I'm trying, I'm trying. And I hope you don't act like this when you're feeling better. "You should rest." She debated with herself if she should try further healing but decided against it. She couldn't do anything else for him until she had her memories again.

There was only one other person in Challen who could help her: Margaret gran Granell, the current Spring Avatar. Gwen had to get to the One Oak as quickly as she could. Maybe that was what the voice she had heard was trying to tell her. The Four knew she didn't understand the rest of it.

"I'll have them bring in hot chocolate and soup for you," she said. "You keep resting."

"But…but you're an Ava Spring. I thought you could heal someone with a touch."

Guilt stabbed her. "I'll heal you as soon as I can."

"What do you mean?"

She hurried out of the parlor without replying.

Father had insisted she take the carriage over to William's estate to make it a formal visit. Now she wished she had her mare with her so she could ride straight to the One Oak. The only problem would be explaining to her father and her future mother-in-law why she was leaving before the wedding, especially without telling them about her difficulty with her healing magic. If word spread an Avatar had lost her magic, people would worry, maybe even lose faith in the Four. But Gwen would face that season when it arrived and not a heartbeat sooner.

She ordered the driver to take her home. Once she was on her way, she alternated between rubbing her forehead and looking out the window for further signs of Chaos Season. Thankfully, this one seemed to be limited in reach. The fields on the lo Havil estate were full of workers removing stones and spreading manure. Other workers repaired barns, fences, or other buildings. *A pity the Four don't have an Avatar who could repair buildings the way we can heal people, plants, and animals. That would make dealing with Chaos Season so much easier.*

Once the coach halted in front of the family house, Gwen jumped out without assistance from the driver and said, "Bruce, please have my mare saddled and brought out for me."

He raised an eyebrow. "Lady lo Havil, if there's somewhere you need to go, you could have me take you there."

For a moment, she was tempted to take him up on his offer. It would be a more comfortable and more appropriate way to travel. However, her father would notice the coach's absence sooner than he would her own. "No, thank you. That will be all."

She strode into the house as fast as her skirts would allow. Father would definitely wonder where she was when she failed to appear for supper. Perhaps she ought to leave him a note to explain her departure so he wouldn't worry. It was her duty to go to the One Oak as soon as she could, and he ought to understand that. Whether or not he could make Lady Shellinda see reason was another story.

When Gwen entered her suite, her maid, Daisy, was already laying out a new gown for dinner. Gwen waved it away. "I won't be needing that one, Daisy. Please give me my riding outfit. And…" She peered into her wardrobe. She ought to bring something suitable for meeting the other Season Avatars, but her formal outfits wouldn't travel well stuffed into a satchel. Yellow was the Goddess of Spring's color, so she had to wear it. The only problem was selecting a dress she could don without help from a maid. "I'll take the blue-and-gold dress, along with anything else I might need overnight."

"Overnight?" Daisy didn't move. "Begging your ladyship's pardon, but your father didn't say anything about a trip any farther than to your intended's."

"It's an emergency."

"Is it your Aunt Gabri?"

Gwen was very tempted to say it was, just to get Daisy moving, but she knew Father wouldn't tolerate such dishonesty. She sighed. "It's Avatar business, Daisy. Please hurry, or I won't reach Lake Verdan before dark." Even if her healing magic was working properly, it wouldn't help her find food or shelter by the roadside, the way a Summer's or Fall's magic could.

"Lady lo Havil, it's already too late for you to reach Lake Verdan today. Can't you wait until tomorrow to travel?"

She shook her head. "I must go where Spring bids me, and She told me I'm needed at the One Oak."

"One of the Four spoke to you?"

"In my head." She rubbed her hand. She could still feel part of the shard in there, moving around. If that had really been the Goddess of Spring's voice she'd heard, then something was very wrong. Gwen resolved to ride for as long as her mare could manage at night. The full moon would help, and the road to Lake Verdan wouldn't be hard to follow.

While Daisy packed, Gwen searched her reticules for stray chals. Funny how she had so many clothes and jewels but little spending money. If she felt more confident about her healing ability, she could barter her talent for food and shelter along the way. But if her magic was working properly, she wouldn't need to make this trip. Perhaps Lucy, the cook, would be willing to give her some food for the road. Avatars always needed to eat to fuel their magic.

"One moment, Daisy." Before the maid could close her satchel, Gwen slipped in her sketchbook and some colored pencils. Perhaps drawing would help her remember something.

Daisy clenched her hands in front of her waist. "What should I say to your father when he asks about you?"

"I'll be home as soon as I can." Hopefully William would recover by then, or at least not get worse. Once she recovered her healing abilities, everything would be fine.

Gwen slipped down the back stairs for the servants, causing a housemaid to shriek in alarm as she passed. It was the fastest way to the kitchen, though, and she was less likely to run into her father this way.

At dinnertime, the kitchen was a flurry of activity, with Lucy single-handedly directing how the main course—game birds—should be laid out as she prepared a sauce. The cook smiled at Gwen. "Can't wait for dinner, dear? I have bread or apples for you."

"I'll need much more than that, Lucy. I won't be able to stay for dinner." Gwen sniffed the air regretfully. The smell of meat and an apple tart made her stomach rumble.

"By All Four, what do you mean?"

Maybe a half-truth would be easier for everyone. Gwen reached for a piece of bread. "William was caught in a Chaos Season and has snowsickness. I need to go to the One Oak before I can help him."

Lucy released her spoon. "You do? You've always managed splendidly on your own."

The bread in Gwen's mouth made it difficult to speak. "Not this time," she said once she managed to choke it down. "I need food for the journey."

"But why leave now? It's late."

She looked Lucy in the eye. "Because Spring told me to."

"Well, I never heard the Goddess before, but I'm not an Avatar. I'm a Fall child anyway." Lucy wiped her hands on a dishtowel. "Let's see what I can give you, dear." The cook sampled, stirred, and directed serving maids as she crossed the kitchen to the pantry. Gwen devoured two more pieces of bread before Lucy returned with a bulging sack. "I wish the Four wouldn't ask this of you, but I'm sure Bruce will take good care of you. Should I pack a sack for him?"

"No need. I'm riding."

Lucy gasped. "Lady Gwendolyn!"

Gwen dashed out before Lucy could chastise her further. She stopped only to grab her warm, waterproof cloak and change into riding boots before heading out to the stables. No sign of her mare—or Bruce. Maybe he'd gone straight back to William's estate to pick up her father. She wasn't sure if her father had ridden over there or not.

She peeked into the stable and found a stableboy feeding the horses. "Please saddle Violet right away."

He looked puzzled, but he said, "Yes, my Lady," and fetched the mare. At least someone around here listened to her without question.

As he led Violet out, the mare widened her nostrils, sniffing the air. Gwen wondered if another Chaos Season was about to happen. A Winter Avatar would have a better sense of that. She would just have to hope she could find shelter for both herself and her horse if Chaos Season struck.

The stableboy glanced at the sun sinking behind the trees. "Will you be all right, my Lady?"

"As long as I stick to the road."

After mounting, Gwen walked her mare down the long drive leading to the main road. She would have liked to go faster, but it wasn't safe in the dim light. When she reached the stone wall marking the edge of the lo Havil estate, she stared at it for a long minute before leaving it behind.

CHAPTER THREE

Aunt Gabri

Although the moon was close to full, it didn't provide as much light as Gwen would have liked. Violet, aptly named for being shy, veered away from every shadow. Gwen soothed her with running explanations of what they were seeing. For once, she wished she was a Fall Avatar and had a magic link with animals. This journey would have been much easier if she was. At least the Fip usurpers kept the road in good condition, so Violet would be less likely to stumble. Still, Gwen kept a close eye on the road and guided Violet away from anything that might damage her hooves.

The air chilled rapidly after the sun went down. Gwen halted to adjust the cinch and eat an apple, giving one to her mare too. Then back to the steady pace, watching the fields give way to forest. Occasionally the road split off to lead to a hamlet of field workers' houses. Some of them were abandoned, their inhabitants gone off to seek their fortune in the capital city of Wistica, or ever farther abroad. Gwen was glad William's family didn't live along this road. Their servants—or her father—might be about, and the thought of having to explain to them why she hadn't finished healing her fiancé made her stomach feel like she'd eaten rocks for dinner.

A pair of yellow eyes gleamed at her from the bushes beside the road. Violet snorted and backed up, fighting for her head. "Easy, girl." Gwen pressed her legs against the mare's sides. The animal appeared too small to be a wolf, but Violet must have smelled something she didn't like.

"You don't want to run, Violet." Gwen patted the mare's neck. "You'll get us both hurt if you do—"

A twig snapped. Violet turned her head as if she meant to bolt back to the stable. Gwen struggled to prevent her from doing so. Then an owl hooted. Violet jumped to the right and smashed Gwen's leg into a tree.

"Freeze it!" Gwen's yell made Violet flatten her ears. "Sorry, girl, but this is the worst time for you to be playing tricks like this." Gwen's leg ached, an unfamiliar and unwelcome sensation. Normally she could heal herself in heartbeats, but she couldn't risk using her magic when she wasn't sure how to use it. For now, she had to calm Violet before the mare injured herself too. The last thing Gwen wanted to do right now was walk to the One Oak.

It took a lot of sweet-talking, pats on the neck, and another apple from Gwen's supper before she could persuade Violet to move forward again. By then, her ankle had swollen so much she wouldn't be able to take her boot off. All the more reason to keep going for as long as possible.

Gwen crouched low over Violet to keep warm. They pressed on for another hour or so. Finally the strip of forest thinned out, and the buildings of Lake Verdan appeared in the distance. The town wasn't as big as Midpoint, only a line of buildings on each side of the road. It would be a long time before the Selathens brought their steam-driven locomotives here. As long as Gwen could find supper and a bed at the inn, she would be content. Neither she nor Violet were in much condition to go farther.

As Gwen relaxed, she glanced back. A light glowed on the road behind her. Someone else was traveling tonight, and she'd bet her magic it was her father or someone from her father, sent to fetch her. She bit her lip, then urged Violet into a trot. It would be harder to drag her back home if she already had sanctuary in the inn. The innkeeper might not be willing to stand up to her father, but there would be witnesses. Witnesses to hear her confess she could no longer heal. Her mood sank even lower.

A creaking sign with the words "The Four's Rest" was the distinguishing feature of the inn. Ivy twisted over the stone walls, and the steps leading to the front door were worn. Gwen rode past them to the stable and woke the snoozing stable boy. He rubbed his eyes at seeing her. "Lady...why, it's Lady lo Havil! What are you doing here this time of night?"

"Hoping you'll assist me with getting down."

Gwen grimaced as she put weight on her injured leg. By the Four, her magic had better return soon. "Check Violet carefully," she told the stable boy. "I want to make sure she's fit for travel in the morning."

She tried not to limp as she entered the inn. Inside, the dark woodwork was scratched. Two long tables with benches filled the common room. Candles dripped wax spots on the tables. A serving woman handed mugs of ale and lamb stew to several tradesmen clustered by the fireplace. It was the kind of scene that would have appalled Lady Shellinda for being common. Gwen was too hungry to care.

Everyone turned to stare at her as she made her way to the fireplace. "Stew, please," she said as she sat at an empty table. "And a room for the night." She fingered the reticule hidden under her cloak. "Can you send the bill to the lo Havil estate?"

Footsteps sounded behind her. "That won't be necessary." Her father's voice.

Gwen turned to face him. Weariness showed in his eyes and slumped posture, but as soon as he saw her, he straightened, and the expression in his eyes grew hard.

"Gwendolyn lo Havil, thank the Four I found you. What were you thinking, running off like that? William's still not well!"

"I know, Father." She took a deep breath, bracing herself as she was forced to confess her failure in public. "But I need help from the One Oak to heal him."

The room fell silent, as if even the fire wanted to listen to her.

"You need help dealing with snowsickness?" He raised his eyebrows. "Didn't you heal one of the coachmen of that over the winter?"

"Yes, but—"

"Lady Shellinda is furious at you for leaving her son in anything less than excellent health. She wanted to break the engagement on the spot. I told her there must be a good reason why you left so suddenly. But I can't think of a single reason why you would ride a skittish horse by yourself at night without doing more than telling a couple of servants you had to leave."

Gwen drew her cloak around her. Sitting close to the fire made her realize how chilly she'd been on her ride. "Father, we need to discuss this someplace private."

Fatigue settled over his features again. Father beckoned Gwen down the dark hallway and into a nook filled with cloaks. The smell of wet wool made her wonder if another Chaos Season had occurred here.

Father picked a spot away from the cloaks and leaned against the wall. "All right, Gwendolyn, tell me why you didn't heal William. That's not like you, any more than this mad nighttime dash."

She described almost everything that had happened since she found the shard. The only things she omitted were William's improper behavior and the fact that the shard was still buried in her palm. By the time she was done, her leg ached so much she had to fight to keep tears from her eyes.

"And you think the Goddess of Spring told you to go to the One Oak?" Her father asked when she was finished.

Gwen nodded.

"But you...didn't see Her? You only heard Her in your thoughts? Maybe it wasn't real."

"She is real! She gifted me with magic lifetimes ago!"

Her father looked away. Most people didn't remember their previous lives. Only the Season Avatars did, so they could retain everything they'd learned about their magic and Challen.

"It would be better for the estate if you get married before you become a Season Avatar," he said. "William can run the estate while you're defending us from Chaos Season. Besides, once you're married, you won't need a chaperone. It wouldn't surprise me if Lady Shellinda thinks you ran away to meet a lover."

"Father!" Gwen straightened, putting weight on both legs before she remembered her injury. Pain made her gasp.

"Gwen? What's wrong?"

"Violet crushed my leg against a tree on the way over here."

"Why didn't you heal it? You always do."

"By All Four, didn't you understand a word I said? I don't remember how to heal! Only the current Ava Spring can help me."

"I...I didn't believe it. Here, let me help you to the common room." He came to her and supported her on her weak side. "Well, we'll have to spend the night here, then. I hope the rooms are adequate."

Gwen's father didn't say anything to her as they returned to the public area. He ordered enough stew, bread, and cheese to sate even her appetite. The innkeeper had no wine, but the rough ale helped dull the leg pain to a bearable ache.

"Get some rest now," Father said after they made their way upstairs. The room was as small as her closet, but the straw mattress looked appealing in her fatigue. "We'll figure out what to do in the morning."

One thing was certain, Gwen realized as she struggled with her boots. She wouldn't be riding in the morning.

* * *

"Gwendolyn, I still wish you'd told me what happened before setting off on your own," her father said over thin oatmeal the next morning. "And I don't know how we're going to appease Lady Shellinda and William." The lines around his eyes grew deeper as he spoke. "But even I can tell you've lost your magic. Avatar business comes first, especially when the Goddess is involved." He stirred some dried fruit into the oatmeal. "So you can go to the One Oak, as long as you return for the wedding once your magic is working properly."

"Thank you, Father." Gwen composed herself to look suitably grateful. If he'd forbidden her to go, she'd have snuck off as soon as the servants were distracted. This was better. "The only thing is, it may be a few days before I can ride."

"It's still not suitable for you to travel alone. You should have someone accompany you."

"Who? Daisy?"

"She should stay at home to help prepare for the wedding. I was thinking Aunt Gabri."

"Aunt Gabri?" Gwen tried to hide her dismay. "She hates travel! She barely even leaves her house!" Was that why he'd suggested her, to force Gwen to return home?

"I know, but she's the closest female relative you have, and she has no obligations, like me with the estate. We can drive over to her house as soon as we're done eating."

Thank the Four Aunt Gabri's house wasn't too far out of the way to Midpoint. The detour would add another day to the journey, but the delay would give Gwen's leg more time to heal on its own. Maybe, if she was lucky, her memories would return too. Even if they did, she still needed to visit the One Oak. She wanted to talk to the Ava Spring and figure out why she'd lost her memories to begin with.

Father arranged for one of his grooms to bring Violet home, then they set out in the lo Havil coach. Gwen propped her leg up on the seat across from her and massaged it, trying to heal her leg without using her memories. It tingled, but the swelling and bruises didn't fade. Father stared out of the window as she worked. By mid-morning, the wind picked up, and dark clouds rolled in.

"How much farther?" she asked.

"Not too far, but we won't beat the rain." The driver urged their team of horses to a faster pace. In this storm, they could get lost, or the chaise could get stuck in the mud. She prayed to the Four that there would be no thunder to make the horses bolt.

The storm ended as quickly as it sprung up. After another couple hours of riding, the carriage turned down a dirt road lined with apple and pear trees. Cottages peeked through the orchard. Aunt Gabri's house, though smaller than the lo Havil's, stood out from the cottages like a violet in the snow. Instead of being built from brick or stone, it had wooden sides that were painted lavender. Even the shutters were dark purple. Three stories high, it rose above the other building as if it disdained them, even though it was in need of repair.

A middle-aged local woman who acted as Aunt Gabri's companion let them in. "Lord and Lady lo Havil! This is a surprise. Let me make sure the mistress is in...."

"Of course she's in," Gwen's father said. "When does she ever go anywhere? Please take my card up to her immediately." He glanced at Gwen. "My daughter is on an urgent mission and requires her aunt's help."

The companion ushered them to the formal drawing room. So many lace doilies covered the furniture it looked as if a group of frantic spiders had decorated them. The room smelled musty. Gwen sat on the edge of a hard chair. How hard would it be to persuade her stay-at-home aunt to escort her to the One Oak? If she did agree to come along, how fast would they be able to travel? Aunt Gabri didn't ride very well and would insist on another slow, heavy coach. The maid returned with tea and almond cake, but the refreshments didn't sweeten Gwen's mood.

Aunt Gabri entered the drawing room. She matched the outside of her house in a lavender gown and amethyst necklace and earrings. The high collar and long sleeves hadn't been fashionable since before Gwen was born. Aunt Gabri probably still insisted on wearing a full corset underneath, laced so tightly it was a miracle she was able to breathe. Even if it was good for posture, Gwen shuddered to think of having to wear something so confining. It wouldn't do for Avatars' work at all.

"Gerad, Gwendolyn, such a pleasure to see you." She grabbed each of them in turn and kissed them on both cheeks. "But why are you here, and why didn't you send word you were coming?"

"It was an unplanned trip." Gwen's father glanced at her. "Gwen will explain."

I have no reason to be embarrassed. I was just doing my duty for Challen. No matter how Gwen tried to justify her actions to herself, she knew it wasn't the stuffy room that made her cheeks warm. She drew herself up straight. "Aunt Gabri, you know I'm meant to be the next Ava Spring someday. I have an urgent mission to go to the One Oak. But Father insists I need a suitable female escort." Gwen took a deep breath. "Will you do me the honor of accompanying me?"

Aunt Gabri's eyes widened. "Me, go to the One Oak! Oh, oh, oh!" She plopped down on an overstuffed loveseat and fanned herself with her hand. "Gwendolyn, dear, I couldn't possibly travel so far."

"It would be less than two days by coach. They're very close to Midpoint."

"But travel...the coach getting stuck somewhere...spending the night in a strange inn, with strangers just waiting for the right moment to slip sleeping powder in your food, so they can sneak into your room while you sleep and rob you...or...or worse!" Aunt Gabri shook her head. "Isn't there anyone else who could take you?"

"There's no one closer, Gabri," Gwen's father said. "And...Gwen's healing magic isn't working properly. She needs to talk to the current Spring Avatar to find out why."

Aunt Gabri peered at her. "Maybe this is a sign you're not the next Spring Avatar after all."

"That's not how Avatar magic works, Aunt Gabri." By All Four, shouldn't she know this? Was she becoming forgetful? Gwen would have to look after her own chaperone. "We are all born on the equinox or solstice, and we remember our past lives. At least, we're supposed to." She stared at her untouched almond cake. "I've lost my memories. How can I face Chaos Season without them?"

Her aunt shuddered. "Chaos Season is so nasty. Worse, it's unpredictable. That's why I don't like to go outside. You never know if you're getting rain, snow, or sun."

"I'm sure the Winter Avatar keeps the weather in order at the One Oak. And the others would reward you handsomely for accompanying me." Gwen smiled at her. "Is there something you would like?"

"If they can't make Challen safe, then what's the point of asking for chals or healing or anything?"

"You need healing?" Gwen perked up; that had to be the answer. "For what?"

"Oh, my knees, and my eyes aren't as sharp as they used to be...."

"I'm sorry, Aunt Gabri. Age is one of the few things an Ava Spring can't cure, even if my magic was working properly."

Now what? Gwen's stomach twisted. There had to be something that would pry her aunt out of the house! Then she thought over her aunt's words. If safety was so important to her, maybe that was the key.

She approached her aunt, took her thin, pale hand, and drew her toward the window. "When was the last time you left the house, Aunt Gabri?"

"I have to think...it must have been the card party at the lu Halls' last moon. They promised me if the wind so much as blew hard, I could stay the night, but the weather was quite fine."

"And did you enjoy yourself?"

"Why, yes, once I knew for certain Lady lu Hall was over her cold and no one else was sick."

"Well, then, if you come with me to the One Oak, you can enjoy the world without fear."

Gwen drew back the curtain, praying to the Goddess of Spring she wouldn't be showing her aunt a blizzard or a tornado. Outside, the trees were covered in apple blossoms, and the lawn was an inviting shade of green. The air was calm, and white clouds in the sky made it appear bluer by contrast. Gwen reached for the window, longing to be out in her season. Then the sky darkened, and the petals on the trees shriveled and died, blanketing the ground as if predicting another snowfall.

Aunt Gabri shook her head and closed the curtain. "See? You can't trust the weather in Challen. Oh, sometimes I wish I didn't live in Challen at all! Surely this country must be cursed..."

"Challen cursed? No!" Gwen threw her arms wide. "Even though I don't know why the Four allow the Chaos Season in Challen, I and all the other Season Avatars are servants of the Four. It's our job to fight the Chaos Season and make Challen safe for you and everyone else. If you really want Challen to be safe, Aunt, then come with me to the One Oak so I can do my part. If you won't, then just hide in your frozen house forever!"

With a gasp, Aunt Gabri sank onto the loveseat. Gwen made no move to touch her. She hadn't meant to get so carried away, but by the Four, she'd spent so many lives defending her country it was automatic to her. Her father was silent, probably stunned by her outburst.

Gwen put her hand over her mouth. "I'm sorry, Aunt Gabri, I shouldn't have said that...."

Aunt Gabri raised her head and stared at her, for once her gaze connecting with Gwen instead of shying away.

"No, Gwendolyn, you're right. You do need to go to the One Oak. And if there's no one else to take you, I guess it's up to me. Oh, dear," she fanned herself, "maybe a sip of something strong first would give me the courage for it."

CHAPTER FOUR

To the One Oak

Liquid courage gave Aunt Gabri flushed cheeks, but it didn't help her leave the house any faster. When she wasn't driving her maid crazy by changing her mind about what she wanted to pack for the trip—and while Gwen wished she'd brought a trunk of clothes, three seemed excessive—she gave conflicting orders to the rest of her staff about how to run the house. Aunt Gabri continued her fussing until bedtime. The next morning, she complained they had to eat too early to digest their food properly. Then Gwen had to reassure her aunt that no, no one would rob them, and that despite the clouds, another thunderstorm like the one the day before was unlikely to return. Finally Aunt Gabri consented to leave her house, even if she swaddled herself in shawls to protect herself from another Chaos Season and glanced around nervously.

Father's leave-taking, on the other hand, was much simpler. He'd borrowed a gelding used by Aunt Gabri's staff for errands. Before riding off, he took Gwen's hands, stared at her for a few moments, and said, "I hope you return ready to do your duty, daughter. Remember the honor of our name and keep it intact. May the Four watch over you."

"And you too," she replied.

"Take good care of your aunt on the trip." Father stepped away from her, mounted the gelding, and rode off without looking back. Aunt Gabri refused to let the coachman help her into the closed-top carriage until he was safely out of sight.

Gwen tried to conceal her impatience, but once they were under-way, she let out a sigh of relief. "If we push hard, we can make it to the One Oak by tomorrow," she said.

"Are you sure? What if we get lost?"

"The roads are well-marked, Aunt Gabri. I'm sure we'll be fine."

Aunt Gabri glanced around as if looking for something else to complain or worry about. She finally sat back against the cushions and rubbed her temples. "I suppose it's easy for a young one like you not to fret," she said. "But I know things never work out the way you think they will."

In other circumstances, Gwen would have considered her soul old-er than her aunt's. But without her memories, she did indeed feel as young as her years.

They rode in silence for a few more minutes before Aunt Gabri sat up straight, a determined expression on her face. "All right then, niece, perhaps you should tell me more about this urgent mission of yours."

"You already know the most important thing," Gwen replied. "I've lost the memories that help me heal people. Without them, my magic is useless, maybe even harmful."

"How could you lose your memories, child? Did you hit your head? And why didn't you heal yourself before you forgot how?"

Gwen flexed her leg. It felt better today than yesterday, but it was still stiff. "It wasn't a head injury," she replied. "Although it did hap-pen after I treated a gardener with a head injury."

"Did his injury affect you?"

"No, that's not how my healing magic works."

"Can't you just go to the university in Wistica to learn whatever you need to know about healing?"

"It wouldn't be enough." Gwen pointed to her own head. "I had access to hundreds of years of treating patients. I've seen diseases we no longer have and injuries so strange you'd swear they were caused by magic. I've seen all types of people, from newborns to the very old. Without this knowledge, I can't direct my magic. I can't even heal a simple cut." Gwen rubbed the scar on her palm. Without access to her memories, she felt like an unfinished drawing. There had to be a way to recover them.

Aunt Gabri stared at her as if she had turned blue. "No wonder you always seemed...older than your years."

Gwen wondered why the Four had sent her to a family who didn't understand Avatars.

They rode in silence for a while. After a rest stop, Aunt Gabri pulled a romance novel out of her reticule and asked Gwen to read to her "since reading in a coach gives me such a headache." The story seemed wildly improbable to Gwen, about a Challen woman falling in love with a man from Selath, the country to the west. Selath was a barren, mountainous land with a reputation for killing anyone foolish enough to travel into it, searching for gems, precious metals, and minerals. A group of people who lived on the border between Challen and Selath claimed their ancestors had come from Selath, and they maintained their own customs. One of them was favoring men above women. What Challen woman would choose to leave her country to live in a harsh land and be treated like something less than a servant? Still, Aunt Gabri sighed and swooned over the couple's trials, making Gwen wonder what, if anything, she wasn't getting from the story.

By the time she was ready to stop reading, her mouth dry and her head aching, the scenery outside the coach suggested they were nearing Midpoint. The endless fields became interspersed with more houses and other buildings, the coach bounced about less often as the dirt road gave way to a paved one, and traffic became heavier, slowing their progress. When they reached an inn on the outskirts of the city, it was well past noon, and Gwen's stomach was protesting so much she wanted to dash out of the coach and fling herself onto the nearest plate of food. Instead, she kept her mouth closed so she didn't snap at her aunt when she took a long time descending from the coach. Aunt Gabri blinked in the heat, fanning herself with a lace fan as old as her dress.

"Thank the Four we made it safely to Midpoint," she said. "But how do we get to the One Oak?"

Gwen glanced around, half-expecting to remember a landmark. The buildings were old enough to have been around for a century or two; they were tall and narrow, each one bearing some repeating design on the woodwork or along the windows. She didn't recognize the buildings or the street names. It didn't matter, she told herself. It shouldn't be too hard to hire someone who knew the way to the One Oak.

Gwen's aunt insisted they take their meal in a secluded room off the main dining hall reserved for ladies of quality. The food was better than normal inn fare: noodle soup with Selathan spices, chicken in a cream sauce, roasted vegetables, fresh bread, and fruit tartlets for dessert. Aunt Gabri kept saying, "Gwendolyn lo Havil, where did you learn your manners from? No lady eats that much or so fast!"

Gwen wiped her mouth with a linen napkin. "I'm sorry, Aunt Gabri, but I'm starving."

"Well, if all Season Avatars eat like you, it's a good thing they stay at the One Oak instead of inflicting their manners on others."

Gwen was sure there had been huge parties held at the One Oak during her previous lives, events that were considered to be almost as prestigious as attending a coronation at the palace in Wistica. She remembered dreaming about such things before she'd lost access to her previous lives.

When she was finally full, she said, "I need to talk to the driver and see if he knows the way to the One Oak. If he doesn't, maybe someone here does. Do you want to come with me, or do you want to wait in the parlor and have me fetch you when we're ready?"

Aunt Gabri stared through the door at the parlor. "Some chocolate and a chance to sit quietly would be nice. But your father would never forgive me if I let you be abducted by some ruffian." She sighed as she rose, then she gasped. "Oh, dear! Gwen, look outside! We'll never be able to travel in these conditions!"

Gwen checked the window. The hot day–too warm for spring–had turned into its opposite: pelting, icy rain. By All Four, when did that happen? The inn walls were thick enough to keep the chill out, but she shivered just the same. They were so close to the One Oak; if the Season Avatars couldn't control the weather here, what did that mean for the rest of Challen?

"It doesn't matter, Aunt; we have to go."

Not knowing where to start, Gwen approached the innkeeper and explained her problem. The stocky bearded man didn't seem too impressed by her claim to be a Season Avatar. "Lady, I get young people claiming to be Season Avatars coming here every moon. Unless you can prove it, don't waste my time."

Even if she couldn't heal, she could still read auras. Faint colors surrounded everyone, the color of their birth God or Goddess. This man's aura was a dull red.

"You were born in the fall," she announced.

He stared down his beaky nose at her. "I was. End of Harvest Moon. But anyone can make a lucky guess."

Gwen calmly faced the dining room. "The server by the fireplace is winter-born." She pointed at the other tables. "I see two summers, a spring, a fall, another winter…."

"Enough." The innkeeper still frowned. "Lady, you may be a genuine Season Avatar, but unless you're a Winter, you can't get to the One Oak. The weather surrounding the Season Avatars' estate has gone crazy the last couple of weeks. It's Chaos Season there all the time now."

"Something must be wrong! That's why I need to get there!"

"The snow is so deep on that road your coach will get stuck. If you're that set on going, you'll have to ride the rest of the way."

If she was alone, Gwen wouldn't have minded so much. Having to bring her timid maiden aunt along complicated the situation.

"Fine," she snapped. "Just tell me where I can hire some horses."

"There's a good stable on the next street."

Gwen wrapped her cloak tightly around her and set out to find the stable. Aunt Gabri must have decided Gwen's virtue was at no risk in this weather, for she elected to stay at the inn. Although Gwen's cloak had a hood, it didn't offer much protection when the wind blew into her face. It was almost as if the weather itself didn't want her to complete her journey. Perhaps that was a clue to the problem; perhaps something had happened to the Avi Win. However, he was married to the Ava Spring; if her husband was ailing, wouldn't she try her hardest to heal him? Gwen frowned. What if the Ava Spring was unable to heal her husband? That would mean either he was mortally ill, or else the Ava Spring's magic was fading. Who would be able to help Gwen?

The stable was warm and dry, a pleasant contrast to the street outside. The smell of horses and hay seemed comforting after her walk. No wonder the head of the stable, a small, middle-aged woman with a red nose and a no-nonsense attitude, shook her head when Gwen requested to hire two of her steadiest horses. "It's abuse taking them out in weather like this," she said. "And where were you planning to go?"

"The One Oak."

"That wouldn't be a bad ride normally, but my hunch is it'll only grow worse the closer you get."

Gwen feared that too. "Well, it's not going to get better until someone talks to the Season Avatars, isn't it?"

"Why would they listen to you? Are you next in line?"

Gwen nodded.

"I bet you're not an Ava Win, though, or you'd be doing something about this sleet yourself. If I don't hear back from you after two days, I'm sending a message to the One Oak." The stable master coughed for half a minute, then walked down the aisle between the stables, inspecting each horse. "Not an Ava Fall either? Blaze has been favoring his right front leg."

"Sorry, I'm an Ava Spring."

"Can you do something to make me feel better? I can't seem to stop coughing. Excuse me." The stable mistress turned away, pulling out a sturdy handkerchief.

Gwen hesitated. She wanted to help this woman, but she wasn't sure she could. If she was honest, would this woman lose faith in the Avatars and the Four?

The woman coughed again, this time hard enough to make her bend over. Gwen hated seeing anyone sound so miserable.

"I'll do what I can." *Help me, Spring. I don't want to make her feel worse.* "May I touch your nose?"

"Are you sure you want to?" The stable master grinned wryly.

"My magic works best when I make contact with the afflicted area."

Gwen came forward and laid a single finger on the woman's nose. Normally she would be able to sense the various tissues that made up a body, but her impressions were muddled. Blood cells appeared where skin should be, and vice versa. She touched her own nose with her other hand. This time she could feel the internal structure properly. Using that as a basis, she studied the lining of the woman's nose. Should she make it dry up? What if she did so permanently and left the stable master worse off than before?

Freeze it. Magic poured from her into the woman's nose and throat, freezing the tissues. Desperately, Gwen thawed them, then yanked her magic back before she gave this woman snowsickness too. "How do you feel, Dama?"

The woman sniffed experimentally, then smiled. "Thank the Four, I can breathe again!"

Maybe Gwen had been able to help her after all. Honesty compelled her to say, "I'm not sure if I cured your illness."

"You didn't?" The woman raised her eyebrows.

Gwen hung her head. "I—I need to consult with the current Ava Spring."

"No one becomes an expert overnight, Ava."

But I am an expert. At least, I was. Gwen forced herself to keep her frustration off of her face.

"For your help, I'll draw you a map with as many landmarks as I remember," the stable master continued. "You might not be able to see much in this weather, so any guide might be useful. I can lend you a better cloak too."

Half an hour later, Gwen proceeded back to the hotel, leading both mares behind her. Her partial success made the hail seem less onerous. Aunt Gabri, however, took one look outside and moaned, "No. By All Four, Gwendolyn, it's impossible now."

"It's not going to get better if we just wait here."

"Of course it will."

"Chaos Season never stops until the Avatars make it stop. I have to find out why the Avatars are permitting this."

Aunt Gabri gave her an imploring look and wrung her glove. "I'm a terrible rider. What if the horse spooks and runs off with me?"

"The stable owner gave me the calmest horses she had. All you have to do is stay on and follow me. Surely you can manage that?"

Aunt Gabri shook her head.

Gwen glared at her. Aunt Gabri's dress wasn't sodden, her leg didn't ache, and her boots weren't squelching with water, but of course she had to be the one to complain. "Very well, Aunt Gabri. You stay here and toast yourself by the fire. I wouldn't want you to risk yourself. When I get to the One Oak, I'll write to Father and tell him what an excellent chaperone you were—right up to the point where you abandoned me on the last stage of the journey."

"Gwendolyn lo Havil, you wouldn't—"

"I am. I don't care what you choose to do, just let me go."

Guilt weighed her down as she strode out the door, but she refused to look back. Yes, she was disrespecting her elder, but she was a Season Avatar first. Why was it none of the people who were supposed to know her best understood that? She sighed. Season Avatars weren't supposed to be alone or work alone. Maybe after recovering her memories, she could meet the people from her birth year. Then she wouldn't have to bear the burden of her magic by herself.

The mounts waited patiently in the inn's crowded stable, still saddled and ready to go. Gwen fetched her satchel from the coach, then reviewed the map one more time, memorizing it. She debated if she should take both horses with her or leave one behind. While it might be useful to be able to switch mounts if the roads were as terrible as the stable owner had predicted, she might wind up losing one.

"Gwendolyn! Wait!"

Aunt Gabri stood in the stable doorway. She already looked pale and bedraggled, as if she'd swam through a flood, but her expression was determined, if grim.

"Your father asked me to take you to the One Oak, so I shall, even if it kills me. And if it does, may the God of Winter freeze you."

Gwen couldn't help but smile. "Thank you, Aunt Gabri. Don't worry; it'll be fine."

The weather certainly wasn't. Although the streets were empty, sheets of rain made it hard to tell where they were going. Gwen leaned forward, hunching as close to her mare as she could not just for warmth, but to urge the animal into something faster than a walk. Though to be fair, not even the speediest hunter would have managed more than a trudge in these conditions. The streets in Midpoint were paved, as was the road leading out of town. The road wasn't as well-maintained as the streets were; the mare clambered through snowdrifts. Every time she did, Gwen's lower limbs and feet were chilled. All she could hear from Aunt Gabri behind her were moans and prayers to the Four.

As the trees around them grew thicker, Gwen lifted her head. They were getting close; she could almost remember individual trees and the twists along this path. The oak trees provided some shelter from the wind and rain. The wind had broken branches along the path, forcing the mare to step even more carefully. Gwen rubbed her neck encouragingly. "There's a hot bran mash for you at the end of this road—"

CRACK! Gwen tightened her grip on the reins. The mare side-stepped a little before settling down. Gwen looked around herself. That thunder had sounded very close by. She could even smell the remnants of the lighting in the air. Why was the Avi Win allowing such violent weather so close to the One Oak?

A couple of turns later, Gwen saw a tree fallen over the road. Although the trunk wasn't as large as some of the other trees in this forest, the conditions were too risky to jump the horse over it.

"Maybe the Season Avatars don't want company!" Aunt Gabri shouted as she finally caught up.

"Nonsense." Or was it? Gwen couldn't worry about that now, not when she was so close. "Let's go around this way."

Gwen guided her horse around the tree. It was taller than she had expected, and she lost sight of the road. For a moment, she panicked. Then she squinted. Was that the One Oak? She turned her mare, following nothing more than instinct. Then suddenly they found the road, the rain died, and she got her first good view of the One Oak, her home in all of her previous lives.

It could have been a castle. Built of stone, it towered above the trees. If the weather had been clear, she would have had no trouble finding it. It wasn't spread out and full of windows like her family's house; this building was much older, with narrow windows and a compact, square shape. She thought she saw greenery on the roof, but it was hard to be certain at this distance. The more she saw, the more she remembered. Each of the four sides was dedicated to a different Season Avatar, with Spring's section at the front. Common rooms, including the library, a work area, and a ballroom, were toward the center. The suites were big enough to accommodate a family for each Season Avatar. Gwen wondered if William would like them.

"Is that it?" Aunt Gabri asked. "It looks so...plain."

"Oh, it's not on the inside, Aunt Gabri. They have paintings by long-gone famous artists, and an atrium, and portraits of every Season Avatar that ever lived. Each new Season Avatar gets to decorate however he or she wants, though you're expected to use a lot of your God or Goddess's color." She clucked to her horse, making her move again. "Come on, let's go!"

"Why exactly do they call this place the One Oak? It's more like a Thousand Oaks!"

Gwen wasn't sure if this was another complaint or her aunt's attempt at humor. "Every Avi or Ava Sum grows an oak tree from an acorn to maturity. It's a way for them to connect to Challen and channel their magic. That's why we Season Avatars spend most of our time here."

"You poor thing." Aunt Gabri shuddered, but it was hard to tell if it was because she was drenched or because Gwen would be tied to this place. Given her own tendency to stay close to home, Gwen suspected the former.

"Well, that's why they make it so nice inside. I really think you'll like it—"

Gwen broke off as she spotted something small and black launch out of a window toward them. As they rode closer, it resolved into a crow. The bird circled overhead, cawing a few times before returning back to the One Oak.

"Don't tell me the Season Avatars keep dirty animals inside their house." Aunt Gabri looked shocked.

"That's not just any animal; that's the Ava Fall's anilink. She bonds with it the way the Avi Sum uses his tree." Gwen's stomach tightened. "And now they know we're here."

.

Three Season Avatars

Now that Gwen was moments away from meeting the current Season Avatars, she realized she was unprepared. She must look a fright, all drenched and mud-spattered as she was by the journey. Even her spare clothing was probably soaked. Standing here, looking up at her once and future home, made her wonder how they would receive her. It wasn't just about figuring out how to restore her magic. If the Season Avatars were letting Chaos Season rule right outside their home, then something was wrong. Would they be able help her? More importantly, how would this affect Challen?

"I suppose we should ride up and announce ourselves," she said, more for her aunt's benefit than her own.

"If they know we're here, I hope they set out some hot chocolate and scones for us," she replied. "I'm wetter than the Chikasi River!" She peered around. "I thought you said the One Oak was on the river, Gwen."

"You can see the river from the other side of the house. Come on." Gwen sent her mare into a walk; the horse put more effort into their uphill climb as if sensing shelter and companions were nearby. "The sooner we arrive, the sooner we can eat and dry off."

The forest gave way to a lawn and garden. The ground was saturated, but the grass, shrubs, and flowers all seemed healthy and vibrant with life, even if some of the taller plants had blown over or snapped in the wind. That probably meant the Avi Sum was still working his magic, at least in a limited area around the One Oak. The path was well-maintained too; every piece of stone fit together perfectly.

The path widened into a broad circle in front of the One Oak, empty as if expecting more guests to arrive by coach. Two grooms, one middle-aged, the other in his twenties, awaited them. The servants wore plain, serviceable clothing, which made the white bands around their upper arms more noticeable.

White? Mourning? Gwen remembered her dream. *By the Four, no....*

"Welcome to the One Oak," the older groom said, helping Aunt Gabri dismount. "Do you have business with the Season Avatars? We weren't expecting anyone, but Brighteyes led us out here."

Aunt Gabri blinked a couple of times. "Who's Brighteyes?"

"The Ava Fall's anilink, Lady."

The crow cawed; Gwen searched and found it—or him—perched on a window ledge. He bobbed his head up and down before ducking inside the house.

When Aunt Gabri didn't say anything else, Gwen slid off her mare and handed over the reins to the younger groom, who smiled briefly at her before turning his attention to the horse. Gwen faced the other groom. "I'm Lady Gwendolyn lo Havil, the next Ava Spring." She wanted to ask who had died, but she wasn't sure she wanted to know the answer.

"Welcome to the One Oak, Ava." The groom bowed his head. "Your predecessor will be missed."

"The Ava Spring is dead?" The one Avatar she needed to talk to, dead before they could meet. The Goddess of Spring had been right, but why would She permit this? Gwen traced a compass rose over her heart. "May she have good sleep and a gentle rebirth. What happened?"

"A riding accident, Ava. Her horse stumbled and broke its leg. She fell off and snapped her neck." He shook his head. "The God of Winter always seems to harvest the Springs through accidents. I guess that's because they'd heal anything short of something quick and lethal."

Gwen shivered. How many times had she died like that?

"Best we get the horses and the ladies inside." The groom shifted the reins of Aunt lo Havil's horse to his other hand. "The inside staff will take good care of you, Ava, Lady."

Sure enough, the door was already open, with a footman in a white coat waiting to escort them inside. Gwen wondered if the staff here were normally so quick to wait upon guests, or if they had already guessed she was the next Ava Spring.

Once they were inside the entrance, Gwen stopped to survey it. The marble floor brought back memories, but the rest of it looked unfamiliar. "What happened to the wood paneling and carvings?" she asked.

The footman's right eye twitched. "The walls have been painted pale yellow for as long as I remember, Ava and Lady—"

"Lo Havil." Gwen searched through her reticule until she found a calling card that was still pristine. She placed it in the center of a silver tray on a stand. "They must have decorated since my last life here." A pity she remembered trivial things like decoration when she needed healing memories. Maybe some of them would return if she stayed here long enough. "I just heard about the Ava Spring. I'm so sorry her season ended so soon, especially since I'd hoped to talk to her. Will another Avatar see me?"

The footman picked up the tray. He tried to keep his expression neutral, but he stared at Gwen for just a heartbeat more than he should. "Which Avatar?"

"Whoever is free." Could any of them help her?

"Of course." He lingered over the last word, as if unsure which title to address her with. "If you ladies will follow me, I'll escort you to the reception area. You can freshen up while I see who can receive you."

Aunt Gabri gawked as they passed down a hallway covered with floor-to-ceiling paintings done centuries before. Gwen tried not to be so obvious with her examination. So many things brought back memories, yet others jarred her. She wished she had some time alone to wander through the One Oak and become reacquainted with it.

The footman led them to a sitting area. The sofa, loveseat, and extra chairs were all upholstered in a plaid fabric featuring equal amounts of red, yellow, blue, and green. Accents around the room—blue vases with force-grown red roses and yellow tulips, green shades on the windows—picked out the same shades. The room felt like it was balanced as an equal tribute to All Four Gods and Goddesses. A reception area like this one should see lots of visitors, but the flowers were drooping as if they'd been left unattended.

"If you would like to dry off—" the footman gestured toward a door on the other side of the room. He quickly lit a fire in the fireplace. "Someone will bring you hot chocolate and some sandwiches soon. Please make yourselves comfortable."

As soon as he had left, Gwen investigated the door he had indicated. To her delight, an indoor water closet was installed there. She changed into her other dress, then pinned her blonde hair into a bun, catching all stray hairs. Her reflection in the mirror above the basin looked tired, older than her eighteen springs. The Season Avatars were older than her father, maybe even old enough to be her grandparents. Her appearance had to be perfect so they would accept her as their equal.

Aunt Gabri looked a little less unhappy than she had on the trip. She stood in front of the fireplace, holding her skirt out so the heat could dry it. "They don't spare the chals around here, do they,

Gwen?" She lowered her voice. "Just how much do you think they're worth? Will you really get a share of all this?"

"The Season Avatars set up a fund centuries ago to keep this estate running." Gwen stared into the fire, remembering monarchs from the past who'd longed to get their fingers into the Season Avatars' fund—or divert the tithe paid to the Avatars by the citizens of Challen into their royal coffers.

"Well, now I understand why Season Avatars don't need to travel much. Everything you could possibly want comes to you."

A maid appeared with the promised hot chocolate and sandwiches. The chocolate was thick and rich, with heavy cream floating on top, and the sandwiches were stuffed with meat and cheese. Gwen devoured three of them, then sat and watched the fire. Her stomach was content; however, as much as she wanted to curl up and drowse for a while, she couldn't stop wondering why the Season Avatars hadn't arrived yet. It shouldn't take a footman that long to find them, even in a house this big. She rolled off the loveseat and pulled the bell cord in the corner. A woman said, "Couldn't wait to take over, could you, with our Margaret scarcely cold in her grave?"

Gwen spun around. A woman stood in the doorway, arms crossed over her bosom. Gwen would have guessed her to be not more than a decade older than herself. It was always hard to tell the age of an Avatar, as the Spring Avatars could slow down the aging process. The pure white silk dress the woman wore indicated deep mourning, and the crow on her shoulder had to be the same one that had spotted them earlier. She must be the Ava Fall, with magic affecting animals. Gwen didn't need to look at her aura, redder than any she'd ever seen, to confirm it.

Gwen sunk into a deep curtsey. "Ava, it's an honor to meet you. I'm Gwendolyn lo Havil—"

"Yes, yes, I received your calling card." The Ava Fall's eyes never warmed. "Of course, anyone can come in here and claim to be a Season Avatar, but proving it is another story."

Blood rushed to Gwen's cheeks. She straightened to her full height. "How dare you accuse me of lying! I thought you were nobly born, like me."

"That doesn't mean anything. So, if you are a Season Avatar, which one are you, then?"

"Spring."

"You would have to be a Spring. So, heal me."

The Ava Fall advanced toward Gwen, who remained silent. If she explained her powers were blocked, this woman was unlikely to accept that. The scent of wine struck Gwen. Aunt Gabri turned away, but Gwen asked, "What do you need me to heal you of, Ava? Too much wine?"

"It hurts my head, but numbs my heart." The Ava Fall sunk down on the closest chair. "By All Four, why be sober again? We all saw it happen but couldn't reach Margaret in time. Our link wasn't active, but we felt something disappear just the same. Dealing with her horse on top of that...." She shuddered. "And all for a frozen shard."

Gwen gasped. "A shard?"

"Buttercup stepped on a piece of pottery that penetrated not just her hoof, but part of her leg." The Ava Fall stared straight ahead. "No matter what I did, I couldn't heal it. I swear it swam up Buttercup's leg like a fish up a stream. I don't even know where it came from. It doesn't match anything we use here. None of the servants recognized it either."

"Did it look...very old? Ochre? With strange markings?"

Now the Ava Fall glared at her. "What do you know about it?"

Gwen extended her hand, palm up. "I have something similar embedded in my hand, and it won't come out. Since it cut me, I can't access my memories of healing. I'm lucky to remember parts of the One Oak's history."

The Ava Fall stilled. "You were cursed by a shard too? Where did it happen?"

"On my family's estate, northwest of here, near Lake Verdan."

"That's a long way away to find another piece of pottery just like the one we found here. It can't be a coincidence."

"Where could they have come from?" Gwen asked. "And who would target Avatars?"

"I have no idea. But if the shards are as old as they look, they could be from someone's pottery collection, like the one in the Winter Wing."

Gwen raised her eyebrows. "Pottery? Who collected that? I don't think anyone did. None of the Wins seemed interested in that sort of thing."

The Ava Fall smiled wanly. "No, no one is. It was a test. Ugh." She rubbed her forehead. "Are you sure you can't heal? Margaret would have flushed this wine's effects from me in a heartbeat."

Gwen raised her injured hand. "Maybe after I figure out how to treat myself first. I was hoping the Ava Spring could help me. But now what do I do?"

The Ava Fall reached for a sandwich and devoured half of it before replying, "Without Margaret, our Season is done. We can't link and send our magic out to protect Challen, and you can't link with us. You have to find the rest of your quartet and take over."

"But my magic is limited!"

"Maybe the four-fold link will break your curse. I don't know what else would. Certainly not our own magic."

"Especially since you can't even control the weather around here, Ava," Aunt Gabri snapped. She flushed as Gwen and the Ava Fall looked at her. "It's true, Ava. We couldn't drive our coach up your road."

"Ah, that's Dorian's fault. He was married to Margaret. Without her to balance him, he can be a little...unstable."

That was bad news. An Avi Win out of control could cause more damage than an Ava Spring who couldn't heal. Maybe the Ava Fall was right. Gwen would have to find the rest of her quartet and assume her traditional role. She had to admit the thought of returning to this home and meeting her three life-to-life companions again excited her more than her upcoming wedding. Maybe the four-fold link could restore her magic. Even William would have to admit the welfare of Challen came first before her marriage and children.

She sat up straight. "You're right, Ava. I hadn't expected to be needed so soon, but when the Four call us, we must answer." *Even if I'm not ready for this task either.*

Aunt Gabri gaped. "What about your wedding, niece?"

"I'll write to William and explain everything to him. He'll understand I have to put Challen first."

Aunt Gabri tsked. "Better put him first, Gwen, or there may be no wedding."

"Gwen is right, Lady lo Havil," the Ava Fall said. "We Avatars have to put our service to the Four, to Challen, and each other over everything else." She turned to Gwen. "Have you found any of the other Avatars from your year yet?"

Gwen shook her head. "Can't you help me?"

"That would have been Margaret's job, identifying the new Avatars." Sophia straightened up. "The Hall of Records in Wistica sends us information about future Avatars when they're born. We'll have to search through her office for the records." She frowned, tapping her fingers against the armrest. "Dorian would know best where they might be, but...he's in no shape to help us, I'm afraid. You'll see for yourself at dinner. In the meantime, I'll have a maid show you to your room. Someone is probably tending to your wardrobe as we speak—"

"Excuse me, Ava, but what about me?"

"Both of you may call me Sophia. 'Ava' makes my head hurt even more. If I know our butler, he already has you two assigned to adjacent guest rooms." She stood, and Gwen knew their interview was over. "Dinner will be served promptly at seven. Don't feel the need to dress formally. Even in normal times, we don't dress for dinner unless company is here."

Gwen wondered if she was considered company or the newest resident.

As promised, a maid waited outside to escort them to their rooms. Gwen guessed they were heading toward the center of the house, to neutral territory. Here, the walls were white with gold trim. Her room was similarly decorated with gold trim, countered by the dark, heavy furniture over a century old. White lace curtains and a runner on the dresser gave the room a more feminine touch. Part of her wished she could move into the Spring Wing, but it wouldn't be seemly so soon after Margaret's passing.

"Would it be possible to bathe?" she asked.

The maid bobbed her head. "Certainly...Ava." She blinked as if she couldn't believe there was another Season Avatar at the One Oak. "There's a bathing closet down the hall."

"A bathing closet? When was that put in?"

"It's been there as long as I've been working here, Ava."

Given the maid's age, that meant the bathing closet had been installed within the last fifteen to twenty years. No wonder Gwen didn't remember it. Even the bathing closet was beautiful, with a porcelain bath and hand-painted tiles depicting the full cycle of seasons. Opening the pipe allowed heated rainwater to flow into the tub. Gwen allowed herself to soak for a while, soothing away the misery of the journey to the One Oak. It would be easy to enjoy the luxury of the One Oak and forget about the rest of the world, but she knew she couldn't do that. For one thing, her father would expect a message from her telling him she'd arrived safely. And William.... Gwen lowered herself into the water. She wasn't looking forward to writing that letter.

When Gwen was done, the maid—whose name was Sylvia—assisted her in changing into her other gown and putting up her hair. Gwen retrieved her sketchbook from her reticule. "I'd like to visit the Portrait Gallery," she told Sylvia.

The maid hesitated. "You don't wish to rest, Ava?"

"No, thank you. I'm much too excited to rest. Besides, maybe I can find some more clues about my fellow Season Avatars there."

Sylvia lowered her voice. "The Avi Win might be there, Ava, and he...he hasn't been himself since the Ava Spring was taken from us."

Gwen straightened her shoulders. "I need to talk to him anyway. Don't bother showing me the way; I want to see if I remember it."

She slipped down the hallway past Aunt Gabri's room. At the end of the hall, Gwen descended the staircase to the main floor. She paused, trying to remember whether she should turn to the center of the house or retrace her way toward the main entrance. Everything had been redecorated since her last life, and the memories of how it should look clashed with the reality. Gwen rubbed her eyes, irritated at her confusion. Finally she followed a hall and discovered the Portrait Gallery at the end.

The Portrait Gallery extended past the atrium. It had no windows, but skylights in the ceiling allowed sunlight in to illuminate the paintings. Since the day was still cloudy, a pair of Delns electric lights burned on the side of each portrait.

No one in the very first group looked familiar to her, so she moved from painting to painting, scrutinizing the features of each Season Avatar. While her group was more likely to be toward the end of the gallery, Gwen enjoyed the chance to relive history. Some of pictures triggered memories; many didn't. The strongest memories came from the third-to-last portrait. A red-haired man, a brown-eyed woman with a fox, and a blonde Ava Win. Gwen stared longest at the Ava Spring in the picture, the woman she used to be. Here she had green eyes and light brown hair. She stood closest to the red-haired man; had they been married? She couldn't remember for certain.

With a sigh, Gwen read the names on the golden plaque next to the portrait. Avatars didn't run in families, so the birth records were her only hope of tracking down the other Season Avatars. She would sketch a copy of the painting anyway. Maybe she'd recognize these souls later based on some physical features they carried over from each life.

"By All Four, who are you?" a man asked.

As soon as Gwen turned to face him, she knew this must be Dorian, the Avi Win. His aura was such a deep blue it was hard to make out the furnishings surrounding him. His white suit gleamed more brightly in contrast. His hair was pure black and thick, and his eyes dark as well, but his expression seemed immobile, as if his face had frozen when his wife died.

Gwen sank into a deep curtsy. "I'm Gwendolyn lo Havil, Avi." The stillness on his face warned her not to reveal that she was an Ava Spring. "I only just found out about the Ava Spring. I'm sorry for her passing."

"How could you be when you never knew her?" Dorian stood in front of his own group portrait, staring at a blonde woman who must have been Margaret. Cold radiated from him, enough to make Gwen's skin on her arms prickle despite her long sleeves.

"I met her briefly when I was a child. She belonged to all of Challen, didn't she? Just like the rest of us Season Avatars."

He turned his head, examining her. "Aren't you a little young to be telling me that?"

"Aren't you a little old to be forgetting it?"

She shouldn't have said that; she should have covered her mouth and eaten her words. From the glare he gave her, he was considering freezing her to death right then and there. Would her healing magic return in time to save her?

He stepped toward her, close enough to catch her by the arm. "Who are you to challenge a Season Avatar?" He spoke quietly, as if icicles were forming in his breath. Gwen could imagine the God of Winter questioning a dying person with such a voice.

Gwen swallowed. "I'm one too."

"Which season? It better not be—"

"Dorian," another man called out, "come prepare for supper. There's someone Sophia wants you to meet..."

He strode forward confidently, as if he was used to dealing with irate Season Avatars. He would be; his aura was the deep green of an Avi Sum. He had the same general coloring as Sophia, with dark hair and eyes. His skin was a shade darker, as if the God of Summer had given him a perpetual tan. The jacket of his mourning suit was buttoned unevenly, and he peered around him as if he had trouble finding Dorian and Gwen.

"Oh, there you are." His gaze passed over Gwen to Dorian, then, after he blinked a few times, returned. Something about his expression made Gwen think he did that all the time. Maybe he kept his mind more focused on his plants than his surroundings. "And there she is. Dorian, this is the next Ava Spring...."

"What?" Dorian's face contorted, and Gwen jumped back before he blasted her with frost. "How can you even say such a thing, Charles? Margaret's not been gone for a moon!"

"I know that, but you know how the Four are. As soon as one season stops, the next one arrives."

"This is different." Dorian turned away from them and laid a hand on the group portrait, over his wife's face. "This end was wrong. We lost her too soon, and she can never come back the way she was...."

"She will, Dorian. You'll find her again. That's the good thing about being a Season Avatar; we'll all be reincarnated with her someday." Charles took Dorian's arm. "Come. We three need to talk."

Charles led Dorian off. Gwen crept backwards silently, grateful for the distraction the Avi Sum had provided but feeling as if she had left something undone by not facing the Avi Win herself. If she couldn't manage these Season Avatars, what would happen when she found the ones she was supposed to work with?

It'll be easier when we're all the same age—or just moons apart. I'll be the oldest, and I'll have tradition on my side. Spring always leads the Season Avatars.

She could already see how losing Margaret had set the older Season Avatars adrift. Gwen hoped she wouldn't need her healing magic to control her quartet.

CHAPTER SIX

Spring's Study

Sophia's introductions at dinner proved anticlimactic. Aunt Gabri's eyes grew wide as the plates when she met the two men, and she blushed and grew pale at turns. Dorian grunted at her, making her stammer. Charles's apologies only seemed to increase her nervousness. She stared down at her plate, eating little and saying nothing. Gwen pitied her but didn't have a chance to defend her, not when Dorian demanded as soon as the servants left, "What are you doing here?"

Gwen hoped Sophia hadn't told the other Avatars her magic had vanished. "I need to find the rest of the Season Avatars I'm supposed to work with, so I need their birth records. Otherwise, I have no way of predicting what class and gender they are this time."

"Yes, you do," Sophia said with a slight smile. "You know Fall always has female Avatars. She dislikes men for some reason. The Summer and Winter Season Avatars could be male or female. Once Dorian—" she glanced at him—"gives us access to Margaret's office, we can find the birth records."

He stared at her for a couple of moments as if not comprehending what she said.

"Dorian." Only a faint edge in her voice betrayed her impatience. "What did you do with the key to Margaret's study?"

"There are things in there she wanted kept private, Sophia. Can't you respect her wishes?"

"She's past all that now. We still have a job to do."

Dorian jerked his head in Gwen's direction. "Not for long, if you let her have her way."

Charles shook his head. "You know we can't send our magic throughout Challen without Margaret. We have to find the new Season Avatars who can link with Gwen."

"And then do what, hand over the keys to the One Oak as well?"

The soup had frozen over, so Gwen set her spoon down. Was that what was bothering Dorian, the fear of losing his lifelong home? She cleared her throat. "The three of you will be welcome to share the One Oak with us for as long as you wish," she said. "It's big enough for all of us, and I'm sure we could use your guidance."

Dorian turned to study her, the hostility in his eyes fading for a moment. "Margaret...Margaret would have done something like that."

Perhaps this was going to work out. Gwen smiled encouragingly at him.

"But are you going to share the weather too?"

"Share the weather?" Gwen stared at him. What did he mean by that?

"You don't understand weather magic. None of you do." Dorian rose, pointing first at Gwen, then at the empty spot at the head of the table. "Two healers? Wonderful; there's never enough magic to heal everyone in Challen. Two users of animal or plant magic? There might be some overlap, but it can be managed. But two Avi or Ava Wins can't work weather magic together. It makes the Chaos Season worse instead of better. So, when—or if—you find the Ava Win, what will you do with me?"

Gwen stared at him, mouth open. Yes, losing her own magic was worse than losing a limb. But Dorian had to know this would happen, so why wasn't he better prepared for it? Wasn't he supposed to put the interests of Challen ahead of his own?

"No one is kicking you out of the One Oak tomorrow, or even next moon," Sophia said. "It's going to take some time before Gwen finds the rest of her group and they're ready to take over from us. You'll still have plenty of time to use your magic. So can't you let us into Margaret's study?"

He stared at her without answering. The soup had thawed into unappetizing chunks. Even though the roast ducks and vegetables were still warm, Gwen had no desire to eat with the tension between Dorian and Sophia hovering in the air.

Charles finally shrugged and said, "Why don't I just break the door down?"

"You know he can do it," Sophia said to Dorian. She didn't seem surprised by Charles's offer, making Gwen wonder if the two of them had planned this ultimatum together.

Dorian drew his thick eyebrows together. "Fine, have it your way. I'll look for the key."

"You don't know where it is? Why didn't you just say so?"

"It's probably in one of her reticules. How am I supposed to keep track of them all?" He reached out and tore a wing off of the nearest bird. "I'll have the maids look through them tomorrow morning."

Sophia inclined her head formally. "Thank you, Dorian."

Charles leaned over toward Gwen. In a stage whisper, he said, "There's always one rebel in every quartet. Good luck managing yours."

"There is?" Her question came out louder than she intended, and the other Season Avatars chuckled.

Gwen steeled herself to ignore their amusement at her expense. Soon she would know the names—and hopefully locations—of the three Season Avatars she would work and live with for the rest of this life. The question was how well they would get along, or if they would be as uncooperative as Dorian. She pictured in her mind the red-haired man and two women from her past life, but memories of their personalities refused to materialize.

* * *

Gwen woke the next morning feeling groggy. Half-forgotten dreams tore at her mind, making her struggle to remember who or when she was. When consciousness fully returned, she rushed to get ready for breakfast. Maybe today she'd find some key to unlocking her memories.

Dorian presented himself at the breakfast buffet with a topaz-encrusted keyring. "One of the maids found it last night."

Sophia reached for it, "Thank you, Dorian—"

"Not so fast. I'm coming with you. I want to make sure you don't disturb anything."

"Perfect," Sophia countered. "You can help us search."

"I didn't agree to that."

"Suit yourself." Sophia threw her hands in the air. "Just let us do what we need to do. You're making this much harder than it has to be."

Staring at Gwen, Dorian said, "It doesn't have to be at all."

Gwen narrowed her eyes. Was that a threat?

"Oh, stop being so childish," Sophia said. "Or is your magic strong enough to take on Chaos Season all by yourself?"

Dorian scowled, still clutching his wife's keys. But once breakfast was over, he led them up two flights of stairs to the Ava Spring's private study. Gwen didn't want to upset him again, so she tried to suppress her reactions. Still, everything was there: the round stained-glass window of daffodils, violets, and lilies in the sitting room; the honey-colored pianoforte in the corner; and the painting of a cherry orchard in bloom done by one of Challen's first great artists, Stephan p'Minnd. She knew as soon as she saw it that it was a favorite of hers, and she studied it while Dorian sorted through the keys until he unlocked the study. When Gwen heard the door click open, she followed the others inside.

Bookshelves lined the room, but only a few shelves were filled. Some of the books they held appeared centuries old—or at least covered with a century's worth of dust. One wall was covered by a map so detailed Gwen thought she might find her family's estate marked on it. However, the most important piece of furniture in the room was the secretary desk. The rolltop was still up, exposing what appeared to be a hundred cubbies. Folded letters, many plain, but others bearing ornate seals, were scattered across the surface, although some were stacked in a crooked pile. Quills and ink had been gathered in a corner of the desk. A dish of nuts and a moldy cup of chocolate had been pushed into the other corner.

Sophia wrinkled her nose. "Really, Dorian, you should have let the maids clean this mess up sooner." She pulled a bell rope in the corner.

He didn't respond to her. "It's like she just stepped away for a few moments before coming back," he muttered, selecting a quill and examining it. "Why isn't she coming back?" He glared at the ceiling. "You tell me why she isn't coming back, Four!"

Sophia pulled the chair far away from the desk, then guided Dorian over to it with far more care than he seemed to deserve. He sank into it, still engrossed with the quill.

"You must have really loved Margaret." Gwen felt awkward intruding on his grief, but the previous Ava Spring's presence still dominated the room, making it hard to ignore Dorian.

"She was my sunshine," he said. "We came here when we were only seventeen for training. I thought at first she was bossy, and she... well, I won't tell you what she thought of me." The tips of his ears turned pink. "But after our first Chaos Season, we understood each other much better...and we've been together ever since." Dorian sighed. "I don't know what to do with myself anymore without her."

How sad, yet how romantic. Gwen wondered if William felt the same way about her. She'd been too busy to think about him much the last couple of days. Would that change after they got married—if they still got married?

Sophia drifted over to Dorian and laid a hand on his shoulder. "Are you sure you want to do this, Dorian? We can take care of it ourselves."

He shook his head. "Being here reminds me of her."

After a couple of moments, when it became apparent he was going to sit there without helping them, Gwen and Sophia started to search for Margaret's records. Gwen dug into each nook of the desk, discovering everything from dead spiders to odd buttons and quills too short to use. Sophia matched keys to the desk drawers. She pulled each one out; after Gwen finished her task, she joined Sophia in sorting through piles of faded letters and account books. But they didn't find any birth records.

"Are you sure Margaret had them?" Gwen asked after they finished. "Could she have sent them back to the Record Hall in Wistica?"

"No reason to do that. They would have made copies for her; they wouldn't let the originals leave the building."

Perhaps it would be easier for Gwen to travel there. At least the workers there would be sure to have the documents on hand. But the records had to be somewhere in this room, and Gwen couldn't walk away from them without looking harder.

"Could she have put them somewhere else?" She looked at both of the older Season Avatars, hoping they would give her some insights into Margaret. "Where did she put special documents? Did she have a secret hiding place?"

Dorian and Sophia stared at her for a long moment. "You're an Ava Spring, Gwen," Sophia said gently. "Do you really think you could keep something like that out of the link?"

Gwen flushed before she had a chance to control her physical reaction, but she stuck her chin forward. "Depending on what we were doing or thinking, possibly."

Would Margaret have had a reason to keep the birth records secret from her other Season Avatars? That didn't make sense; the other three had a right to access the records in Wistica too. Then again, why would they bother? The only reason Gwen could think of was if they were curious about their successors, but Sophia and Charles hadn't seemed to care about that in the wake of Margaret's death. Dorian, on the other hand, wanted to protect his own status as the Avi Win. Maybe Margaret hadn't wanted to upset him by letting him know his successor was growing up somewhere in Challen.

If Margaret's own fellow Avatars couldn't figure out what she did with the records, then I guess I have to. I may not be able to heal like a Spring, but I can still think like one. Gwen rose and paced around the room, studying the décor and furnishings. If the birth records were meant for her as the next Ava Spring, then they might be hidden in something spring-related, like flowers or the color yellow. Or healing...

Gwen stopped as she read a book title: *An Introduction to the Human Body, with Illustrations.* That was something she needed to read even if it didn't have the birth records. Was she imagining things, or was it less dusty than some of the other books? The binding was worn, as if it had been frequently consulted.

She examined the cover, then flipped through the book. A page fluttered to the floor. At first, it appeared to be just a letter, but Gwen's heart raced when she glanced at the signature and seal. She didn't know the name, but the seal—a book guarded by a sword—was from the Records Hall in Wistica.

"Is that it?" Sophia asked.

Gwen edged closer to the window. The letter was dated three years ago; the ink hadn't faded much—it must be a special blend—but the handwriting was cramped. Even so, she was able to pick out her own name, followed by the date of her birth and the location of her family's estate. She knew all that; where was the information she needed?

She studied the next paragraph, holding the paper at different angles to make sure she didn't misread a letter. "For Summer, we have another Ava by the name of Jenna Dorshay," she read out loud. "Born to Frank and Jenny Dorshay, farmers, living outside of the town of Bull Rock, in the northeast section of Challen."

"A farmer's child." Sophia nodded. "It makes sense. Charles's father was noble, but he loved breeding plants in his garden. The Four like placing us in areas where we can gain some practical experience before coming here."

"Where is Bull Rock?" Gwen asked.

Sophia prodded Dorian until he looked away from the quill. "Can you find Bull Rock, Dorian?"

Grumbling, he rose and studied the map on the wall for a couple of heartbeats before tapping a dot. Gwen leaned in close to read the name. From the size of the lettering, Bull Rock had to be even smaller than Lake Verdan. But Bull Rock was close to the One Oak, probably a day by horseback, longer by carriage.

"If she's not far from here, you'd think she'd come herself, instead of making me go after her," Gwen said.

Dorian looked up. "Could be the roads are bad, or she has other things tying her there. Spring would be a busy season for her."

"Would you happen to know anything about the roads?" Sophia asked a little too sweetly.

"Do you expect me to control every cloud and wind burst by myself?"

"I'm sure you'd try."

Gwen edged away from them, trying to concentrate on the letter. The next part didn't sound right. She could make out the name—Kay Seltich—and her place of birth—Wistica, Winter Quarter. But her current location was unknown. Even stranger, she was listed as the next Ava Win, not the next Ava Fall. Had the letter writer gone out of order for some reason?

Gwen read the final paragraph: "Unfortunately, we have no records for an Ava Fall. There were absolutely no births in Challen on the Fall Equinox fifteen years ago."

She rubbed her eyes, but the words didn't change.

Impossible. The Four would never incarnate only three from a quartet. Perhaps there had been a mistake in the record-keeping. Maybe the midwife had gotten the date wrong if the girl had been born close to midnight. Maybe the child's birth record hadn't been sent to Wistica, even though Challen law required it. This was an important birth, almost as important as a royal child. Why would anyone not want that acknowledged?

"Still can't find the records?" Sophia asked.

Gwen smoothed away her frown. "I have two of the names, not three."

Dorian turned toward her. "Which one is missing?"

"The Ava Fall."

He shrugged. "Not my season. Are you done in here? Good. I'd like to be alone for a while."

He pulled the chair up to the desk and examined his wife's belongings as if they contained a clue to the reason behind her death. Still clutching the letter, Gwen followed Sophia back to the hallway.

"What do I do now?" Gwen asked the older woman.

"Well, if I were you, I'd find the other Avatars and bring them back here."

"I don't even have all the names!"

"I'm sorry." Sophia lifted her hands. "If the Hall of Records doesn't have them, then they can't be found."

Gwen placed her hands on her hips. "That's it? You're not going to do anything else?"

Sophia closed her eyes and turned her head away from Gwen. After a few heartbeats, she said, "The only anilink I can sense is Brighteyes. Like Dorian, my magic won't reach across Challen anymore either. Brighteyes can tell the other crows to look out for someone your age with magic, but even though crows are smart, they're not as smart as a person."

It was a small hope, but it was all Gwen had at the moment. She retreated to her room to figure out what to do next.

* * *

"Gwen, stop pacing and come help me with this puzzle," Aunt Gabri said. "Your eyes are much younger than mine."

"I've got to figure out why there aren't any records regarding the Ava Fall." She twitched her skirt out of the way as she passed close to the table where her aunt was working. "It's important."

"You keep driving and driving yourself without a break. Do you really think the Four insist you work all the time and never have any fun?"

Puzzles weren't Gwen's idea of fun, but she couldn't figure out where the missing Ava Fall was when her aunt kept talking. She sighed as she drew up a chair.

They sat in a small parlor not far from their rooms. The curtains were drawn, shutting out the grey rain. Gwen wondered if the weather in the rest of Challen was this miserable or if Dorian was doing a better job of restoring spring. The shelves and paintings lining the walls made her feel closed in and only increased her desire to pace. The puzzle Aunt Gabri had found wasn't much of a distraction. It was scenic enough, a view of Wistica from the harbor, but she needed to be in the city talking to the record keepers, not looking at pictures of it.

"Why would anyone not want to mark the birth of a Season Avatar?" She picked up an edge piece and tried it at the bottom of the puzzle, but it didn't fit. "We do important work. Challen wouldn't be livable, let alone prosperous, without us to tame Chaos Season."

"There's more to Challen than the Chaos Season and the Season Avatars," Aunt Gabri said.

Gwen stared at her. "You barely step out of your house because of Chaos Season, Aunt Gabri. What do you know about Challen?"

"More than you think I do, niece. I attended the university in Wistica when I was your age. I even made some long-lost friends there and met your uncle."

Aunt Gabri stared off into the distance. Gwen wondered if she was remembering her youth or the Chaos Season that had killed Uncle Hal. Finally Aunt Gabri sighed and said, "How are you at history?"

"As good as anyone else, I guess." Gwen tried another spot; still no match. "I know my Season Avatars and monarchs—"

"Interesting that you put the Season Avatars ahead of the kings and queens. I don't think His Royal Majesty would approve."

His Royal Majesty came from the same family who had conquered Challen, the family that provided Avatars for the Fip God of War. How could a Season Avatar approve of that? "I respect the monarchy," Gwen said carefully. "I just serve the Four first."

"Do you think he would see it that way?" Her aunt grinned unpleasantly. "Or would he worry you threaten the crown? The Season Avatars have done so before, you know."

Gwen's cheeks grew warm. "The Fips should have left Challen alone. Why do they need to conquer the world?"

"You see, Gwen? The king has reason to keep an eye on the Season Avatars, after all."

Gwen looked up from the puzzle. "You think he thinks the next Ava Fall was a traitor, and so he doesn't want her to take her rightful place? You think he suppressed her birth record?" She lowered her voice. "Now you're the one talking against the king!"

"Maybe he did, maybe he didn't. You have to look at everything, Gwen." Aunt Gabri glanced at the pieces, selected one, and snapped it into place on her first try. "See, you have your own puzzle, but you're missing one of the pieces. Sometimes you can figure out what goes where by looking at what goes next to it."

"I don't have enough information yet." She retrieved the letter from her reticule and reread it. Something came to her. "Aunt Gabri, if the Ava Fall is a missing puzzle piece, then do you think if I find Jenna and Kay, I'll figure out how she fits into the quartet?"

Approval shone in her eyes. "It's possible."

"Then that settles it." Gwen rose. "I'll talk to the Season Avatars right now and see if they can lend me a coach in the morning to take us to Bull Rock."

Another piece fell from Aunt Gabri's hand. "Tomorrow? So soon?"

"Why wait? Challen needs new Season Avatars, and I need to restore my healing magic."

"What if they're already on the way to the One Oak, just like you were drawn here? Someone should stay behind and meet them."

"Sophia can handle that."

Aunt Gabri groaned. "Gwendolyn, how long is it going to take to find all the other Season Avatars?"

"How can I know when we have no idea where the Ava Fall or Ava Win are? Meeting Jenna will be simple compared to those."

Aunt Gabri pushed the puzzle pieces away from her. "It's just...when your father asked me to accompany you to the One Oak, I thought it would just be a few days, maybe a week, before I could return home. This could take moons. I should be home reading novels and drinking chocolate."

"You can always do that. Just think, when you return home, you'll have lots of stories to tell the neighbors."

"Yes, lots of stories about uncomfortable carriages and dirty inns. No, thank you."

Next she'd be protesting that her old bones needed to rest some more before chasing Gwen around Challen. It was a pity Gwen couldn't do more to help her with that—or her aunt's homesickness.

"If you really want to go home, I won't stop you," she said. "Maybe Sophia would come with me instead, or I can hire a maid."

Aunt Gabri shook her head. "Your father would scold me for the rest of my life if I abandoned you now. No, I know my duty. That doesn't mean I'll like it, though."

Gwen sighed with relief. If getting from the lo Havil estate to the One Oak had been more challenging than she'd realized, traveling across the entire country would be more than all her previous lives had prepared her for. It was good to have a companion, no matter how reluctant.

She leaned over and kissed her aunt's cheek. "Thank you, Aunt Gabri."

Her aunt's eyes shone, and Gwen realized maybe she had felt left out, being a normal person surrounded by Season Avatars. She wondered if William would feel the same way when they got married...or if they got married.

"Oh, by All Four." She sat down again. "Would you believe I forgot about the wedding next moon? I'd better write to William and ask him to postpone it."

"If you do that, he might cancel it altogether." Aunt Gabri's eyes grew round with horror. "Then what would your prospects be, with that stain on your record?"

"A stain on my record?" Gwen wanted to blurt out how lewd William had been before she left, but before she could continue, her aunt nodded.

"Dashing around the country when you're supposed to be preparing for your wedding. The gentlemen will think you don't take marriage seriously."

Gwen let out a harsh laugh. "I'm supposed to let the country go to ruin so I can make sure my trousseau is complete?" Even Aunt Gabri had to see the problem with that.

Aunt Gabri shook her head. "Are you willing to ruin your family's future instead?"

Speechless, Gwen stared at her aunt for a string of fast heartbeats before rising and exiting the room.

Ruin the lo Havils' future? Honestly! Her full skirt caught on a knickknack, which fell to the floor when she tugged the cloth free. *I'm not pledging myself to Fall and becoming a spinster. Avatars can marry. I should have no problem conceiving and bearing children— when I'm ready for them.*

Gwen swallowed as she stopped by a mirror in the hall. Her expression was too unhappy to be that of a bride.

Even if I am a Season Avatar, I'm still a woman too. It's not that I don't want to get married; I just don't know if I want to be married to William. At least he won't have to worry about me cheating on him with a Season Avatar when we're all women.

She would have to write him and explain the situation before embarking on her trip to Bull Rock. Depending on how he responded, she'd have to decide if it was worth going through with the marriage or upsetting her family and William's by breaking the engagement.

CHAPTER SEVEN

Bull Rock

Although the Season Avatars didn't travel as much as they used to, they still maintained fine carriages. The coach-and-four that would carry Gwen and her aunt to Bull Rock featured the Season Avatars' insignia—an acorn, an oak with green leaves, a tree in autumn foliage, and one with bare branches—on the doors. More acorns and oak leaves were carved into the trim. Inside, the deep blue cushions protected them from the jouncing far better than the thin pads in public transport—or even the lo Havil carriage. The interior had been painted with a sky scene so detailed Gwen could identify which hawks were soaring into the clouds. Despite the luxury, as they made their way toward the road, Aunt Gabri clutched the door handle so tightly Gwen wondered which would fall off first, the handle or the fingers.

"Don't worry, Aunt Gabri." She smiled, but her aunt didn't copy the gesture. "This trip should be much easier than the one here. Since it's an official mission from the Season Avatars, I have permission to spend their chals as necessary. The coachman knows the way to Bull Rock, and I'm sure I won't have a problem identifying Jenna in such a small town. What can go wrong?"

"What about the weather?" Aunt Gabri lifted the shade covering her window.

Dorian had promised before they left that he'd ensure proper weather for this time of year, though Gwen suspected part of the reason he did so was because of Sophia pressuring him. By All Four, if he was so obsessed with using his weather magic, why not do it properly? Still, when her aunt shut her eyes, Gwen peeked out the window herself. Sunny and clear, though perhaps a trifle more chilly than she would have preferred. She was grateful for the coat Sophia had lent her. Made of waterproof wool, it was lined with silk and stuffed with soft down, suitable for withstanding the worst of Chaos Season.

Soon I'll be standing in the middle of it with my fellow Season Avatars—or should I call them sister Season Avatars? I hope they're easy to get along with, not like Dorian.

"You say this Jenna we're supposed to meet is a farmer's daughter?" Aunt Gabri asked. "I hope she's not too dreadful. She'll have no idea how to get along in polite society."

Gwen grimaced. That could be awkward, not so much in their group, but when they held balls and parties at the One Oak. The current Season Avatars might not show much interest in entertaining, especially after losing their leader, but once Gwen and her companions conquered their first Chaos Season, she intended to celebrate.

Gwen took a deep breath. "Actually, if you study the biographies of previous Season Avatars, you'll see that they come from all different backgrounds, from the poorest to the richest."

Aunt Gabri looked scandalized. "If you really serve the Four, why don't They ensure all Season Avatars are nobly born? Isn't that a reward for virtue?"

"We're sent to lives that will help us understand our magic and the needs of Challen better. Jenna needs to work with plants, so she'll get plenty of practice on a farm."

Secretly, though, she was grateful she'd been born to a noble life this time. It would make it easier for her to lead the others with the advantage of natural rank, and she could help them with proper etiquette when the time came.

The trip back to Midpoint was much shorter than the one from it had been, now that the weather was cooperating. They halted briefly to provide for the horses and purchase some still-hot stuffed pastries for lunch. Gwen promised the stable mistress a groom from the One Oak would return her horses, along with thanks from the Ava Fall and a wallet of chals. Aunt Gabri's coachman transferred their luggage to the Avatars' coach and set off for home. He carried letters for Gwen's father and William. Gwen wondered when—or how—one of William's letters would find her. Had he recovered from his snow sickness? Did he still care for her?

The route to Bull Rock veered away from the path to Lake Verdan. Gwen watched the scenery for a while, but the corn and wheat fields here looked very much the same as they did back home—all mud and standing water. She finished reading her aunt's romance novel out loud and started another, much the same.

"Don't you have any set outside Challen?" she asked.

Aunt Gabri started. "Huh? What?"

"Do you have any books about other countries? I'll never see them, so it would be nice to learn more about them."

"I don't think so. You should have said something when we were back in Midpoint. We won't be able to find any books in the middle of a cornfield."

It didn't look like there was anything out here. With the sun sinking toward the horizon, it was time to start wondering where to spend the night. Before Gwen could ask, the coachman, James, turned off of the main road onto a dirt path.

"I know the farmers who live here, young Ava," he said. "Their house isn't as fine as the One Oak, but they'll be willing to put you up for the night for a few chals—and maybe some magic."

Gwen shifted uneasily on the seat. Chals might have to do. Aunt Gabri complained about the bedbugs and rats and other pests that were bound to keep her up all night, but Gwen didn't respond. Instead, she stared out at the rain-soaked fields, too wet for plowing or sowing. Dorian needed to resume his duties as soon as possible.

James brought them to a wooden farmhouse. A stocky woman whose lined face told stories about her lifetime of chores came outside, followed by a pair of girls and a toddling boy. Her sleeves were rolled up, exposing her marriage tattoo—and a thumb-sized mole with a jagged edge. She greeted James, then stared at Gwen and Aunt Gabri. "You're not the regular Season Avatars," she said.

"No. I'm the soon-to-be Ava Spring, Lady Gwendolyn lo Havil. This is my aunt, Lady Gabri lo Havil." Gwen stared at the woman's mole. "Your pardon, Dame, but how long have you had that mole?"

"You mean my farmer's mark?" She squinted as she rolled her arm to look at it. "I think I first noticed it last summer. Why?"

"I'd like to examine it." Gwen clenched her fist, and the embedded shard shifted under her skin. Freeze it, she shouldn't have said anything. What if she couldn't treat the woman successfully? But everything about that mole looked wrong to her.

"After I get you settled and finish dinner," the woman said as she shooed the children back into the house.

Gwen sat at the long wooden table and sipped hard cider as she waited, fingering the shard as she tried to figure out how to work around it.

The farmers served her fried eggs, fresh bread, and potatoes. Gwen gobbled it down until she noticed the woman had given her the biggest portion. When she forced herself to turn down another serving, the children devoured the leftovers.

"Thank you for the dinner, Dame," Gwen said. "Now, you must let me repay you by checking your arm."

The woman sighed. "If you must. Elsa, clear the table."

Gwen grabbed the woman's arm with both hands and examined it magically. Some details, like the woman's bones, were clearer than others, like her skin and blood. Gwen shifted her grip, and the view changed. Now she couldn't make out the woman's wrist, even though it was right under her hand.

Of course! That's the hand with the shard! Gwen released the woman's wrist, and she was able to study the mole without interference. Something about it felt separate, wrong. Gwen tried to isolate it so she could grow new flesh around it and remove it from the arm. However, although she managed to encase it in new growth, it wouldn't come off. She tried several times, but she had to stop before she made the bump too large.

"I'm sorry, Dame. This is a stubborn one." She smiled weakly, resisting the urge to wipe her hand on her dress. "Maybe I can try it again in the morning."

"That's all right...Ava." The woman rose. "Of course, if the fields are dry enough tomorrow, I'll be needed out there."

Gwen wished she could help with that, or with anything else. But at least she'd achieved a partial victory. She could manage some healing with her unaffected hand. Gwen prayed to the Goddess of Spring that she'd delayed the woman's disease enough so that she would still be alive once Gwen recovered her healing magic. If she ever did.

* * *

Gwen woke to find the farmer and his wife already in the field, with the oldest girl left behind to serve breakfast. The travelers were on the road not two hours after dawn. The weather promised to be spring-like; Gwen prayed it would last. They should reach Bull Rock by lunchtime. Hopefully the hamlet would have an inn where they could eat—and where Gwen could inquire about Jenna.

"What do you think this farm girl will be like?" Aunt Gabri asked. She stared out the window as if she found the unchanging farmland more interesting than the answer.

"If she's the reincarnation of the last Avi Sum I worked with, then she used to be Jacob Raddes."

Aunt Gabri sucked in her breath. "*The* Jacob Raddes?"

"I doubt there was more than one. What do you know of him?"

"He was quite the rake! From serving girls to noblewomen, they say he bedded them all!"

Gwen blushed so quickly she couldn't stop it. Her aunt's words triggered a flood of memories, discovering Jacob with another woman in some hidden corner of the One Oak. The locations and the women changed, but not him or his promises to stop. But he always was so contrite afterward, so eager to make it up to her, sharing so much pleasure through their link she couldn't help but take him back....

"I don't know why his wife would put up with such a thing, unless she was one of the Season Avatars."

Gwen ungritted her teeth long enough to say, "Yes, she was."

Aunt Gabri peered over at her. "Are you all right, dear? A touch of indigestion from that farmer food?"

"I'm perfectly well, Aunt Gabri."

Gwen turned to contemplate the farmhouses herself. She wished she'd thought to bring along some biographies about Jacob and the other Season Avatars she'd worked with. How trustworthy were her own memories? How much would Jenna be like Jacob? Had she learned her lessons from her previous life, or would she repeat them? Gwen firmed her mouth. At least she couldn't marry Jenna this time. Maybe it wasn't fair to judge Jenna by her past-life actions before they'd even met. The Four in Their wisdom had decreed they should be Season Avatars together again. Gwen just hoped They'd also given her the fortitude to endure Jenna for another lifetime.

The sun was directly overhead by the time they reached the outskirts of Bull Rock. The only way Gwen could tell was by the sign next to a large rock. As they drove by, Gwen studied it. From the back, it did look a little like a bull with lowered horns. "This would be a better place to find an Ava Fall, to tame that bull."

Aunt Gabri stared at her blankly, as if she didn't understand the joke. Gwen didn't bother explaining it.

Bull Rock was even smaller than Lake Verdan. The street was dustier, the stores fewer, and the buildings in need of repair. Only a few people were in evidence: the elderly or those incapacitated in some way and unable to farm. She winced as she saw a one-handed youth awkwardly sweeping a storefront. Even when Gwen's magic was working, she couldn't replace a maimed or amputated hand. The windows bore thick shutters instead of curtains, and the buildings were solid, ready to endure anything the Chaos Season thrust upon the hamlet.

James slowed the coach. "Ava, where do you want to stop?"

"If they have an inn or pub, try there first. If not, then the general store." Food first, then talk with the locals to find Jenna. It shouldn't be hard to find her in such a small town; she'd stick out like a rose in a vegetable garden.

James stopped the coach at the biggest building, in the middle of the main street. The few people on the street gathered around as Gwen and her aunt descended from the coach. Gwen automatically scanned the crowd for someone with a Season-Avatar-strong aura—without success. The auras were a mix of colors from all the seasons, but none of them matched Charles's aura. Gwen hadn't expected to meet Jenna the instant she set foot in Bull Rock, though it would have made her task easier. Perhaps someone here could help her.

Gwen tilted her chin up. "Excuse me." She raised her voice. "I'm looking for Jenna Dorshay. Can any of you tell me where to find her?"

She caught a few mutterings: "Don't know a Jenna by that name," "Could she mean..." "No, that was another Jenna." "That's not even her name; it's Henna."

"The Dorshays don't live in town," an old woman in the back of the crowd called out. "Their farm is four or five miles that way, by the pond." She pointed to the left.

"Thank you." Gwen gave the woman a chal. "Come on, Aunt Gabri. Let's eat something before we drive out to the farm."

"Not another dirty place with animals running about," Aunt Gabri complained as they entered the pub.

The only sign of dirt in the pub was the smoke-stained fireplace at the end of the room. Five tables with three or four chairs each filled the room, making Gwen wonder how small this town was. What did they do for entertainment at the end of a long day? How did they celebrate the solstices and the equinoxes if there was nowhere to gather?

The owner of the pub, a middle-aged woman named Bettina, ushered them to the table closest to the unlit fireplace. Her hair was pulled back in a severe bun, and her dress covered everything save her face and hands. Her smile, though hospitable, seemed forced as she apologized over and over for the poor fare her humble place provided, unworthy of such fine ladies as Gwen and her aunt. It was enough to make Gwen lose her appetite.

As Bettina struggled to open a wine bottle, she asked, "If I may be so bold, ladies, what brings you to our small town?"

"I'm looking for someone." Gwen scrutinized the pub owner. "Jenna Dorshay. Do you know where I could find her?"

The knife slipped, almost slicing open Bettina's hand. "That...that wench! By All Four, why would you look for her?"

"She's the next Ava Sum, and it's time for her to visit the One Oak."

The bottle crashed on the floor. Bettina's face flushed red, then grew pale. "Sally! Bring the mop!" She turned back to Gwen. "Is it really true? How would you know?"

Aunt Gabri beamed. "My niece is the next Ava Spring."

Bettina curtseyed several times. "I'm so sorry for the mess, Ava. Let me fetch you another bottle." She scurried away.

Sounds like Jenna is no better than Jacob was. Gwen clenched her napkin. This was not going to go over well with Aunt Gabri. As for her, maybe the Four should have mixed up the Avatar quartets and let Gwen work with someone else this lifetime. It would be less awkward for all of them.

Sure enough, a few heartbeats later, Aunt Gabri said, "Gwendolyn, this Jenna...she doesn't sound as if she's suitable to be a Season Avatar."

Gwen stared at the fireplace. "If she has half the magic she did in her previous life, she is."

"But she doesn't sound at all...ladylike. Of course the poor child probably never learned proper manners growing up in a place like this, but still...it sounds like she might not even be decent!"

"I know." Gwen sighed. "Some things never change from life to life."

"You mean...she was like this before?"

Gwen nodded.

"Then you have to find someone else!" Aunt Gabri smacked her gloves on the table.

"Aunt Gabri, there is no one else. Only Avatars are born on days of season change. That's how we tracked Jenna down in the first place."

"But...she'll corrupt you! I can't believe you ran away from your own wedding for this." Aunt Gabri shook her head sadly. "If William won't take you, who will?"

"Hopefully someone who won't be jealous of my fellow Season Avatars before I even meet them," Gwen snapped.

Aunt Gabri's eyes opened wide, but before she could speak, Bettina returned with more wine and apologies. Gwen waved them aside. "All I want to know is where I can find Jenna. Please."

With another melodramatic huff, Bettina said, "Two doors down, in the general store. She's the shopkeeper—"

Gwen didn't wait to hear the rest. She grabbed her reticule and dashed out of the pub. When she got to the street, she turned right, searching for the general store.

I can't believe I'm finally going to meet one of the Season Avatars I'm going to work with. Conscious of more locals gaping at her, Gwen forced herself to walk sedately. No need to be out of breath when she met Jenna. *I wonder what she remembers. I wonder what I'll remember about her. Maybe it's a good thing my memories are vague. It's a new life; I should give her a fresh start.*

Then again, some Avatars never changed.

Gwen looked in the window of the second store, but it wasn't the general store; it looked more like a school. Several young children sat at a table as the teacher paced back and forth, reading from a book. Gwen turned away before the others stared at her. She must have gone the wrong way from the pub. *How embarrassing.* This time, she forced the blush out of her face. Sauntering as if she'd meant to do that all along, she strolled back the way she'd come. The few people out on the street converged in front of what Gwen assumed really was the general store. *Freeze it, I bet they knew all along who I was looking for. They could have told me where she was right away.*

"By All Four, maybe this is the right Jenna!" Someone in the crowd whispered, but Gwen still heard him.

"I told you." An older woman chortled with pleasure.

Gwen paused in front of the crowd. "A little privacy, good people, if you please. I'd like to speak to Jenna alone."

"But we've never met a real Season Avatar!" someone protested. "We want to see magic!"

Gwen tried to shoo them away, but they surged toward her. She stepped back and raised her hands. "Perhaps later you can see some magic." Maybe linking with Jenna would help her recover her talent. "But I really must speak to Jenna first—"

"No! Show us your magic first!"

They swarmed around her, all talking at once so she couldn't follow what a single one of them said. Their combined breath stank, not just from smelly food, but from rotted teeth. If only she could fix them. She could have tolerated one at a time, but the crowd was overwhelming.

"What's all this ruckus?" a young woman said in a carrying voice. "How can I get Robbie to nap with all this noise?"

Everyone fell silent and backed away from Gwen. It was easy to see why; the newcomer stood nearly a hand taller than Gwen, and she carried a broom as if she meant to sweep everyone else away. But what made Gwen suck her breath in was the bright green aura surrounding her.

This was Jenna. Gwen was about to introduce herself when she noticed a small yellow aura nearly disguised by Jenna's.

Jenna cradled a baby next to her heart.

CHAPTER EIGHT

Jenna

By All Four Gods and Goddesses, Jenna hadn't even waited to become a Season Avatar before she started having children. Had she had a fling? It would fit her character, though it was sad she hadn't learned her lesson from previous lives. The friendly introduction Gwen had planned for this moment was overshadowed by the instinct to comment on the child. She bit down on her lips to keep herself silent instead; one ill-picked word could set her entire relationship with Jenna on the wrong path.

Jenna strode forward as if it was normal for her to confront speechless noblewomen. Her appearance didn't fit with what Gwen had been told about her being a farm girl. Although her dress was mourning white, embroidery enlivened the button-down sleeves and low neckline. It was too clean for Jenna to have been working outside. Perhaps she was in town running errands, but then why bring a child with her? Her child rested in a sling that matched her gown. Her red hair had been braided and coiled up; it was a style for someone planning to keep her hair out of her face while she worked, but it was still fancier than something a farm girl would wear. Most of the field girls at

Gwen's family's estate braided their hair and left it at that. A single silver chain glittered at Jenna's throat.

She must be trying to better her station. Perhaps she ....offered herself to someone in exchange for trinkets and fancy clothes. Gwen swallowed, suddenly repulsed by the images in her head. *That would explain the child. But why did she bother selling herself for so little when she stands to share in the One Oak's wealth?*

Jenna halted, staring at Gwen with eyes as green as her aura. "By All Four, who are you?" Her voice was low for a woman. "I feel like I should know you, but I've never seen you before in my life."

"That's no way to talk to a lady," Aunt Gabri admonished from the back of the crowd. When had she left the pub?

Gwen took a deep breath. Neither the crowd nor Aunt Gabri mattered now. There was only Jenna.

"I'm Lady Gwendolyn lo Havil. And I'm your sister Ava Spring."

Jenna's eyes widened for an instant, but she nodded as if she had expected this all along. "Are we needed back at the One Oak?"

Gwen nodded in return, unsure if she should tell Jenna why in front of this crowd.

"It's about freezing time!" The babe stirred briefly at Jenna's harsh words, but it didn't cry. "I've been waiting my whole life to go there. Why won't the Four let us grow up there instead of wherever they put us?"

Gwen's hackles stirred. "We're supposed to learn from our families and our surroundings." *Is she going to question everything?*

Jenna didn't speak, but the scornful expression in her eyes stated exactly how she felt about the life the Four had given her.

Despite Jenna's anger, Gwen stepped closer to her. The instinct to touch her, to link with her, was strong, but she didn't want to do it with so many people watching. "We need to talk. Is there someplace private we can go?"

"Yes, Thomas's store. Come with me."

Jenna led Gwen back through the crowd, which had grown when Gwen wasn't paying attention. Aunt Gabri caught Gwen's sleeve. "Is this the...the girl you were looking for?" she whispered. "I told you she'd be trouble."

"Aunt Gabri, let me talk to her. In private."

Her aunt put on a hurt expression. "I'm your chaperone."

"I don't think she'll put my virtue at risk. Besides, Jenna and I need to talk about Season Avatar affairs."

"I'm still coming."

The crowd pressed around them, so there was nowhere Gwen could send her. Jenna opened the store door wide enough for the three of them to step through, then shoved it closed and locked it with one hand. The noise outside died, giving Gwen a moment of peace to look around.

The store looked bare; a few tins of salt and sugar on the shelves, along with some bolts of cloth in a pattern Gwen wouldn't use for rags, and a bucket of nails in the corner. Advertisements of beautiful women promoting soaps and perfumes adorned the walls, mocking the life of farm women everywhere. Jenna sat down on a tall stool. She opened the neckline of her dress even farther, as if she was going to spill out of it. Flushing, Gwen turned away.

"I thought you wanted to talk, not...flaunt yourself."

"Robbie's upset by all the noise outside. He needs some comfort."

"By All Four Gods and Goddesses, what are you doing with a child, Jenna sum Dorshay?" Gwen automatically gave Jenna the Avatar prefix she would obtain once ennobled. "You knew someday we'd need to assemble and take over from the older Season Avatars. Why burden yourself with an infant?"

"First of all, I'm not a Dorshay any longer," Jenna said. "I'm Jenna t'Reve now."

She got married? This might complicate things. Gwen peered at Jenna, looking for her marriage tattoo. Her sleeves were still down, so it didn't show.

"Where's your husband, then?"

Her face was shadowed for a moment. "With the God of Winter."

"I'm...I'm sorry." Gwen stared at Robbie again. The child was less than a moon old, and Jenna's dress was full white. "Did he get to see the baby?"

Jenna shook her head. "He knew the child was coming—that's why we got married—but one night when we were in bed being intimate—he just—he grunted, and his face grew red, then he got very still and heavy—I couldn't move him..."

"That's enough." Gwen shuddered, but the part of her not frightened by details involving the marriage act was trying to figure out what had happened. His heart, perhaps?

Aunt Gabri tsked. "Shame on you getting things out of order, girl. You could have at least prevented that."

Gwen swept her gaze between her aunt and Jenna, not sure who shocked her more.

Jenna rubbed her son's back. "The plants I need don't grow very well in Bull Rock. Sides, it seemed right at the time."

"Even when you knew very well the Season Avatars could summon you to the One Oak at any instant?"

Jenna glared at Gwen as if all of this was somehow her fault. "How come none of you came when I made that rose bush grow as big as a barn last year? Didn't you hear about it?"

Gwen pursed her lips as she remembered back. "I think I read about it in the paper, but I couldn't come. We were hosting a ball that moon."

"How nice for you, hosting a ball. I suppose it was so you could find yourself a husband?"

The thing that irritated her was Jenna was right. That was the night William had proposed. "And you sought a husband in another way. Why?"

Still watching her son, Jenna softly replied, "It was necessary."

Her sudden change in tone made Gwen want to press for details, but before she could, Jenna continued, "So, why are you here now?"

"The current Ava Spring is dead. We have to find our other two Season Avatars so we can replace the old ones. They can't reach across Challen anymore without Margaret."

Jenna nodded. "I see. I guess we should go, then." She looked around. "But what do I do with Thomas's shop?"

"Is there anyone here who can look after it for you?"

"I don't know. My brothers and sisters are needed on our family farm. They're all younger than me anyway."

"What about the child?" Aunt Gabri asked.

"I'm sure the Season Avatars can hire a wet nurse to look after him," Gwen said.

Jenna drew her eyebrows together. "But I'm his mama. I look after him."

"But we still have to find the Ava Fall and Ava Win, and I don't know where they are. We have to go to Wistica next and look at the records so we can figure out where they might be."

"Wistica! How grand!" Jenna removed her son from her bosom, rose, and did a little jig. "Did you hear that, Robbie? We're going to the capital city!"

"Didn't you understand what I said? Wistica is only the start of our trip. The other two Season Avatars could be anywhere in Challen. We can't drag a baby with us!"

Jenna pressed her lips together, then said, "Well, I can't leave him with someone else for moons on end either. A child belongs with his mother."

Gwen sighed. "Then stay at the One Oak with him. As a new mother, you should recover your strength."

"And miss the chance to see Wistica and the rest of Challen? I'm not that delicate. The Four will have to freeze me first!"

Eyes still closed, Robbie let out a yawn. He took after his mother, though there was something about his face that seemed familiar.

Gwen didn't think she had ever met someone named Thomas t'Reve, so she couldn't be seeing the father in the son. She had to admit Robbie was cute, even if his mouth was dirty, but she still didn't want him along on this trip. A baby this young would slow them down and be inconvenient in countless ways.

Aunt Gabri stepped forward. "He's adorable. May I hold him?"

Jenna settled him into Aunt Gabri's arms. Gwen stared for a couple of minutes as her aunt fussed over the baby, who seemed to enjoy the attention. *Who would have thought Aunt Gabri liked babies so much?*

Jenna protectively watched Aunt Gabri with Robbie. Gwen took advantage of the distraction to study the next Ava Summer. She knew she ought to know Jenna better; she ought to remember details from their lives together. But her memories were too muddled to be trustworthy. Perhaps the link would provide some clarity, if not better recall.

"Jenna," Gwen said softly as she approached her. "We should link. We can get to know each other a little better." *And see if we can start the introductions over, so we get off on the right foot this time.*

"What? Link? Now?"

"Why not?"

"We don't have the others." Jenna glanced around the store. "And there's nowhere here in town where my magic is needed."

"I could use your help to heal people here," Gwen said. "I can't do it without you."

"Really?" Jenna raised her eyebrows. "Why not? Don't you remember how?" She said it with a slight smirk that made Gwen's hackles rise.

"What if I said I was cursed?" she snapped, stopping herself just in time from spitting the words into Jenna's face.

"Cursed? There's no such thing as curses! That's outside the Four's magic."

"I know that." Gwen hugged herself. "That's why I don't understand what's going on. All I can figure out is that I got a pottery shard stuck in my hand, I can't heal it out of me, and I have a better feel for healing when I use the other hand. Even that isn't going as well as it should. I tried to heal a farmer's wife with a skin tumor on the way over here, and I couldn't get rid of it, just seal it off before it spreads. If it does, and I can't get my magic back, she'll die, along with all the other people I'm supposed to save."

Jenna sucked in her breath. "By All Four Gods and Goddesses, I didn't think we could lose our magic. If we don't lose it when we die and are reborn, what could interfere with that?"

"I don't know. I thought linking might bring it back."

Jenna backed away. "Or linking might make me lose mine, and then what happens to Challen?"

Robbie started to wail.

Gwen hadn't thought of that. The last thing she wanted to do was spread this curse. But if it wasn't safe for her to link with the rest of her Season Avatars, they wouldn't be able to drive the next Chaos Season from Challen and restore it. Everyone would suffer for her foolish mistake.

"If that's the case, only the Four can help us now," she said.

Aunt Gabri passed a much smellier baby back to Jenna and said, "Gwen, dear, you should go to the Temple in Wistica and pray there. Isn't that supposed to be a holy place?"

Gwen nodded. "It would be fitting to visit the Temple while we're there."

Avatars had been leading the soltrans there since the Four had chosen them hundreds of years ago. As long as their other duties didn't interfere, they traveled down the Chikasi River from the One Oak to Wistica for every solstice and equinox. Gwen knew the Goddess of Spring could hear her wherever she was, but perhaps going to the Temple would be enough to break the curse and remove the shard.

"Are we going to sail down the Chikasi River?" Jenna beamed so brightly Gwen wished her joy was directed at her. She felt it ought to be, even if she couldn't explain why.

Gwen bit back a sarcastic response and asked, "How soon can you be ready to go?"

"I don't have much to pack." Jenna spun around, looking at the store. "What do I do with Thomas' store? Robbie should be able to come back and run it when he's old enough, but I won't have time for it when we become Avatars."

Robbie wouldn't inherit anything from the One Oak or the Season Avatars' estate. It would be handy for him to have something of his own when he was old enough. Would a run-down store in a small town be worth anything by then?

"Find someone to take over, at least for now," Gwen said. "I want to be on the way to Wistica as soon as possible."

"I'd rather have some time to rest," Aunt Gabri muttered. "All this bouncing in carriages day and night is hard on an old woman's bones."

Gwen brushed her objection aside; she could soothe her aunt later. "Isn't there anyone here who can take over, Jenna?"

"Thomas' brother, Tyre," she said flatly. "He wants this store for himself." She rearranged perfectly folded bolts of cloth with her free hand. "You may as well hear it from me, since I'm sure someone will tell you if they haven't already. No one thinks Thomas is Robbie's father."

"Is he?" Aunt Gabri leaned closer, as if relishing the prospect of gossip.

"Thomas was excited about becoming a father. He was looking forward so much to seeing Robbie."

Gwen sighed. Not a straight yes-or-no answer. Hadn't Jenna always been like this, no matter what name she bore? She was sure she remembered that much from her previous lives. She took a deep breath. "If my healing magic was working properly, I could touch both Robbie and Tyre and tell if they were related. But now I'm not sure that will work."

Something flickered in Jenna's eyes, but Gwen couldn't tell if it was relief or fear.

"What if he insists on a test anyway? What will you tell him?"

Gwen rubbed the stubborn shard in her palm. She didn't want to lie, but she worried how people would react if her blocked magic became common knowledge. "Is there some way we can compromise?" she asked. She paced for a couple of moments as she thought. "What if the One Oak pays him a fee to run the store until Robbie is of age?"

"What if he takes the chals and still refuses to give up the store later?"

That was so many years in the future Gwen didn't think it worth worrying about. She had enough problems in the present. "I'm sure the older Avatars have lawyers who can deal with that for us," she said. "After all, if taking care of the store frees you to be an Avatar, then the estate will arrange it."

"You make it sound so easy," Jenna said. "Tyre won't let it be that simple." She shook her head. "He just won't."

Gwen wondered if that had something to do with Jenna herself. Her memories weren't as clear as they should have been, but she didn't think Jenna had ever been easy-going.

"We don't need to worry about the next season until the soltrans," she said. "Let's get ready to leave."

Jenna went into the back to collect a few things. When she was out of the room, Aunt Gabri frowned. "I've never seen a farm girl talk back so much to one of her betters. You'd better take a firm hand with her, Gwen, or she'll try to run the Avatars instead of you."

Gwen didn't respond, but she thought to herself, *All the more reason to leave here and seek out the other two Season Avatars. We always did get along better in the whole group than we did alone.* Or did they? She wasn't sure anymore.

Jenna returned a few minutes later carrying a couple of bags and with Robbie secured in a sling. She opened the shop door and beckoned for Gwen and Aunt Gabri to follow. The crowd from before hadn't dispersed; if anything, it seemed even larger. Gwen caught a few whispers: "That's her! Isn't she grand? Are they both Season Avatars? You mean Jenna was right?"

Jenna shifted her son to her shoulder. "Tyre!" she called. "Come here. We need to talk."

A middle-aged man pushed his way to the front of the crowd. Gwen compared his features to Robbie's. Only the noses seemed similar. He shot Jenna a hostile look that made Gwen's hackles rise. Jenna might be irritating, but she was a sister Season Avatar. Gwen would support her – or have to support her – no matter what.

Before Tyre could speak, she forestalled him. "Are you Tyre t'Reve, brother of Thomas t'Reve?"

"Yes. I'm much closer to him than she was." Now he stared at Gwen. "And who are you? What are you doing here?"

She drew herself up to her full height. "I'm Lady Gwendolyn lo Havil—"

"The next Ava Spring." Jenna finished Gwen's sentence as smoothly as if they'd rehearsed it.

"I've just come from the One Oak in search of Jenna Dorshay, now Jenna t'Reve. She is the next Ava Sum, and it's time for both of us to take our place."

The crowd murmured at that. Gwen caught a few references to the other Season Avatars as people speculated about them. She wasn't sure if she was supposed to announce Margaret's death, so she didn't.

Now came the tricky part. She turned to Tyre. "Sir t'Reve, the Four require your assistance on behalf of Challen. Will you take over the running of your sleeping brother's store for Jenna and her son, Robbie, so she may go to One Oak?"

He stared at Jenna, not her, for a few heartbeats. Then, he said loudly, "She has no right to the store, not for her, not for her bastard. He's not Thomas's, or I'm an Avatar myself."

The crowd sucked in its breath.

"The Four do not require additional Season Avatars," Gwen said as levelly as she could manage, hoping she was right. "They simply need you to run the store until Robbie is old enough to decide what to do with it."

Tyre stepped closer to her. "You're a mite free to talk for the Four, Ava. And what's in it for me?"

"I will ask the One Oak to send you a stipend each moon for your time. It will be more than adequate, I assure you."

For a few heartbeats, Gwen thought he would accept their offer, and everyone would be satisfied. But then he glanced at Jenna again, and his expression darkened. "You're an Ava Spring, right? Well, then, prove that Robbie is Thomas's, and I'll do it for him." He jerked his head at Jenna. "Not her."

By All Four, how do I handle this? If Jenna was innocent of nothing more than anticipating her vows, then everything would be fine. Gwen wished she could be sure of that. Something about Jenna's behavior made her think this test would condemn her, not save her. She didn't want to accuse her sister Season Avatar, someone she'd worked with in many previous lifetimes. Maybe that would be enough to stave off Tyre's request.

Gwen smiled at him. "You do understand, Sir t'Reve, that I've known Jenna and worked with her as a Season Avatar in other lives. Would it be enough for me to vouch for her?"

Jenna's eyes widened in surprise.

Tyre shook his head. "Not for me. I want proof."

"What if I can't give it to you?" How could she get out of this without revealing her magic had been cursed?

"You're the next Ava Spring! If you can't do it, who else can?"

"No one," Gwen snapped. "The current Ava Spring is with the God of Winter now."

Shocked cries sprang from the crowd. Even Tyre looked taken aback for a few heartbeats. Then he drew closer to Gwen and whispered, "Please, Ava, I just want to know."

His pleading moved her more than his anger had, but it didn't solve the other problems. Gwen sighed. "I shouldn't have said anything about the Ava Spring, Sir t'Reve. I'm really not...ready to do what you want of me. If I ... attempt this, you must not speak out against Jenna, no matter what I find." She hardened her gaze. "If you do, your stipend will be cancelled."

He studied her for a moment before nodding.

"Come." Gwen beckoned Jenna and Tyre back inside the store. "This should be done in private."

Jenna's face was pale, and she hesitated for an instant before letting Gwen touch her son. That was enough to tell Gwen the truth. She laid her good hand on Robbie's petal-soft cheek for a moment anyway, just long enough to sense his essence but hopefully not long enough to give him her curse. She automatically reached for Jenna before remembering that was risky too. Finally, she said, "Sir T'Reve, let me take your hand."

Although his skin was rough, it didn't have the calluses Gwen would have expected on a farmer. She wondered what his profession was. She studied his essence for a few moments before switching to Robbie again. If she dared touch both of them at once, this comparison would be much easier.

Gwen was hard put to describe how she could sense the similarities and differences between Robbie and Tyre. There were no terms for the patterns she felt in their skin. What mattered was how much the patterns matched. She knew the closer they matched, the more closely related the two were. There were some matches, but not as many as she might have expected. Did Robbie match Jenna more? Were the differences between Robbie and Tyre due to differences between Thomas and Tyre? By All Four, what if Thomas and Tyre weren't really brothers? Then none of this would matter.

She broke away from them and squeezed her fists, trying to rein in her frustration. The bump in the palm of her hand only made it worse.

Her voice sounded tighter and higher-pitched than normal as she said, "I can't say for sure one way or another."

Tyre and Jenna glared at each other for a few heartbeats.

"I'll tend the store," he said, "but only for the stipend, not for Robbie."

"Fine." Jenna leaned forward as if charging into battle. "But if you take a single chal that doesn't belong to you, I'll send vines—"

"Jenna, that's enough," Gwen said. "Your season here is done. Better to welcome the new season than cling to the old."

"That's true." She smiled. "This new season has to be four times better than the last one."

Gwen had her doubts about that.

CHAPTER NINE

Lady of the Waters

Gwen and her aunt managed to find a tolerable place to spend the night, and they left the next morning with Jenna and her son. A strong wind battered at them for much of the trip, not enough to cause an accident but enough to keep their rest breaks short. Gwen and Jenna sat opposite each other, and Gwen wore a pair of gloves to prevent her from accidentally linking with Jenna. Jenna chattered about Robbie and Thomas and her family. Aunt Gabri gradually thawed under the onslaught of words, but although Jenna made Gwen smile occasionally, the conversation seemed superficial without a link or shared memories from previous lives to draw them together.

Jenna stared out the window as they drove past the lane to the One Oak. "Aren't we stopping at the One Oak first before going to Wistica?"

Gwen shrugged. "Why delay? It's more important to find the next Ava Fall and Ava Win before Chaos Season strikes again. For all we know, it's affecting another part of Challen right now, and we can't do anything about it." She fingered her palm. Sometimes the shard pressed against her as if it was trying to move into her arm, but so far she'd managed to hold it back. She wasn't sure what would happen if it moved further into her body. Very few things could kill an Ava Spring, but this might.

Aunt Gabri cleared her throat. "Gwendolyn, what if William sent you a letter there?"

Unable to control her flush, Gwen watched the path retreat behind them. There was still time to turn the coach around and check. But it was already after lunch. If they stopped now, they wouldn't have time to catch the last steamboat to Wistica tonight. Delay here could mean lives lost elsewhere. William would have to understand that her duty to Challen came first.

Gwen leaned back in her seat. "Continue to Midpoint as planned, James. When you return to the One Oak, please have any correspondence forwarded to the Avatars' House in Wistica."

"Aren't we staying at your father's house?" Aunt Gabri asked.

"We're on official Season Avatar business, Aunt Gabri. The staff at the Avatars' House will be better able to help us."

Aunt Gabri sighed. "And what if your father is expecting us at his residence? Or back at his estate? What about your wedding, child? Only the Four know when it will take place. If it ever does."

The comment stung more than Gwen thought it would. While she tried to figure out how to respond, Jenna shot her a look of sympathy. She leaned forward and said, "When we're in Wistica, will we have time to shop for clothes?"

Gwen seized the change of subject. "Yes, all of us need new clothes. It'll take several days to investigate where our other Avatars are and where this shard came from, and that will give us time to order new clothes in our colors." She glanced at Jenna. "Made in the capital city of Challen, no less."

"The center of society and fashion."

Gwen and Jenna grinned at each other. For once, they seemed to be sharing the same thought, even without the link.

Aunt Gabri groaned. "And just how many more days do you expect me to be cramped in this coach while we travel to Wistica, Gwendolyn?"

"None." Gwen pointed out the window. "There's the river. We can take passage on a steamboat down to Wistica. It'll be faster, and we can walk around on deck during the day and have our own berths at night."

"And we can be seasick the entire time," Aunt Gabri muttered.

"But we'll be on a river," Jenna said brightly. "Wouldn't you get riversick?"

Aunt Gabri glared at her and didn't speak until they arrived in Midpoint. James drove them straight to the docks. Six of them protruded into the river. At each one, a boat painted in one of the Four's colors was tied up, with crew busy loading cargo or cleaning the decks. Well-dressed passengers and observers crowded the walkway as if this was a holiday. The closer they got to the boats, the more apparent the smell of smoke became. Beyond the boats, the river stretched wider than Gwen had expected; even with her keen vision, the opposite shore was only a smudge against the water's deep blue.

Aunt Gabri cleared her throat. "How do you know all those boats are going to Wistica? I wouldn't want to be sailing along and then suddenly find myself in the middle of Selath with no way to get back home!"

Gwen had assumed they would all sail straight to Wistica; it hadn't occurred to her that they would travel anywhere else. "Then we should ask someone. But whom?"

"How about him?" Jenna pointed to a man in one of the more ornate uniforms they'd seen so far, with several stars on his gray jacket. He appeared to be one of the captains, so he should know the boats' itineraries. Unfortunately, he was also talking to several other important-looking crewmembers. Gwen watched them for several heartbeats, but when the group showed no signs of breaking up, she fussed with her dress until it didn't look as if she'd been stuck in a coach for days on end. Then she marched up to him. Although she approached him from the side so he could see her, he continued rattling off sailing terms she didn't understand. She stared at him, willing him to look at her. Finally, one of the other men nudged him, and he turned in her direction.

"Yes, Lady?" His tone was balanced between politeness and dismissal.

Gwen put her own edge into her voice. "We need to get to Wistica as soon as possible. Which boat will get us there the fastest?"

One of the other men chuckled at her question.

"I'm not the ticket seller, Lady. You have to arrange passage in the stone cottage at the end of the dock." His voice warmed slightly as he added, "But you'd do well to ask for *Lady of the Waters*. We leave in two hours, and I want all passengers on board in one."

Gwen nodded before shepherding her group to the cottage. Inside, it was a single room, with maps of the Chikasi River lining the walls. Illustrations of the various boats that sailed from here also decorated the walls, with their sailing schedules listed underneath. Gwen pushed past a couple of other travelers as she searched for the *Lady of the Waters*. It was red, dedicated to the Goddess of Fall. Since they still needed to find the Ava Fall, Gwen hoped that was a good omen.

"How long will the trip to Wistica take?" she asked the ticket seller.

"About two days."

She marveled at the speed. By land, the trip would take two weeks.

"Mind," the seller added, "the river conditions make all the difference between a fast passage and a slow one—or even a failed one."

Aunt Gabri turned pale. "Surely you don't mean those boats can sink!"

"Not very often, Lady. The last one we lost was caught in ice during a sudden Chaos outbreak."

Gwen prayed Dorian was performing his duty. "We were recommended to take the *Lady of the Waters*. Do you know anything about that boat? Or its crew?"

The seller nodded. "They're experienced and reliable. They'll get you there in good time."

His expression was open, so Gwen decided to trust him. "Passage for all of us, then."

"Which class?"

"First, of course."

The ticket seller frowned. "I'm truly sorry, Lady, but there are no more berths left in First Class."

Gwen frowned. "Are there any other boats leaving for Wistica today with First Class berths?"

The ticket seller consulted his book, then shook his head. "Seems like all the nobles have been summoned to the capital."

"Whatever for?"

"That I don't know, Lady." He stared at her. "Though if I were to guess, rumors have been flying about the One Oak and Chaos Season."

Margaret. Word has gotten out about Margaret. How were the nobles going to react at the news one of the Season Avatars was dead? They were probably all worried about Chaos Season destroying their wealth. Gwen wondered if her father and William's family were on the way to the capital too. They would also take the steamboat. She hadn't seen them on the dock, but they could have left before her.

"Do you have space for three people anywhere?" she asked.

"What about Robbie?" Jenna added.

"Babies stay with their mothers," the ticket seller said. "And I can put you on the *Lady of the Waters* if you're willing to travel Third Class."

Gwen turned to Jenna and Aunt Gabri. Both of them frowned, but Gwen spread her hands in appeal. "You know we need to get there as quickly as possible. It can't be that bad."

"It'll be dirty and uncomfortable," Aunt Gabri proclaimed. "Worse, what if someone we know sees us there? Lo Havils shouldn't have to travel Third Class! We'll be humiliated!"

"Well, shouting about it in the ticket office won't help."

Jenna sighed. "Gwen's right, Lady lo Havil. We can't afford to wait. If Chaos Season returns, we might be delayed, or even stuck here. We can't track down the other Avatars from Midpoint." She glanced over at the picture of the *Lady of the Waters*. "On the way back, I really want to travel First Class. I won't be able to leave the One Oak much once we're installed."

Gwen nodded at Jenna as she purchased the tickets. They spent the next hour buying pillows and extra blankets; a picnic basket with bread, hard cheese, and dried fruit; and a couple bottles of wine from a nearby open market catering to travelers. Sophia had given Gwen a letter of credit, so she could have all the bills sent to the One Oak. James helped them bring everything to the boat so they could get settled, then left for the One Oak.

The boat was in good repair and seemed fit for a monarch. Carved otters decorated the railing and other spots on the ship. Down below, however, once they moved past the doors leading to the private first-class berths, they found that the third-class berths were all in one long part of the boat. Hammocks hung in three tiers from the ceiling to the floor. They had been assigned a set near the back of the boat.

Aunt Gabri gingerly pushed the hammock on the bottom and watched it swing back and forth. "I don't see how I'm supposed to fall asleep in this. I'll get dizzy."

Jenna eyed the rope ladder leading up to the higher hammocks. "I hope I can climb this with Robbie."

It looked as if Gwen would have to be the one sleeping on top. "If you take the middle hammock, I can hand Robbie to you once you're settled."

"That's fine." Jenna immediately sat on the lowest hammock and started nursing her son. At Aunt Gabri's outraged gasp, she said, "Better now than on the deck, don't you think? I'm not missing the launch."

"We need privacy." Aunt Gabri pressed her lips into a firm line.

Sighing, Gwen clambered up to her bunk. "Could you hand me some blankets, please?"

After taking a couple of minutes to find her balance, Gwen managed to hang the longest blanket over a pair of hooks. There was no window, so once the blanket was in place, it was nearly impossible to see. But the gentle rocking of the boat and the smells of wood and wool were comforting. Gwen allowed herself to hope that the trip might not just be bearable, but even pleasant.

When Jenna was decent again, she and Gwen returned to the deck. Despite the smoke and steam fouling the air, a sense of excitement prevailed as other passengers bid farewell to their loved ones and crew members scampered around obeying the captain's orders. Finally, the gangplank was drawn back into the boat, the ropes holding her to the dock were pulled free, and the *Lady of the Waters* proceeded at a stately pace away from Midpoint. The air freshened as they moved. Gwen and Jenna leaned against the railing, observing the people and the changing scenery along the river. They didn't speak, but words weren't necessary. They didn't need to link to share the excitement.

They stayed out there until it was almost sunset, then Jenna went below to tend to Robbie and bring some food out so they could eat on the deck. Most of the other passengers had the same idea, so they had to search for a private space. They ended up sitting on some bales of wool near the back of the boat.

"This must be so hard on you, traveling beneath your station," Jenna said as she unwrapped some bread. Her snide tone was only half-hearted.

"Funny, you seemed awfully disappointed when we had to take Third Class berths." Gwen discreetly tucked another layer of skirt between her lower limbs and the scratchy wool.

"Who wouldn't be?" Jenna stared at the river as if she'd never seen so much water in her life. "Did you do a lot of traveling before this?"

"We'd travel to Midpoint once or twice a year on special shopping excursions, and twice I accompanied Father to Wistica when he attended the Assembly or visited his friends. Most of the time we stay close to our estate so he can manage it." Gwen sighed. Would things have been different if her mother had lived? Maybe her father would have brought her to Wistica more often.

"Did you like Wistica?" Jenna asked.

"Oh, yes. There's so much to see there. It's much dirtier and noisier than the country, though."

Jenna munched on her meal and didn't comment. Gwen copied her while observing the other passengers. Most of them were men, merchants or nobles by their clothes. Quite a few of them appeared to be from Selath; the Selathens tended to have dark skin and hair. A few of them clung to the sides of the boat as if its gentle rocking was too much for them. Others brandished mugs of ale or cups of wine, talking loudly. A woman accompanied herself on a guitar as she sung a love ballad. The longing she sang about echoed in Gwen's heart, even as she tried to figure out what she longed for. Her family estate? William? Thoughts of the One Oak resonated within her, but it still didn't seem like enough.

"Jenna, did you love your husband?" Gwen asked when the song was over.

She dropped her bread in her cup. "Thomas? Honestly, maybe not at first. But I grew fond of him. The house and store felt empty when the God of Winter claimed him. Why?"

Gwen wondered if she would grow to love William after they were married. She didn't want to talk about him with Jenna, even if she wasn't sure why. She remembered what she'd sensed in Bull Rock when she'd examined Robbie and Thomas' brother. She lowered her voice. "Robbie isn't Thomas's, is he?"

Jenna stared at her. "What makes you say that?"

"Robbie doesn't have enough in common with his supposed uncle."

"I thought you said your magic wasn't working properly."

"It's not. But I can still tell."

The silence between them seemed to stretch into forever. Gwen resented the interruptions of music, water splashing, and other conversations.

"Why didn't you say anything back in Bull Rock?" Jenna finally asked.

"I wasn't sure then." *And I'm supposed to support my sister Avatars no matter what.* Didn't Jenna feel the same way? They'd been reincarnated together life after life; they should know each other as well as their own selves by now. Gwen knew that if she didn't have that frozen shard buried in her hand, she'd have much better recall of her lives, so Jenna's memories must be intact.

Robbie fussed and spit up milk. Jenna massaged his belly for a moment before picking him up and cradling him. All the while, she ignored Gwen as if she wasn't there. Gwen watched them, jealous of their bond.

"Who's his father, then?"

Jenna jerked her head to look at her. Her cheeks were redder than apples. "I…I'd rather not talk about it."

She couldn't have been forced, could she? She had her magic to protect her, even if she hadn't called upon the Goddess of Fall. If Fall Herself failed the women of Challen, then the country was in desperate straits indeed.

Gwen rubbed the shard. "Maybe if we linked…."

Jenna abruptly rose. "Freeze it, Gwen, it's none of your business who fathered Robbie. You keep that shard of yours away from me and my son before you poison us too."

She flounced off.

Gwen stared after her, too shocked to do anything else. Why was she so touchy about this? Did she think she could keep Robbie's heritage a secret forever? Sooner or later, it would come out in the link. Unless they never linked…but no, they would have to do so eventually, shard or no.

By All Four Gods and Goddesses, if dealing with one Season Avatar was this hard, how would Gwen manage when all four of them were reunited? She must have done it in other lives; would she be able to do it in this one?

Gwen watched the water flow past the boat and the moon rise over the river. When weariness forced her to her hammock, past her sleeping companions, she still had no answer.

* * *

Chaos Season descended on Gwen in the form of a tornado. She reached for the other Avatars, but they had abandoned her.

"Give up, little Avatar," a woman's voice mocked her. The voice came from everywhere, but it was too cruel to be Spring or Fall. "Even your gods are subject to Time. How do you think you can stand against Me?"

"You're lying!" she shouted. "The Four are supreme in Challen!"

"If that's true, why did They let Fip conquer it? Why don't They let you use your magic on your own? Oh, that's right, you've lost your magic. You should have never had it to begin with."

The tornado halted within arms-length of Gwen, as if blocked by a glass wall. "That's not true, Gwendolyn lo Havil," Spring said. Like the other woman, she was invisible. "You're my strongest and wisest Avatar. You can escape from this trap. Someone in Wistica can help you…."

Glass shattered as the tornado reached for her….

Gwen sat up, bumping her head on the ceiling before she remembered where she was. A chilly breeze woke her completely. Where was that breeze coming from? There were no heaters in this section, but all the people packed into the cramped quarters gave off enough warmth to compensate.

Too disturbed by her dream to fall back asleep, Gwen shifted in her hammock, trying to get comfortable. Each time she moved, the rocking unsettled her. After a few moments, she decided to get up and go to the deck to clear her head. She could commune with Spring better without the distraction of the sleepers around her. Even if Spring didn't respond, experiencing Her season would calm Gwen.

Gwen climbed down and slipped her traveling dress over her chemise and petticoat. Jenna stirred, still cradling her son. They looked so peaceful together, as if they were all each other would ever need. Gwen swallowed as she remembered her dream. Maybe it was a warning from the Goddess. Maybe she was doing something to drive the other Avatars away without realizing it. Or maybe just the frozen shard was enough to scare them away.

Scowling, she stomped up to the deck. A pair of lamps hung at the front of the boat, but back here the only lights came from the moon and stars. Gwen waited for her eyes to adjust before making her way to the side. Sticks and small logs bobbed as the *Lady of the Waters* churned past them. Other debris came up to the surface as the boat stirred up the water, but they sank quickly. One piece of flotsam, however, didn't sink but floated in the boat's wake, following them as if tied on a string.

Out here, with the passengers below and the crew in the engine room, Gwen finally felt free enough to weep. Her healing magic was blocked, no other Ava Springs were alive to help her, and even her sister Avatar wouldn't link with her for fear of losing her magic too. She didn't need bad dreams to tell her Chaos Season would ruin Challen during her turn of service. What was the point of continuing this journey? Even if she found the Fall and Winter Avatars, they wouldn't want to link with her either. Their whole quartet was doomed to failure. Had Spring reincarnated another set of Season Avatars, a set better able to handle these problems? Gwen eyed the water again.

Maybe she should throw herself overboard and give herself to the God of Winter. Surely in her next life, she'd be free of this curse. That was, if Winter didn't freeze her forever for killing herself. Would He do that to an Avatar? The Avatars had reincarnated over and over for centuries without interruption. So much was different this time Gwen didn't know if the usual rules still applied.

She studied the water for a few more minutes before she noticed the floating debris was moving faster than the boat. Now it was only a few arm-lengths away. It was slightly curved and upside down. Maybe air was trapped underneath, but that wouldn't explain how it was moving so quickly. With her vision now fully adapted to the dark, Gwen could see some familiar markings on the surface. She'd seen them on the shard now stuck in her skin.

By All Four…. Gwen shook her head, sharpened her vision, and checked again. Her sight was true. There was another piece of cursed pottery in the river, and it would bump against the boat any heartbeat now. That couldn't be natural, or the will of the Four. If this thing was chasing the boat—or her—she had to stop it before it hurt more innocent people.

Gwen searched the deck for something she could throw at the shard. Then she remembered how fragments of it could still be dangerous. If she broke it, would the pieces sink or continue pursuing her? More pieces meant more risk to everyone. Best to keep this shard intact if possible.

I need to trap it. But with what? There wasn't even a bucket on deck. There might be a spare one next to the sleeping berths below. Suddenly Gwen knew how to keep this shard from hurting anyone else. She'd need Jenna's help, though.

Scritch…scratch…. Dear Four, the shard was climbing up the boat! Gwen backed away from the railing slowly, trying to feel where she was going while watching for the shard. She encountered the opening to the deck below sooner than she expected and stumbled. Only her quick reflexes saved her from hitting her head. As she took her first step, the shard heaved itself over the railing.

No time to waste now. Gwen bolted down the steps and straight for Jenna's hammock. "Jenna, wake up!" she whispered as loudly as she dared.

Jenna continued to snore.

Gwen shook her shoulder. Her fingers grazed Jenna's neck. Images flooded her mind of a couple making love in a sumptuous room. The man looked familiar, but she couldn't see the woman's face. *Freeze it! I linked with Jenna without thinking about it! I hope I didn't curse her...* She sent a mental command to wake up into Jenna's dream, then removed her hand.

"Mumph?" Jenna wasted precious heartbeats tossing about before opening her eyes. "Ginny, is that you? Have you forgiven me yet?"

"Ginny?" Gwen froze. That had been her name in her last life. Why was Jenna dreaming about it? How unfair that her memories were muddled.

Clunk, clunk.

"What was that?" Jenna asked.

"It's the shard!" Gwen reached for Jenna but drew back before touching her again. "There's another frozen shard after me, moving on its own. We have to trap it in a bucket so it doesn't hurt anyone."

"I knew that wine had fermented too long."

"Jenna, it's true! I saw it in the water, then it was next to the boat."

Clunk. The shard, still intact from what Gwen could see, tumbled into view.

Jenna attempted to push herself into a sitting position, but her hammock rocked instead. "You sure someone's not playing a trick on you?"

"No one else knows about the shard in my hand." Gwen glanced around, trying to find the extra bucket. She couldn't see it, but she supposed she should be able to smell it. Reluctantly, she sharpened that sense. A foul odor came from the far corner.

As she ran for the bucket, the shard bounced down the rest of the stairs.

"By All Four!" Jenna cried. "Is that thing moving on its own?"

Robbie whimpered. Aunt Gabri and some of the other female passengers stirred and muttered complaints. The few awake enough to look around focused on Jenna. Behind them, the shard advanced toward Gwen. It rolled onto its narrow side and wove between trunks and discarded boots.

Gwen scooped up a half-full bucket of night waste, wrinkling her nose at the smell, and dumped the contents into a second bucket. Some splashed onto her hands and gown, but she couldn't spare a heartbeat for disgust. She grabbed the lid and stepped toward the shard. What would happen to her if a second shard became embedded in her skin? Her hands shook at the thought. *You have to do this, Gwen,* she told herself. *At least you have innate healing magic to protect yourself; everyone else has nothing.* Still, with every step, she prayed to the Goddess of Spring to aid her.

She was still several feet away from the shard when it rolled onto a boot and launched itself at her face. Reflexively, she blocked it with the lid. Too late she remembered breaking the shard would make it more dangerous. But it bounced off, still in one piece, and spun as if considering its next target.

"Get it, Gwen!" Although Robbie still wailed, Jenna had come forward without him, holding a patched petticoat.

"What is that?" A woman about Aunt Gabri's age asked.

"A rat," Jenna replied.

The women who were awake started screaming, rousing the rest of the occupants. Although Gwen didn't want to explain the truth to them, she wished Jenna had come up with a better lie, or at least one that wouldn't upset the passengers.

"There!" Even as she spoke, Jenna pounced on the shard, trapping it under her petticoat before it could touch her. Gwen followed with the bucket. As smoothly as if they'd done this in previous lives, Jenna used the rest of the cloth to push the shard into the bucket while Gwen closed the lid. Jenna took the bucket from her and pressed on both lid and bucket. "That ought to hold it."

Gwen tested the lid. As she'd hoped, Jenna had fused the wood lid and bucket so the shard couldn't escape. Working with dead wood stretched the limit of an Ava Sum's magic; Jenna looked more exhausted than she had been before she'd gone to bed. She staggered back to her hammock, retrieved Robbie from a befuddled Aunt Gabri, and nursed him.

"Everything's under control," Gwen told the other passengers. "Go back to sleep."

As they settled down, she gave Jenna some bread and cheese from their food basket. Jenna devoured it in heartbeats. Using magic always made Avatars hungry; Gwen had eaten two complete chickens by herself one time after a trader had brought illness to Lake Verdan. Healing everyone had drained her so much she'd slept for an entire day after her feast. It had been a difficult job, but at the time, it had felt like a triumph to beat the illness down. She wondered when she would get to use her magic like that again.

"Thanks," Jenna said after she finished the last of their watered wine and laid down, stroking Robbie's fine hair as he closed his eyes and leaned next to her. Jenna didn't seem quite so trusting of Gwen, but she must have forgotten about their argument earlier. Had she realized Gwen had accidentally linked with her? Maybe not.

It doesn't look like linking with her affected her magic, Gwen mused as she put the bucket in her hammock. She didn't want it next to her, but it didn't seem safe to leave it anywhere else. *I'll watch Jenna for the next couple of days to make sure nothing happened.* Maybe then Jenna would be willing to link with her—if she wasn't upset about Gwen waiting so long to tell her about it.

Gwen tried to get comfortable, but between wondering about what she had seen in Jenna's dream and listening to the shard rattle in the bucket, she had a hard time falling asleep.

CHAPTER TEN

Wistica

Gwen woke late the next morning, after everyone else had gone on deck. The first thing she did was check the bucket. The shard was still rattling around inside; Gwen was astonished it hadn't smashed itself to bits. As if that wasn't disturbing enough, the bucket had fallen on the floor and was rolling about every time the shard moved. Gwen made herself as presentable as possible, then grabbed the bucket and hurried to show Jenna.

Jenna had found a warm spot in the sun and spread out a blanket. She sat there stretching Robbie's limbs. As soon as Gwen explained the situation, she grabbed the bucket, holding it away from her son. She frowned as she examined the bucket. "I hardened that wood last night to make it stronger," she said. "It's a good thing I did, or it would have broken out by now. I can feel the inside is chipped and splintered. There's not much else I can do."

"Maybe you can put the bucket in our food basket and harden that too," Gwen said. "I think as soon as we disembark, we should do something about this shard."

Jenna gestured at the river. "Or you could put it back where you found it."

Gwen shook her head. "No. It might escape and come after us again. Or someone else. You have the best magic to deal with it."

There were other Avatars for other countries, each with a different type of magic. Besides the native Season Avatars, the only other Avatar in Challen was the Avatar of War from the royal Fip family. His magic wouldn't be helpful. If anything, he would try to turn the shard into a weapon.

"Maybe if we knew more about when and where this shard came from, we would know what kind of magic this is," Gwen said. "It looks ancient. I don't remember anything like this from another life. Do you?"

"I thought you couldn't remember anything." Jenna frowned.

"Nothing useful."

Jenna stared at Gwen, then said, "What do you consider useful?"

"Healing, mostly."

"Still nothing from your personal experiences?"

Gwen struggled to suppress a flush. Her glimpse of Jenna's dream had triggered some scandalous thoughts. "Never mind that. You don't remember light red pottery, do you?"

She laughed. "Why would I bother with something like that? People are more interesting than things."

Gwen drew closer to her. "And how far back do you remember?"

"Clearly? Three, maybe four hundred years. Farther back, things get mixed up!" She flicked a bug off of her son. "I don't remember pottery like that."

"Then maybe it's really old, or comes from somewhere outside Challen." Gwen stared at the bucket. "Either way, the best place to find someone who knows something about this pottery is at the University of Challen. We should go there immediately when we arrive in Wistica."

"Immediately? What about our house, or the seamstress?" Jenna gestured at her patched dress. "Who will take me for an Avatar when

I'm dressed like this? And just because you're wearing silk doesn't mean it's not wrinkled and stained from the trip."

Gwen had to admit she longed for a hot bath and a fresh outfit herself. "As long as that bucket doesn't break, Jenna. You'd better take charge of it."

Gwen extended the bucket toward Jenna, but she refused to take it. "Are you sure that's safe to have so close to Robbie?"

"How sure are you your magic is strong enough to keep it from escaping?"

Jenna frowned as she sealed the bucket inside the picnic basket and treated the wood. Gwen tested it, rapping on it and scratching the wood with her nails. It seemed strong, but she could still hear that frozen shard scraping away at the bucket for the rest of the day and well into the night.

* * *

The next morning, Gwen could tell they were getting closer to Wistica; more houses, farms, and other buildings appeared along the river banks, and a variety of boats competed for free patches of water. By midmorning, the first—or last—houses in the Spring and Summer Quarters were visible. The city houses rose several stories high, as if to look down on the rest of the city. Jenna held her baby up to see the city, but she frowned once they began passing the nobles' estates.

Gwen joined Jenna at the railing, careful not to get too close. "Something wrong?"

"Can't you see it? Look at the cherry trees."

"Which ones?"

"It doesn't matter. Check out that one." Jenna pointed at one on the riverbank. "It should be blooming, not bare. And the grass is too brown."

Gwen frowned and drew her cloak closer around her shoulders. "You think it's Chaos Season?"

"Chaos Season always comes when it's least wanted," Jenna recited the old proverb. "Here, hold Robbie." Before Gwen could protest, Jenna thrust her child at Gwen and leaned forward so far a sailor yelled at her. She ignored him, turning her head as if searching for something.

"I can't feel Chaos Season—yet," she said as she pulled back. "Can you?"

"With this shard in my hand, I'd be lucky to tell that snow is cold." Gwen slapped her hand against the railing, but all it did was make her palm sting.

Jenna laughed. Was she mocking the curse? Or did she like Gwen's sense of humor? Gwen raised the corners of her lips. When Jenna smiled broadly, her own expression became more real for a moment. The shared feeling strengthened Gwen's resolve.

"Once we learn more about the pottery, we have to go to the Record Hall," she said. "The sooner we find Fall and Winter, the better prepared we will be for Chaos Season."

* * *

"I do hope we'll be able to stay in Wistica for a while, Gwendolyn, instead of tearing about the country," Aunt Gabri said as they disembarked in the Summer Quarter of Wistica. "I could use a chance to put my feet up and enjoy a pot of chocolate."

Gwen shrugged. "It all depends on where the other two Season Avatars are, Aunt Gabri. They could be in this city; they could be at the other end of Challen." She beckoned a young street boy over and presented him with a chal. "Find us a carriage, please."

No official sign marked the entrance to the Spring Quarter, but none was necessary. The streets were wider and cleaner than in the Summer Quarter. The houses were taller, each with distinct architecture and fenced off from the street. Jenna stared at it all, exclaiming and pointing out new things to Robbie.

The Season Avatars' official residence in Wistica was in an older section of the Spring Quarter, almost next to the Fall Quarter, where the civic and merchant buildings were. It might no longer be considered a fashionable location, but it would be a good base for them to visit the University of Challen and the Hall of Records. Gwen frowned when she saw the gates to their house closed. Hadn't Sophia sent word of their arrival? Maybe she didn't know when they would come to Wistica. Still, the servants should have been watching for them.

The coachman rang the bell several times. A stable boy with a white armband finally came out to inspect their coach before letting them into the courtyard. "Sorry, my ladies," he said, "but the Avatars aren't here."

"They are now," Gwen said. Since she didn't want to risk passing on her curse, Jenna demonstrated her magic by touching a plant in the garden and making it flower.

"You're part of the next quartet?" The stable boy bobbed his head several times. "We were told the Ava Spring was with the God of Winter now. What sad, strange times these are."

"Strange?" Gwen asked.

"Aye, Ava." He hesitated before granting her the title. "We've had to keep the gate shut since a man has been spying on the house."

"How old is he?" Maybe he was the missing Fall Avatar. But if Fall had decided to incarnate one of Her Avatars as a male, Gwen would expect Chaos Season to start dropping roses and chals on the city.

"I'd say mid-thirties, or even forty."

Not one of their Avatars, then.

The stable boy glanced out the gate. "He's come by here several times in the evening, staring at the grounds as if he's trying to memorize them. He walks around the wall and examines it. I don't know if he wants to repair the wall or climb over it in the middle of the night and steal all the valuables. I hear there are items in the house that date back to the Annexation."

There should have been even older items here, but the original house, as old as the first group of Avatars, had been razed during the Fip Invasion of Challen. Gwen suspected but couldn't confirm from memory that the Fips had destroyed the house on purpose, to retaliate against the Avatars who had led the resistance until the Four commanded them to stop.

"What does he look like?" Jenna asked, leaning toward the stable boy.

He thought about it for a moment. "About average height and weight, dark complexion, like a Delnsman. He always carries a satchel with him."

The interest faded from Jenna's eyes, and she turned away. So, she was looking for a specific man. Perhaps Robbie's real father? Gwen would have liked to ask further questions of both Jenna and the stable boy. The latter was already unloading their belongings, however, so Gwen grabbed the picnic basket with the shard and followed Jenna into the house. Aunt Gabri trailed her.

The butler, a tall, thin man who must have been part Fip, frowned as Jenna invaded the parlor. Gwen handed him her letter of introduction from Sophia and waited for him to read it. He handed it back to her, still frowning. "Are you the Lady lo Havil the Ava Fall spoke of?"

"I am. This is Jenna t'Reve, the next Ava Sum. And my aunt, Lady Gabri lo Havil," Gwen added as Aunt Gabri sank into the loveseat.

"Yes. So I see." He eyed them as if judging whether to turn them back out. "And this is all you brought with you?"

"We were hoping to order some new clothes while we were in Wistica," Jenna said.

"Yes, that would be an excellent idea." He clapped his hands, and a maid scurried into the room. "Send a messenger to the Golden Thread and tell Dama N'idde to send three of her finest seamstresses here at once. We will need one wardrobe in gold and another in mourning with green touches, plus something suitable for a chaperone."

She nodded and left.

Gwen cleared her throat. "I know our gowns are worse for travel, but they hardly qualify as a state of emergency. We have a great deal of work to do in Wistica, and I don't want to waste days on fittings."

Jenna glared at her as if she didn't agree.

"I assure you, young Ava, Dama N'idde and her seamstresses will work through the night if necessary to make sure all of you are presentable in time."

"Presentable?" Jenna asked.

"In time?" Gwen asked simultaneously.

"Have you reported your arrival here in Wistica to the king?" the butler asked.

"By All Four, we just disembarked." Aunt Gabri stretched. "My stomach is still unsettled from the trip."

"Of course, Lady lo Havil," the butler said. "But I'm sure you'll understand that His Majesty will want to meet the next set of Season Avatars as soon as possible. You'll have to report to him as soon as your wardrobes are ready."

Jenna gasped.

The butler glanced at her, then added, "Though we may need some deportment lessons first."

Despite the flush in Jenna's cheeks, she stood straight and tall as she said, "If the Four wanted me to grow up as a farm girl, They must have thought my plant magic was more important than manners."

The butler stared at her, but she didn't cower. He finally let out a sigh so quiet Gwen doubted anyone else had heard it. "I can tell you are quite different from the current Avi Sum, young Ava. Which reminds me; where is the rest of your quartet?"

Gwen stepped forward. "We don't know. We're here in Wistica to search the Hall of Records for them." She squeezed her hand. "We also need to inquire at the University regarding antique pottery."

"Antique pottery? Have you had a chance to read *The Wistica Word* yet, young Ava?"

"No, and please call us simply 'Ava.' Our souls are as old as any other Avatar's."

Jenna smiled. "I don't mind being young. Someday, Gwen, I hope you learn to be young too."

The butler's mouth twitched. "As you wish, Ava. I'll fetch you a fresh copy of the newspaper and send messages to the Hall of Records and the University. Please enjoy lunch and the fittings in the meantime. If you need anything else, my name is Master Marten."

He showed them to the dining room across the hall, then departed. A maid came and offered to take Robbie for a while; her smile looked strained as Jenna issued a list of instructions while Robbie howled. A few minutes after the maid left, a footman appeared with a newspaper on a silver tray and offered it to Gwen. While Jenna studied the paintings on the wall and reminisced about previous lives, Gwen skimmed for articles about Chaos Season, the Avatars, or shards. Margaret's death was the first story, but it didn't mention the shard that had injured her horse. A second article wondered about the new Season Avatars who were expected to report to the One Oak. Gwen scanned the column, hoping someone else had some information she could use but worrying she'd overlooked an obvious clue. Her name was mentioned, as was Jenna and her rose bush, but no one else. Even Kay had been overlooked. The Four weren't making this quest easy for her.

As she'd feared, Chaos Season had struck several times throughout Challen, particularly in the western half of the country. Five people had been killed, while several others were badly wounded. Gwen grimaced as the shard shifted under her skin. If only she could do something, but even if she wasn't cursed, she was in the wrong part of the country.

Another article caught her attention: "University Acquires Rare Intact Pot From Pre-Annexation Days." Gwen caught her breath. Could the shard be that old? Someone had sketched the pot, but although the pattern looked familiar, the picture was in black-and-white, not color. She skimmed the article for a description. Unfortunately, no one bothered to mention the color, only that it had been donated to the University by a visiting Delnsman named Kron Evenhanded. He was giving a public lecture this very night about and life in Wistica before the Annexation.

Gwen whooped, and Aunt Gabri and Jenna stared at her with wide eyes. Gwen didn't care if they thought her unladylike. "Jenna, look at this!" She thrust the newspaper at her. "The Four must have arranged this for us. We must go!"

CHAPTER ELEVEN

The Water Clock

Jenna moved her lips as she stared at the paper. "Do you think it's safe, Gwen?"

"Safe? Why wouldn't it be safe?"

"Those shards came from somewhere." She set the paper down on the table with a thwack. "What if the Delnsman sent them? And what kind of name is Kron Evenhanded anyway? He must have made that up. Maybe he's an Avatar for Delns, and he wants to steal our magic!"

Uneasiness stirred within Gwen, but she had to investigate the best clue to her curse, no matter how risky it was. Besides, Jenna had to be wrong. "Delns doesn't even have a God, let alone Avatars," she reminded Jenna.

"Well, maybe they finally realized how useful we are and are trying to create their own Avatars." Jenna rubbed her hands, a determined look in her eyes. "You're going to go no matter what I say, aren't you? I'd better go to the courtyard after lunch and prepare a fighting stick."

"Why not send for one from the Temple?"

"They're too old, and just for the soltrans. The fresher the stick, the better for my magic."

At the start of every new season, the Avatars traveled to Wistica to perform the soltrans ceremony on the ancient Temple grounds. It was one of the few pre-Annexation buildings still intact. Gwen didn't think the Four fought each other in ritual combat the way the Avatars did, but the common people loved the show.

Aunt Gabri roused herself from her window seat. "A fighting stick? Jenna t'Reve, you may not be my niece, but I forbid you to carry something like that in public! That's disgraceful!"

"I do it twice a year at the soltrans. So does Gwen."

"That's different." Aunt Gabri shot Gwen a stern look. "I don't think the Four meant for you to be...hooligans!"

Gwen set the newspaper aside. "Aunt Gabri, Jenna is only trying to protect us."

She sniffed. "Your fiancé should be here to take care of that for you."

Gwen and Jenna exchanged she-can't-be-serious looks. Avatars could look after themselves. Or was this another subtle dig for Gwen to get married?

The servants brought them a late lunch of soup, bread, cold chicken, fish, young vegetables, and a fruit tartlet. Gwen and Jenna ate so much Aunt Gabri muttered something about fittings on a full stomach. But the fitting proceeded more smoothly than Gwen had expected. The seamstresses brought along several outfits in different colors and styles for each of them, not just ball gowns, but day and dinner dresses and even some riding outfits. Gwen found it a welcome change to forget about her duties for a while and chat with Jenna about fashion. Aunt Gabri argued with her seamstress, complaining that the dresses showed too much skin these days.

"How about something with a corset, to keep the young women standing straight?" she asked.

Gwen gasped. "No, Aunt Gabri. Those aren't healthy. We need to breathe."

"And move about, especially tonight," Jenna added. "Do you think something like this will do, Gwen?" She turned about, displaying a moss green dress with a square neckline and a short train. "I know I should be wearing all white, but …we're in Wistica."

Jenna sighed, and even without a link, Gwen could guess what she was thinking: this was her first visit to the capital of Challen, and she wanted to experience everything to the fullest before settling down at the One Oak.

Aunt Gabri glared in Jenna. "Here in Wistica, it's more important than ever to show you understand proper manners, farm girl."

Jenna put her hands on her hips. Her face reddened like a tomato ripening as they watched.

Even though Aunt Gabri was technically correct, Gwen decided it was better to pacify Jenna. "Jenna is here to represent Summer, not Winter, Aunt Gabri. She has to wear green at Court. If the seamstress can remove the train, this dress would also be suitable for tonight."

"Just suitable?" Jenna sank into a graceful curtsy, so low Gwen could see the swell of her heavy breasts. They stirred faint memories from previous lives. *Why should I care? I know we've served together in previous lives, even if I don't remember them well. I hope we'll be friends this time, but that's all we can be to each other.*

Gwen kept her gaze focused on Jenna's face. "I'm sure many gentlemen will find it more than suitable."

Jenna's face fell. "Maybe I should pick something else."

Why was she upset? "No, no, it's beautiful. You look beautiful."

"Are you sure?"

"Of course. You would be beautiful in rags."

"Not that you should wear rags to such a public event," Aunt Gabri admonished.

"If you think I should wear it then." Jenna turned to examine herself in a full-length mirror a maid had brought in. "What about you, Gwen? Let me help you pick one." She grinned as she approached

Gwen and whispered, "I'll find you something that will give your fussy aunt something to fret about."

"That doesn't sound like a good idea," she whispered back.

"You never think my ideas are good. This one is." Jenna gestured at a dress Gwen had admired earlier. It had gold embroidery over lemon fabric, but its neckline, although not as low as Jenna's, dipped more than Gwen felt comfortable with. "Go ahead. It was made for you."

Gwen let the dressmaker help her into it. It was loose at the bust and hips, but otherwise it fit well. "I can have this ready after dinner if you would like, Ava," the dressmaker said as she pinned the sides.

Aunt Gabri pursed her lips. "And maybe add some lace at the neckline?"

"No. No lace," Gwen said. "It doesn't go with the gown." Besides, with Jenna to goad her on, she liked the idea of wearing something daring.

By the time the fitting was done, it was time for dinner again. Afterward, a maid assisted Gwen into her new dress and pinned up her hair in an elaborate braid. Gwen hadn't brought her jewelry on this trip, but the dress was rich enough to stand on its own. Jenna looked just as splendid. As for Aunt Gabri, she hadn't found anything ready to wear, so she wore one of her old dresses, something twenty years out of date with a corset and lots of lace. Gwen didn't tell her it made her look even older.

Jenna gripped the handle of the picnic basket with both hands. "Should we bring the shard or leave it here?"

"Is there any way you can transfer it to something smaller, like your reticule?"

Each of their dresses came with a matching reticule. Jenna opened hers, then shook her head. "It's silk. I can't work with it."

"Better bury the shard under as much wood as possible, then."

After Jenna protected the shard as best as she could, a short carriage ride brought them to the University. The stone buildings were so ancient they bent the streets to their will, forcing them to curve instead of running straight. The driver let them off in the courtyard, and they passed through an arch. Aunt Gabri perked up as she looked around at the buildings. "That's where I studied poetry," she said as she pointed at one. "And over there is the library. Each floor has books in a different language."

Nobles and commoners alike streamed toward the main hall where the lecture would be held. Inside, children hawking cones of nuts and cups of chocolate and tea drew attendees away from the ticket window. A maid who'd accompanied Gwen and Jenna stood in line for them while Gwen surveyed the crowd to see if she recognized anyone. If William was in Wistica, he didn't seem to be attending the lecture tonight. Not surprising, as he preferred hunting and drinking to anything more cultured.

"How close will we be sitting?" Gwen asked the maid when she returned.

"I'm afraid all the boxes have already been reserved, Ava, but I was able to find you three seats close to the front. I'll stand off to the side."

"I hope they're not too close, or I might switch places with you," she said.

"Oh, no, Ava!" The maid, who was about Gwen's age, blushed. "Master Marten would be most furious with me if he ever found out! He'd send me away."

A couple of people chatting close by turned to look at them. Gwen hid her hand with the shard under her reticule. "Never mind. I was only joking. Please show us where we'll be sitting, then bring us chocolate and nuts."

The seats the maid had found for them were off to the side, below the boxes. Two rows of people separated them from the stage. Gwen wondered if it was safe for them to be there—or anyone else, for that matter. A table stood next to an empty podium. Several ancient statues and pieces of jewelry were displayed on it, but no pottery.

"Do you think he'll bring the pot out?" Jenna asked.

"If he does, how will we protect the audience?"

Jenna looked grim. "I should have brought a fighting stick after all. Maybe the chairs—"

The audience around them hushed as a woman with salt-and-pepper hair, wearing a black robe over her gray gown, stepped to the podium. "Lords and ladies, tonight we have a special treat for you. Our newest lecturer may be from Delns, but he knows more about pre-Annexation Vistichia than anyone I've met. Please welcome Kron Evenhanded!"

Polite applause broke out as a man in his late thirties or early forties came out, adjusting his sleeves as if they were uncomfortable. His dark, wavy hair, brown skin, and sharp nose made him appear like an historical figure himself. Carrying no notes, he walked past the podium and peered into the audience as if he was searching for someone. Gwen fought down the impulse to duck.

"Eight hundred years ago, Vistichia was a much different place from this modern-day Wistica." He spoke fluent Challen with an accent Gwen didn't recognize. "Ordinary people lived in mud-brick houses, sharing walls with their neighbors. Women spent hours every day grinding corn or other grains for flatcakes to feed their families. Men fished in the Chikasi River or sold goods in the marketplace. Children assisted their parents instead of attending school." He hesitated. "All those people are long gone now, of course, reborn into other lives. Perhaps some of you lived in Vistichia during those days. Whether you were here or not, I can make that period come alive for you again."

He returned to the table and picked up each item in turn, explaining what it was and how it had been used. Gwen listened closely, amazed at the details he described. He sounded as familiar with these objects as she was with the utensils at her dinner table. How did he know such things? Even Avatars forgot everyday items from their previous lives. The University official who had introduced him seemed as astonished as everyone else. Why was she so surprised? Didn't this man have a scholarly reputation? Gwen shifted in her seat, too distracted to pay more attention. If this man did discover a pot like the one that had cursed her, she hoped he would bring it out soon.

"It's rare to find pre-Annexation artifacts these days, and many of the ones that still exist are in poor condition." Kron stepped behind the podium for the first time since he'd started speaking. "So, I was… very lucky to find this intact water clock recently."

He pulled out an ochre pot a couple of feet tall. It matched the shard in Gwen's hand perfectly, but as he rotated it, she could see there were no pieces missing. She still flinched as he stepped to the edge of the stage and walked back and forth so everyone could get a better view. Jenna half-rose in her seat despite protests from the man sitting behind her. Nothing happened. The pot didn't try to attack anyone, even when Kron set it on the table.

"Is that a match?" Jenna whispered.

"Yes. Do you think he's lying about it being intact? Look at the back."

Although the water clock was curved in front, with rows of holes in the center of decorative circles, the other side was flat and unglazed, as if it was meant to stand flush against a wall.

"It must have been made like that," Gwen said. "The sides are too smooth for the back to be a repair job." The pattern at the edge appeared to have been cut off. She wished she could study the pot close-up—if it was safe to do so.

Gwen didn't pay much attention to Kron's concluding remarks, but she applauded politely with the rest of the audience. He glanced at her a couple of times. Did he know she was the next Spring Ava, or could he tell she was cursed? Maybe he meant to curse her again.

You can't let that happen, she told herself. *You can't continue like this either. You have to talk to him to figure out how to remove the shard and lift the curse.*

She pulled a calling card out of her reticule and beckoned the maid over. "Please give this to the speaker and tell him two of the Season Avatars wish to speak to him in private."

"At once, Ava." The maid bobbed her head and pressed forward to the stage. However, she wasn't the only one. Servants, scholars, and even a couple of nobles blocked her way, shouting questions at Kron.

"Should we join them?" Jenna asked.

"No. Let's wait." She watched as the maid tried to push past the people blocking her. If Gwen's magic was working properly, she might be able to do something to move things along. All she could do now was pray to Spring.

Perhaps Spring was in a benevolent mood, for the maid managed to slip past a noble and present Gwen's calling card to Kron. His eyes widened as the maid spoke to him. Other people in the crowd turned to look at Gwen and Jenna, whispering, "Avas" and "Avatars."

Gwen rose. "Now we can go see him, Jenna." She lowered her voice. "Got any wood?"

"Should I break an arm off a chair?"

"I don't think that would make a good impression."

The crowd parted for them. Some bowed or curtseyed, but one older man reached for Gwen. "Young Ava, if you're a Spring, I need to talk to you about my digestion—"

"Not now, my Lord. Perhaps some other time."

Kron studied them as they approached. "Which ones are you?" he asked. "I don't recognize either of you."

Gwen narrowed her eyes. Even a foreigner should know better than to be so rude to Avatars. "We haven't met before, sir."

He glanced at her card. "Of course we have, Lady Gwendolyn lo Havil. These names are so different now. Were you... Galia? They say you serve the Goddess of Spring, so you must be Galia."

Galia? It could have been her name in a previous life. How would a Delnsman know that?

Kron turned to Jenna. "As for you...I know you're not Ysabel, so...are you Caye?" He shook his head. "No, you don't seem as quiet as she was. But I have a hard time seeing you as Janno."

Jenna turned pale. "My name is Jenna in this life."

"Well, when I knew you, you were a man. In fact, you were Galia's son."

Gwen and Jenna stared at each other. Such an arrangement wasn't possible. Season Avatars didn't share families. And if they had been born in different generations, they would be part of different quartets. Did Kron really know anything about their past lives, or had the names been a lucky guess?

Names...does he know about Kay? "Caye" is very close to her current name. "Who's Ysabel?" Gwen asked aloud. "Is she the next Ava Fall? She has to be! How do you know of her? Where is she?"

Kron's shoulders sagged. "I was hoping you would help me find her."

CHAPTER TWELVE

Kron Evenhanded

"I think we'd better find someplace private to talk," Gwen said. "We have a lot of questions for you."

He smiled wryly. "I'm sure I have many more for you."

"Is there a suitable place close by?" Gwen asked. The lecture hall was too open for her tastes. Perhaps it would be simplest to bring him back to the Avatars' house. With Aunt Gabri and the servants to chaperone them, no one could object. Then she remembered the water clock. "Do you have to bring that ...object with you?"

"The water clock? I sold it to the University."

"Is it safe to leave it unattended?"

Kron raised his eyebrows. "Once I put it back in its display case. Come." He scooped up the water clock as if it was as ordinary as a teacup, then exchanged a few words with the University official.

She frowned, then announced, "I'm afraid the scholar cannot entertain any more questions tonight. He will be available mid-morning tomorrow for private tours of our collection—in exchange for a donation to support our research...."

Gwen and Jenna followed Kron. He led them down a hallway dark enough to make Gwen nervous. Before she could ask about candles, he said, "I think we could use some light, don't you?" and touched a fixture on the wall. It glowed; heartbeats later, the rest of them lit up.

"By All Four Gods and Goddesses!" Gwen flicked her finger in each of the four directions. "Are you sure you're not an Avi Win? What kind of magic is that?"

"I'm an artificer; I enchant objects. Don't you remember?" He shook his head sadly. "I thought the Four let you retain more memories than that. It's still good to meet some familiar souls from Vistichia."

Gwen shivered as Kron used the pre-Annexation form of Wistica's name.

"That's not a seasonal magic. Which God or Goddess gave you that power?" Jenna asked. "A foreign god?"

"None of them. I come from a time when a few people had magic talents of their own, not given to them by deities."

That sounded like nonsense—or blasphemy. Even the Avatar of War obtained his magic from the God of Fip. How was it possible to come from another time anyway?

Gwen tried to think of a suitable response as Kron led them to a display area. Mosaics hung on the walls, and various ancient objects, from spears to something that looked like a flute, were arranged in glass-and-wood cabinets. The air smelled of vinegar, lemon, and wax. He crossed to the center cabinet and laid his hand along the edge. The door opened. He placed the water clock on the shelf, closed the door, and touched it again. "There. It will only open for me and a few other scholars and officials at the University. I also enchanted the glass so it wouldn't break."

"They know about this...this...non-Challen magic?" Gwen asked.

"They don't know it's magic. I told them it's a new kind of lock I invented." Kron pointed to a metal contraption on the door. "They stick a key in here to open the door."

"And you can enchant anything? Even pottery?"

"Yes. But that's not important now. You need to help me find Ysabel."

How could he dismiss his magic so easily, especially when he'd admitted he might be responsible for the shards? But the Ysabel he kept talking about might be the Ava Fall Gwen was searching for. Gwen decided she needed to learn more about Ysabel first before bringing up the shards again.

"Is Ysabel really the next Ava Fall?" she asked. "How did you learn about her? Even the previous Ava Spring didn't have any information about her."

"Spring showed her to me."

Gwen's jaw dropped. "The Goddess?" Her heart raced. When was the last time one of the Four had spoken directly to an Avatar?

"You're not even a Challen." Jenna stepped forward and casually laid her hand on a wooden cabinet. "Why would one of the Four talk to you?"

"I was married to Ysabel a long time ago, before the Annexation, before the Four came to Challen." Kron's expression didn't change, and his breathing and heart rate seemed unaffected too. Either he was a very good liar, or he believed what he was saying. "Ysabel was named Bella then. She became one of Fall's Avatars, and she was closest to Galia, Janno, and Caye. The Spring, Summer, and Winter Avatars."

Gwen and Jenna exchanged glances. The names fit almost too well. However, nothing else matched the way reincarnation worked.

Gwen took a step forward, past a cabinet of weapons. "Kron, even if you were married to Bella hundreds of years ago, that marriage only lasted until one of you died. We may reincarnate as part of the same group of Avatars, but the Four send us to new lives each time. We grow up in different families, in different parts of Challen. Most of us don't even stay male or female from life to life—except for the Falls. They're always women. Just because Ysabel married you once doesn't mean she'll do so again."

"They say those who are meant to be together do marry each other time and time again." Jenna studied Gwen with shadowed eyes.

"Well, I'm sure Ysabel and I are like that," Kron said. "Otherwise, Spring wouldn't have shown her to me."

"And did Spring show you where Ysabel is?" Gwen asked.

"She only said Ysabel was on the other side of Challen."

Gwen refrained from gnashing her teeth, as that was unladylike. Funny how ladies weren't supposed to show frustration, no matter the circumstances. This was more information than she'd had, but it still wasn't enough to pinpoint where to find the Fall Avatar.

Jenna raised her eyebrows as she glanced at Gwen, then she moved closer to Kron, draping herself against a cabinet in such a way as to show off her bosom. "You keep talking about your time and this time. How come you remember your past life so well? Even we have trouble with details after a few hundred years."

Kron searched his clothing, paying no attention to Jenna. "It was just a couple of weeks ago. Now, where did I put that enchanted quill?"

Gwen indulged in a snort. "No one grows up that quickly."

"Here it is!" He pulled out a heavily folded sheet of paper and a stained quill pen. He set them on a cabinet. "This will capture your words for later." Finally, he looked over at Gwen. "You don't understand, either of you. I wasn't reincarnated the way you Avatars are. I came to this time fully grown, inside that water clock."

Gwen and Jenna raised their eyebrows in unison. *By All Four Gods and Goddesses, he talks quite rationally, but Spring didn't give him a full measure of reason. Dear Goddess, why did you send him to me? Can I trust what he said about the Ava Fall?*

Kron sighed. "I can see you two don't believe me. I can demonstrate, but then I want to know more about Ysabel." His words and tone sounded reasonable, but there had to be a threat behind them. Gwen stood up straight, her cursed hand in front of her. She'd strike him with boils—or worse—before letting him make more shards to inflict others.

He unlocked the cabinet and removed the water clock, extending it toward Gwen. "Feel free to examine it if you like."

Gwen shook her head and stepped backward. Jenna copied her.

"Are you sure? You seemed interested in it earlier. Very well."

He set it on the floor, and the water clock swelled until it was the size of a cabinet, big enough to swallow Gwen, dress and all.

"By All Four." She couldn't help retreating to the door. Gwen had stood in the middle of hail, lightning, and whirlwinds before, but it took all of her courage to stay in the room. She couldn't look like a coward in front of Jenna. Even her sister Ava had abandoned all attempts to flirt and hid behind a cabinet. Time for Gwen to regain control of the situation. "That's enough, Sir Evenhanded!"

"What about Bella?" The water clock loomed like a threat. "What can you tell me about her? Can you take me to her?"

The eagerness in Kron's voice almost made Gwen believe he was genuine. "We don't know anything about Ysabel," she said. "I swear by the Four. So far it's only Jenna and me in this generation. We're here to look for her and the next Ava Win."

"Could I be of assistance?" He sounded hopeful.

"Thank you, but no." She forced a smile. "We can manage on our own. Good night."

She grabbed Jenna's arm—no link formed through the fabric—and dragged her back to the hall, ignoring Kron calling "Wait!" behind them.

Aunt Gabri remained in her seat, face so pale it was almost gray. Alarmed, Gwen risked a link with her untainted hand. Her aunt's heartbeat was erratic. Gwen sent calming magic to it, lulling it back to a normal rhythm. "We'd better get you back to the house, Aunt Gabri, so you can lie down."

"There are plants that might help her," Jenna said. "But I don't know where I could find them here."

"You'd have to visit an apothecary. Even then, it's more likely to be distilled, not the whole plant." It pained Gwen that she couldn't trust her own healing magic for her aunt, but she was glad the Four had provided her with backup.

"I can't believe how improperly you two behaved, Gwendolyn." Aunt Gabri paused to wheeze. "Running off like that to meet a strange man. William will be most upset when he hears about this, mark my word."

"Yes, Aunt Gabri." She couldn't be too ill if she felt able to complain. Still, Gwen couldn't help wondering if this attack would have happened if Aunt Gabri had stayed home.

"And he will hear, mind you, with all the nobles here tonight."

"Yes, Aunt Gabri. Would you like some help getting to the coach?"

She sighed. "Yes, Gwendolyn. That's a dear."

Jenna let Aunt Gabri lean on her. Once they made it outside to the crisp air, Aunt Gabri revived a little. Although Gwen and Jenna exchanged serious glances, they didn't speak until they arrived back at the Season Avatars' house and saw Aunt Gabri safely settled in her room. Once Gwen had assured herself her aunt was stable and given her what healing she could muster, she returned to the drawing room. A decanter of sherry stood half-full, while Jenna wiped her mouth on a lacy napkin.

"By the Four, that's good stuff," she said.

"Better not have too much. It's not good for either you or Robbie."

"I just finished feeding him. Thank the Four I could wear green tonight. I didn't think we'd spend so much time at the university. White's not a good color when you...leak."

Gwen coughed as her own sherry went down the wrong way. When she could speak again, she said, "Better find a wet nurse for Robbie. We'll be busy, and you might not have time or strength."

"I can manage." Jenna stared down at herself as if she didn't believe her own words.

Time to change the subject. "So, what did you think of Kron?"

"Very strange." Jenna crossed to the window and stared at the courtyard below. "He seems to know things about us that we've forgotten, but he acts like he's spoken directly with the Four, and when was the last time They appeared to us? There are only twelve of us Avatars, and we know them all. Plus, he has strange magic. He's not one of us!"

"Well, I can't imagine the Four would allow him here in Wistica if he was truly evil. But the water clock...how did he do that? Did he fool us into thinking it changed size? Did he really come forward in time without dying?" Gwen blinked her eyes, testing her vision. It seemed normal. Maybe Kron had performed illusions earlier. "If he can lock cabinets and make things grow, maybe he can break pieces off the water clock and send them after us."

Jenna shrugged. "Freeze me if I know why. Maybe it has something to do with Ysabel."

"She wouldn't ask him to curse us."

"Of course not. He hasn't even found her yet. Oh, I know!" Jenna clapped her hands. "He's using the shards from the water clock to look for her, only it must have thought we were her because we're all Avatars."

Gwen paced. The carpet beneath her thin-soled shoes felt comforting. Jenna's theory made sense, but it didn't explain why the shards interfered with her magic. She sighed. Did they have to go back to the University and ask him about that? She didn't want to go anywhere near that water clock again.

"You don't see anything unusual out there, do you?" Gwen asked.

"You mean, more shards? No. I thought I saw someone pass a few heartbeats ago, but they're gone."

Gwen came over to check herself. A gaslight stood in front of the gate, providing enough light to prove the street was empty—for now.

"At least one good thing came out of our visit tonight," she said. "We now have a name for the Ava Fall. It should help us track her down in the records tomorrow."

"I wonder why the other Ava Spring couldn't find her." Jenna turned to face Gwen. "But I'm sure you'll succeed. You're very determined that way."

The compliment felt like a gift. Gwen smiled, her worries eased. Maybe her relationship with Jenna was improving to the point where they could link. Then she remembered the bulge in her hand. Finding the other two Avatars wouldn't matter if she couldn't link with them.

"I think I'll check on my aunt before going to bed. Good night, Jenna." She didn't quite know what she wanted to say to Jenna, but she knew her words were inadequate. She could still feel Jenna's gaze on her as she left.

CHAPTER THIRTEEN

The Hall of Records

Gwen rose about an hour after dawn. She chose a dress simple enough for her to put on by herself, then rapped on Jenna's door. Jenna didn't appear for another half-hour, after Gwen had persuaded a maid to start serving breakfast early. Jenna's eyes were red, and she added extra pepper to her cup of chocolate before draining it.

"Poor night with Robbie?" Gwen had slept too deeply to hear anything.

"I thought he could sleep through the night by now. No such luck." She glanced upstairs. "He's still asleep. Do I bring him with me to the Hall of Records?"

"What if he wakes up? If he cries, he'll disturb the other clerks there." Worse, what if he damaged one of the precious records? Gwen shook her head. "Jenna, you're going to have to use a wet nurse sooner or later, or you'll never be able to fulfill your duties as an Avatar."

"But I'm his mama, Gwen. I have a duty to him too." She smiled. "And it's nice holding Robbie close, like we're the only two people in the world."

No wonder Jenna wasn't interested in linking with Gwen; she'd already bonded with her child. Gwen swallowed a bitter lump of jealousy. She couldn't remember much of her mother besides the death, but she would have bet the family estate that her mother hadn't nursed her when she was a baby. It never would have even occurred to her.

"Do whatever you need to do, then." She'd already finished her breakfast, so she stood up. "I'm going to peek in on my aunt, then order the carriage brought around. Aunt Gabri should stay here and rest today. Hopefully if we leave quickly, she won't do more than complain."

Aunt Gabri was still sleeping. Her color was better, and her heartbeat more regular. Gwen touched her gingerly. Her heart had to work hard to push her blood through narrowed veins. Gwen tried to widen them, but her healing backfired and made the problem worse. By the time she managed to undo the damage, her aunt was no better off than before, and sweat—not "glow"—plastered Gwen's hair to her forehead. She whispered, "Sorry" to her aunt and kissed her check.

Jenna waited in the foyer with a fussy baby. "He didn't want to nurse very long," she said once the carriage arrived and they'd settled themselves. "Any idea why?"

"It could be something you ate. Or the change in routine."

"Then a wet nurse might upset him more."

If her magic was working properly, Gwen could have done more to help Robbie—or convince Jenna to wean him and let a wet nurse take over. Jenna would have to sort the issue out for herself.

Outside, Wistica was stirring to life. In the Spring Quarter, gardeners were out doing work, and a few maids draped in shawls and carrying big baskets were on their way to market. The Summer Quarter was more active. Shopkeepers opened their doors and set out wares, while workers and schoolchildren rushed by. The carriage turned onto a street where every building boasted the seal of Challen above the doorway. This area was quieter than the rest of the quarter, as if the government of Challen needed silence for its work. *Or as if they're all entombed in the stone buildings.*

Despite her morbid thought, Gwen kept her face composed as she stepped down from the carriage. Jenna cradled Robbie with one hand and let the coachman take the other to assist her. Once she was ready, Gwen led the way to a building on the corner labeled "Hall of Records." She rapped on the wooden door. After fifty heartbeats, she tried it again. A spectacled balding young man opened the door and stared at her. He glanced first at her, then at Jenna. "Here to register a birth? Didn't the midwife take care of that for you?"

Gwen shook her head. "No, we're here to examine the records."

He tilted his spectacles back. "And you are—"

"Lady Gwendolyn lo Havil, the next Ava Spring. And this is Jenna t'Reve, the next Ava Sum."

The bored expression in his eyes gave way to excitement. "Yes, we've been told to expect you. My apologies, Ladies, I mean Avas, I didn't think you'd be here so early. Please, come in."

He opened the door wide enough to admit them to a dimly lit hall. Although the morning had been cool, the hall was even colder than the outside. The clerk led them down an echoing corridor. Metal doors interrupted the stone at intervals. Each door bore a sign with heavy, old-fashioned lettering: Marriages, 300-400 A.A.; Births, 300-400 A.A.; Estates, 300-600 A.A....

"How far back do your records go?" Gwen asked.

"About seventy years After Annexation, Ava."

"And you can still read the records?"

The clerk's ears turned red. "The originals didn't last, but fortunately they were copied before we lost them."

After leading them up three flights of stairs, the clerk stopped in front of a door labeled Births, 500-600 A.A. Gwen's own birth would be recorded here, along with the answers she'd been looking for.

The room ran deeper than she expected, like an ancient tomb of knowledge. The walls were lined with shelves stacked with bound records, and a single long table dominated the center of the room. Candles in candlestick holders, quill pens, and scraps of paper were set in front of each chair. The clerk gestured at the table. "Please sit, Avas."

Jenna sat at the far end, fussing over Robbie. Gwen lit a few tapers from the central candlestick. After searching the shelves, the clerk returned with two books. "Here are the birth records for the year you were born, the fall and winter seasons."

Since the winter book was on top, Gwen checked it first. The first page was for the first day of Snowmoon, the Winter Solstice. A single name occupied the page; it was written in such an elaborate script Gwen wouldn't have been able to figure out what the letters were if she didn't know what the name was. "Kay Seltich. Mother: Kathri Seltich, Seamstress. Father: Patrick Seltich, Dock Workman. Place of Birth: Wistica, Winter Quarter, Frost Street, 472, Apartment 404."

"I thought you already had her name," Jenna said.

"Yes, but not her family's address." Gwen copied the address onto a scrap of paper and set it aside so the ink would dry. "We can start looking for her there."

Next, she turned her attention to the fall book. If Kron was right, Ysabel would be listed here. She opened the book to the first page, for the Fall Equinox, and stared at it. "It's blank."

"As I explained to the previous Ava Spring, we have no records of any child being born in Challen on that date."

"That's not possible!" Jenna said. "Is it?"

"It's very rare for a day to go by without a birth, Ava. It may take a few weeks for birth records to reach us from the very small towns and the farthest corners of Challen, but we enter each record on the correct page as soon as it arrives."

"Are birth records ever lost in transit?" Gwen asked.

"Not to my knowledge, Ava. Records such as births, deaths, and marriages are very important, second only to the monarch's messages. Every care is taken to ensure that they arrive intact."

Gwen and Jenna stared at each other for a moment. This would have been a good time to link and exchange private thoughts—if Gwen's magic was working.

Jenna looked down at her son in her lap. "Sir, I'm curious. Could you look up my son's birth record? He was born about two moons ago."

"One moment, if you please, Ava." He bowed his head, then withdrew to the back of the room.

Gwen studied the page. It looked pristine to her, but she was no expert. "Jenna, can you tell if there's any ink residue on this page? Maybe they used the wrong ink, and it faded away."

She touched it, closed her eyes, and shook her head a couple of heartbeats later.

"So Kron lied to us."

"Why would he lie about someone he loves?" Jenna opened her eyes. "There has to be another explanation. Maybe Ysabel's birth record got lost before arriving here." She held Robbie over her heart, his head on her shoulder, and rubbed his back.

"Or maybe someone, somewhere, didn't want anyone to know who the next Ava Fall is." Restless, Gwen got up to pace by the shelves. "Without us and our magic, Challen would be as barren as Selath. A foreigner—like Kron—might be acting against the country."

"But wasn't he in that jar until recently, less than a moon ago?"

"Who else would hide the identity of a Season Avatar?" Gwen snapped.

The clerk returned with a book and set it on the table. He bowed and said, "Please pull the bell cord in the corner when you're done with the records, Avas," before leaving.

Robbie spit up, and Jenna dug in her reticule for a rag. "By the Four, I should have known that would happen. I hope my dress isn't ruined." She wiped the wet spot. "Gwen, the two people who know the most about a child's birth are the mother and the midwife. Maybe Ysabel's mother is trying to pretend her child isn't a Season Avatar."

"But why?" Gwen brushed dust off her skirt.

"I don't know. Why would the Four send an Avatar where she's not wanted?" Jenna sighed. "Check the other pages, Gwen. I'll bet my best dress Ysabel's birth was registered on a different day." She chewed her lip for a moment. "Though if I really wanted to hide that my child was an Ava Fall, I'd say she was born in summer."

Gwen nodded. "Good idea. Let me see if I can find the summer book by myself." She searched the shelves until she came close to the right year, then looked for a two-book gap. The summer book was next to it. "How many days back should I check?"

"A week at most."

That left her with a couple hundred names to check. Was one of them Ysabel? What if there were more than one girl with that name?

She skimmed the list, paying more attention to the first names instead of the family ones, when a long surname caught her eye. "Lathatilltin? That's not a Challen name!"

"What kind of name is it?" Jenna asked.

"I'm...I'm not sure." Gwen glanced at the rest of the name, then shrieked. "Ysabel! I found her!"

Robbie wailed. Jenna comforted him and peered over Gwen's shoulder. "Where?"

"Right here." She read the rest of the entry out loud: "Ysabel s'Ivena Lathatilltin. Mother: Mattie s'Ivena Lathatilltin, Pianoforte teacher. Father: Haltin Lathatilltin, merchant and watch maker. Place of birth: Tradetown, Amity Street, House 31. She was born on the last day of Heatmoon, the day before the equinox." Gwen gasped. "By All Four!"

"What? What?"

Gwen's finger trembled as she pointed to the next entry: "Lathtin Hal Lathatilltin. Mother: Mattie s'Ivena Lathatilltin..."

Jenna spoke after a hundred quick heartbeats. "Twins? Avatar twins?"

"They can't be," Gwen said. "That's a male name."

"Don't try to trick me, Gwen; I know twins aren't always the same…" Jenna's eyes widened. "But a male Fall Avatar? Fall barely tolerates men."

"Then this must be the wrong Ysabel." Gwen slowly scanned a full moon's worth of summer birth records while Jenna did the same for fall. But they couldn't find anyone else with that name.

Maybe it was a further ruse, a false baby invented to protect his sister. But anyone caught altering birth records would be sentenced to harsh labor. Who would risk that? Gwen stared at the entry some more, trying to understand its puzzle. She wished she dared throw the book against the wall.

"I'll bet Kron is trying to mislead us," she said. "Ysabel can't be the right one."

"Then how do we pick the right girl out of the rest of the names?"

"Maybe it's…" Gwen waited for a sign, something to point to a different name. Nothing happened. She sighed. "I have no idea. Freeze it, if Ysabel is our only clue, we have to track her down, no matter how impossible it is for her to be an Avatar."

"I've never heard of Tradetown," Jenna said. "Where is it?"

"Let's ask the clerk."

The clerk was just outside the door. Gwen extended the book toward him, but he raised both hands, blocking her from leaving. "I'm terribly sorry, Ava, but no one is allowed to take these books out of their rooms. These are the only copies, and we can't risk losing them."

"I just wanted to show you this entry. Can you tell me where Tradetown is?"

"I think it's near Selath."

Gwen repressed a groan. That was on the other side of the country. They could waste half a moon trying to beat rain from a white cloud. What would happen to the real Ava Fall in the meantime?

"What about that name? Latha ... whatever the rest of it was." Jenna widened her eyes, looking perfectly innocent. "What kind of name is that?"

The clerk straightened up and polished his spectacles. "Most likely Selathen, Ava."

"A Challen woman and a Selathan man?" Gwen said.

"Such unions are uncommon, Ava, but they do happen. Even if both parents were Selathen, if the birth happens in our country, it's noted here. That's the law."

"Thank you, sir." Gwen copied down the information while Jenna stuffed the used rag into her reticule. The clerk snatched the record book as soon as Gwen was done.

"If I could ask you one final question," she said, "do you track when people move?"

"Only if it involves birth, death, marriage, or property, Ava."

"So, if I asked you to tell me where someone was now, you wouldn't be able to do it?"

He shook his head.

"I see. Well, thank you for your time." Gwen withdrew a gold chal from her reticule. "And here's for your trouble."

He bowed several times. "A pleasure to serve the Season Avatars. I only wish I'd been of more assistance."

He led them back through the maze of rooms to the entrance before taking leave of them. Outside, the sun was high in the sky—nearly noon. The air was fresh and warm after the Hall of Records, as if the Four had decided to reward them with a proper spring at last.

"Let's stop by the Temple before lunch," Gwen said. "Maybe the Four will send us an explanation."

They walked a couple of blocks to the Temple. Its dark gray stone stood out against the paler government buildings, and the worn steps leading up to the Temple reminded everyone that this was one of the few pre-Annexation buildings left in Wistica. Since it wasn't a solstice or equinox, only a few worshippers climbed the steps with Gwen and Jenna. The Avas paused at the top. A covered porch gave the Avatars room to battle each other with staffs every three moons. Gwen fancied she saw echoes of herself in previous lives still fighting for her season.

Inside, the central square felt dark, despite a fire burning in front of Spring's altar. Gwen knelt in front of it as Jenna crossed to Summer's wall. *Bright Goddess, giver of life and warmth, help me understand what to do. Is Ysabel really the one we seek?*

She waited. She thought she smelled a faint breeze carrying rain and sun, mud and lilacs and apple blossoms, but it vanished faster than a flower could drop its petals.

"Are there roses in here?" Jenna walked around Summer's altar. "I thought I smelled them. Grass too."

"I definitely smelled spring."

They looked at each other and smiled. Maybe the Four weren't so silent after all. Side by side, Gwen and Jenna circled the room, stopping in front of each altar to curtsey before leaving.

Jenna waited until they were back in the carriage, heading back to the house, before leaning forward and asking, "Why do you think Ysabel is listed with the wrong birthday?"

"Maybe it has something to do with her Selathen father. Selathens shun magic; they think it's evil."

"Chaos Season might be, but not our magic."

"They don't care. To them, all magic is bad, no matter how it's used."

Jenna shook her head. "Then why would the Goddess of Fall send her Ava to start her life in a family like that? And with a male twin?"

"Maybe to protect her. Let's call on Kay's family this afternoon. We need to learn more about her before leaving Wistica."

The ride back to the Avatars' house took longer than the outward trip, since traffic was heavier. Gwen's stomach was beyond rumbling by the time they arrived. The last thing she expected for lunch was a guest—especially when he turned out to be Kron.

CHAPTER FOURTEEN

Kron's Story

"He had your card this time, Ava," Marten explained. "So we were obliged to let him in."

Gwen raised her eyebrows. "This time? Has he been here before?"

"Yes, Ava. The stable boys have noticed him lurking outside the gates on previous occasions."

Oh, By the Four... "And did he bring anything...unusual with him?"

Marten shook his head. "Will you receive him, Ava? I'm sure he knows you're here."

Jenna leaned forward, her breath hot against Gwen's ear. "Maybe we should show him the shard I have trapped. He was right about Ysabel, Gwen. Maybe he'll help you—if you ask."

She planned to demand answers instead. "Have another place laid for him for lunch." Maybe he would be more willing to talk after they'd eaten.

Aunt Gabri joined them despite her pale complexion. She watched Kron as if she shared Gwen's suspicions. Kron wore the same clothes as he had last night, but they still looked fresh and crisp.

"Thank you for agreeing to talk to me again," he said after bowing slightly to each of them. "You left so quickly last night I was afraid

I'd offended you. Your manners and customs are so different from—" he glanced at Aunt Gabri—"from what I'm used to."

Aunt Gabri humpfed as if that wasn't a sufficient excuse.

Kron wolfed down his seafood bisque. "Anyway, are you sure there's nothing more you can tell me about Ysabel?"

"Who's Ysabel?" Aunt Gabri asked.

"She may be the next Ava Fall," Gwen replied. She stirred her soup as she debated what to tell Kron. She and Jenna had found Ysabel's record fairly easily; would Kron be able to do the same? How much access would he, as a foreigner, have to the Challen Hall of Records? While he wouldn't be as welcome as an Avatar, Gwen suspected he could find a way in if he chose, but it might be harder for him to find the exact record. She had the advantage of having more information—for now. Best to use it while it was still valuable.

Gwen took a deep breath and hoped she was doing the right thing. "We've traced her birth record to Tradetown," she said. "We're not sure if she's still there."

"If that's you only lead, you have to start looking there," he said. "When are you leaving?"

"First we have to search for the Ava Win. She was born in Wistica, the Winter Quarter."

"The Winter Quarter!" Aunt Gabri dropped her spoon, spattering soup on the white tablecloth. "That's where the poor people live."

"Avatars come from all social classes, Aunt Gabri."

"Except for Springs." Jenna stabbed a stalk of asparagus as if it had offended her. "You never hear of a Spring that started on a farm, or as a worker."

Gwen fought down the flush burning on her cheeks. "We have to deal with nobles and royals. Best to have the quartet leader understand them." And better to change the subject. "Back to Kay, do we visit her home or summon her here?"

"If she's anywhere in Wistica, you'd think she'd come here on her own," Jenna said. "So, why hasn't she?"

Gwen stared at the rest of the dishes laid out for them: a pair of hens, fish with lemon and butter, stewed vegetables, and hearty bread. She gestured for the serving man to bring her some of everything. "Kay should know she's needed by now." She frowned as she tried to remember how Kay had been in previous lives. "She's dedicated to being an Avatar, isn't she, Jenna?"

"She's always serious about everything, just like you. You're lucky to have me in your quartet. Otherwise, none of you would ever do anything fun."

Gwen ignored the jibe. "So if Kay hasn't come to us, something must be wrong. I think we should visit her house and investigate."

"You plan to go to the Winter Quarter?" Aunt Gabri let out a healthy shriek that made everyone wince. "Are you trying to be the death of me, child? You'll be robbed and murdered!"

Gwen sighed. "Do you honestly think they would set upon an Ava Spring? They'd more likely ask me to heal them."

"Exactly! And when you can't do it, they'll turn on you like a pack of dogs on a wounded rabbit."

The room fell silent. Even the servants froze with dishes and wine-glasses in their hands.

"Galia? I mean, Gwen?" Kron leaned forward. "What do you mean, you can't use your magic?"

How dare he look and sound so innocent? Gwen clanked her knife onto the table, then stood. "You should know all about it, Kron Even-handed, with your frozen shards. Why are you spreading curses throughout Challen?"

"What? Shards? Curses? What are you talking about?"

"You know very well what we're talking about." Jenna stood up too. "We saw your water clock. The back doesn't match the front. Is that where the shards came from?"

He looked back and forth at each of them, his expression becoming more guarded. "You're saying you saw pieces of pottery that look like my water clock? Can you show them to me?"

"I have one embedded in my hand right now." Gwen displayed the bump to him. "And it's interfering with my magic. I'm lucky it hasn't killed me. Another shard caused the other Ava Spring to die when it lodged in her horse's hoof. And a third came after us while we were traveling down the Chikasi River. Jenna trapped it in a wooden bucket."

Kron studied her hand for a moment, then shook his head. "I can't sense the shard you bear. Your magic must be blocking mine."

"Maybe I should get the one from upstairs," Jenna suggested.

"Now? Well, why not?" Gwen shrugged. "I've lost my appetite."

Gwen, Aunt Gabri, and Kron retired to the parlor while Jenna fetched the basket. She hauled it with difficulty, as if it resisted her. Kron came forward to help her set it next to the fireplace. After exchanging glances, the Avatars backed into a corner, behind a wooden table. Aunt Gabri eyed them as if wondering if she should join them.

"Don't worry, Aunt Gabri," Gwen said. "It wants us, not you."

"Humph. I'll believe that when I see it."

Kron examined the basket from all angles before pressing on the rim. The basket cracked, exposing the bucket from the ship. Gwen grimaced at the sudden sharp odor of ammonia, but what worried her were the cracks and splinters in the thick wood. The shard still rapped against the bucket, but the rhythm seemed slower than before.

"What did you do to the basket?" Jenna asked. "I'd swear by the Four that the wood wasn't that brittle."

"It wasn't," Kron replied. "I can make or break things as I need to."

"Please don't break too many things in here. They're all antiques."

"If you say so." He glanced at a porcelain figurine on the mantel. "They all look new to me."

As he focused on the bucket, the smell faded. "Jenna, did you strengthen this wood?" Kron asked.

"I had to, otherwise it would have broken."

"I'm surprised it didn't, if this is Time's work. Yes, I see signs of decay. The Four can keep Time's worst effects out of Challen. That's probably the only reason the bucket didn't break."

"Time?" Jenna whispered. "What is he talking about?"

"I was hoping you remembered something about it," Gwen replied.

Keeping his hands on the bucket, Kron glanced around the room. "I need something metal that's large enough to contain this shard. Something with a lid would be ideal."

Gwen gathered her courage and darted away from the protection of the table long enough to pull the bell cord. Marten appeared a few moments later and listened as Kron repeated his request. "I know just what you need, sir," he said. He summoned a maid to borrow a soup pot from the kitchen. "Will this do?"

Kron nodded, then set the bucket in the pot. Gwen hoped the kitchen tossed the pot out once they were done with it.

"I'll need you to watch this," he said. "Just to make sure this is the shard you were talking about."

"By All Four, how many pottery shards do you think there are in Challen that can move about on their own?" Jenna asked.

"I don't know. That's what worries me."

Before Gwen could ask if there were enough shards to threaten all of the living Avatars, Kron pressed on the bucket, splitting it with a crack. For an instant, all was quiet in the parlor as the rapping stopped. Then the shard rose in the air, spinning as if deciding where to go. Gwen and Jenna reached for the closet objects—pillows from a nearby loveseat—to act as shields. Kron grabbed the shard barehanded. He uttered something in a language Gwen had never heard before. The shard wiggled, and he gripped it with both hands. He threw it into the pot, but the shard didn't shatter. Kron clamped the lid in place. Again he inspected the room.

"You say everything in here is ancient by your standards, correct? Is there anything in here that was blessed by the Four or used in Their Temple?"

The butler had remained to watch the proceedings, so Gwen asked, "Marten, is there anything in the house that fits our guest's needs?"

"Does it matter what it is, sir?"

Kron shook his head. "I'd like something small enough to fit into this pot, but I can work with whatever you have. I may have to damage it, though."

"Are there any old fighting sticks around?" Jenna asked. "We could break one of those to the right length."

Marten shook his head. "We don't keep items like that here, Ava."

"Clothing, then," Gwen suggested. "Part of a ceremonial robe. The former Ava Spring won't need hers anymore."

"I'll have another maid bring something down, Ava."

Everyone stared at the pot as they waited. Once the maid arrived with a saffron-colored gown, Kron tore off part of the skirt. He removed the shard and wrapped it in the skirt. It faded to a yellow so pale it looked white. The material shriveled, and threads snapped until the scrap couldn't even be used as a rag. Kron tossed it away, tore off another part of the gown, and repeated the process three more times. The last time, the cloth remained intact. Kron unwrapped the shard. "I pulled out all the foul magic Sal-thaath infested it with. It should be harmless now."

He set it on the floor, and it remained there instead of flying toward Gwen.

Her shoulders ached with tension; she worked them until they felt less stiff. That didn't help her unsettled stomach. What if this was a trick to lull her into accepting Kron? He might curse Jenna, or the other two Avatars, despite his claim that he'd been married to one of them.

Jenna approached the shard and tapped it with her shoe. It collapsed into dust. "He's right, Gwen."

"What about your magic, Jenna?" Gwen felt the ridge in her palm. "Is it still there?"

She touched a chair back, then nodded. Lucky her. Gwen wondered if pulverizing the shard in her palm would free her from the curse. Instinct warned her it might spread through her body, affecting her health, her magic, or both.

"Where did the foul magic come from in the first place?" she asked. "What's a ...Sal-thaath?"

Kron swept up the remnants of the shard with the rest of Margaret's dress. Marten and the maid watched with wide eyes, but he didn't pay any attention to them. "Not a what, Gwen. Who."

"Who?"

He gave her a sharp look. "You don't remember him? Or Salth?"

"Is that like Selath?" Jenna asked.

"Selath is the barren country to the west of Challen, correct? Yes, that's where Salth lived. Or lives." He sighed. "Of course, she would have to be still alive too. How foolish to hope I could escape from someone with time magic by traveling ahead in time, especially when Sal-thaath came with me."

"And how did that happen? No, wait." Gwen came around to take a seat. "Perhaps it would be better to tell us everything from the beginning, instead of a word here and there."

"Well, you still haven't told me much about Ysabel, and all this talk isn't taking us to her." Kron balled up the fabric. It grew smaller and smaller until it was the size of a marble. He placed it in his pocket. "If we're going to make a second attempt to destroy Salth, you need to know what happened the first time. I'm surprised the Four didn't make sure you keep those memories with you each life."

"Destroy Salth? Honestly, Kron, if you want us to help you, you have to explain yourself. I'm not a parrot."

"Even a parrot would use a title when addressing someone," Aunt Gabri said.

"Oh. Am I supposed to address you as 'Lady' or 'Ava'?" Kron asked. "Your time seems so formal. When we were living together in Vistichia, we called each other by name."

Aunt Gabri's eyes bulged. Gwen raced over to make sure her heart wasn't bothering her again.

"Please tell us what we need to know, Kron," she said. "And please try not to scandalize my aunt, especially when I can't heal her."

"Sorry. Maybe we should let her rest."

Aunt Gabri let out a long, dramatic sigh. "No, I'll do my duty, even if it sends me to the God of Winter this afternoon. Though a sip of sherry might help."

Marten brought in sherry, chocolate, and the cold leftovers from lunch as Kron related how he'd met Bella—Ysabel's original name—hundreds of years ago when her sister had been harassed by a magically powerful boy named Sal-thaath. Kron had attempted to civilize him, but Sal-thaath's mother, another powerful magician named Salth, had raised her son with more arrogance than Gwen had seen from the most self-important noble. Salth came up with a way to extract magic from mortals' souls and planned to test it on Bella. Kron rescued Bella but accidently killed Sal-thaath when he attempted to drain the boy's magic. Somehow, Salth managed to revive him and became more powerful herself.

"At that point, the Four appeared and gifted magic to twelve specially chosen residents of Vistichia," Kron said. "That includes you two and my Bella. But Salth was still angry at Bella and me, even though the Four wouldn't let her attack us directly. Worse, Salth found a way to drain time from other living things to keep her son alive. That's why Selath is such a wasteland."

"It's not a complete wasteland anymore," Jenna said. "Wild grasses grow there."

Kron stared at her. "Is it inhabited?"

"Not really. There are people who live on the border of Challen and Selath, and some of them venture farther in to mine for gems and minerals."

"And what happens to them?"

"They get old before their time," Gwen said softly, "and an Ava Spring can't cure them."

Kron spoke again in a language Gwen couldn't understand before switching to the modern version. "Salth is still stealing time for her son from other people. And if I understand Chaos Season correctly, you could say time gets mixed up in Challen. Salth must be trying to steal time from the people of Challen too."

Gwen frowned at that statement. "If that's true, I should feel it when I heal people injured during Chaos Season. I can't cure wounds directly caused by magic very well, but I've never had trouble helping people during Chaos Season."

"Chaos Season is mostly weather-related," Jenna added. "It also affects plants and animals. They may shift from summer to winter patterns, but they don't age and die."

"Then maybe Chaos Season is a side effect of what Salth is really trying to do." Kron touched the pocket with the cloth and pottery dust. "Or maybe it's linked to Sal-thaath."

"If they lived hundreds of years ago, why aren't they dead?" Jenna asked.

Kron smiled sardonically. "Do you think someone who controls time would die? Salth is powerful—maybe not as much as the Four, but she can challenge Them."

Silence fell in the room as Gwen absorbed that statement.

"As for Sal-thaath," Kron continued, "He came to this year the same way I did, inside the water clock. He wasn't with me when I arrived in the Temple. The Four wouldn't let him into Challen. I think when he escaped from his half of the water clock, the broken pieces were scattered across Challen. That's where the shards came from, Gwen."

She let out a deep breath. "So, you're saying you didn't create these shards, but you brought the boy who made them here."

"Not on purpose. Salth and Sal-thaath tricked all of us the first time we attempted to destroy the crystal house where she stores her stolen magic. She wanted to take my own magic—that, or yours. I managed to send all twelve of you Avatars back to Vistichia first, where the Four could protect you."

Gwen shot Jenna a do-you-remember-any-of-this look, but she shook her head. Gwen tried to keep her own expression from giving away her mistrust. Kron could claim to have saved them in the past, long before their own memories could confirm it, and blame someone else for their current problems. Until she saw this boy, she wouldn't believe Kron.

"I think we need some time to think all of this over." She rose, a signal for the butler to show their visitor out. Outside, the sky had darkened to the deep blue of late afternoon and early evening. Was it too late to call on Kay? No; the situation was urgent. If there were more shards in Challen, Gwen and Jenna needed to find Ysabel and Kay before the shards did.

"I need to make a finder," Kron said. Marten fetched his coat, and he put it on without showing signs of offense. "So I can track down the rest of the shards before others are hurt. I'll meet you once you find Bella."

"An excellent plan." Gwen didn't know what he meant by a finder, but she smiled politely anyway. "Let us know how it goes."

As soon as he was safely gone, Gwen turned to Jenna. "Do you believe any of it?"

"I…I don't know. I never heard of magic like his before."

"Same here. And he admitted the shards came from that jar we saw. That boy sounds like something he invented."

"But I believe him when he says he loves Bella. I mean, Ysabel." Jenna held her head high, as if daring Gwen to disagree with her. "He comes alive when he talks about her. I can hear it in his voice."

"He's still a danger to the rest of us," Gwen snapped. "Marten, have the carriage brought around. On second thought, can you send for a hired one? It might be safer when we go to the Winter Quarter."

Aunt Gabri had been resting with her head bobbing as she breathed, but she looked up at that. "The Winter Quarter! Gwendolyn, you can't go there! It's not safe, especially when it's almost nighttime."

"We've wasted enough time, Aunt," she said. "We need to find Kay and Ysabel as quickly as possible. Please don't feel you need to come with us. You'll be safer here."

Aunt Gabri opened her mouth as if she meant to argue, then closed it. "I...I suppose you're right. How many manservants will you bring with you?"

Gwen and Jenna looked at each other. "Just give me a fighting stick," Jenna said. "As long as I have a plant I can channel magic through, we should be fine."

"I don't think the Winter Quarter has a lot of lawns or flowerboxes." Gwen hadn't ever been allowed in that section before. She hoped she sounded more confident than she felt. "We should dress plainly, so we don't stand out."

By the time Gwen changed into a light blue linen dress borrowed from a maid and put her hair back in a simple coil, the streetlights were already lit. Jenna, wearing the dress she'd worn when Gwen had first met her, seemed confident enough. However, she'd left Robbie behind and bore an oak cane instead. If the cab driver wondered why two ordinary-looking young women needed to travel from the Spring Quarter to the Winter one, or why they traveled with uniformed escort, he didn't ask.

He took them to a four-story tenement building remarkable only for the oak tree out front. One of the biggest branches was gone, a scar in its place. Jenna laid a hand on the tree and closed her eyes for a few heartbeats. "Lightning," she said quietly. "Several years ago. I'd say four or five."

"Lightning perhaps drawn down by an Ava Win practicing her magic?"

"Perhaps." Jenna scratched her head. "The Four don't normally send the Wins to cities, do they? Doesn't seem like the best place to practice weather magic."

Gwen nodded. Too many people could be hurt if a Win made a mistake. "I'm sure They had a reason for it," she said. "Maybe we'll figure out why once we meet Kay and her family."

Gwen and Jenna went inside and climbed to the top floor. The stairs creaked underfoot, and cooking smells, along with less savory ones, drifted past them. More children raced past them, and laundry flopped over railings. Gwen averted her eyes, grateful Aunt Gwen had remained behind. If the steep climb didn't injure her heart, the living conditions would shock her senseless. These people seemed to have even less than the workers on the lo Havil estate. Was this how most people lived in Challen? The Four had made Their Avatars responsible for making sure everyone in Challen had what they needed to live. Of course, that had been before the Fips had taken over the country to grow food for its army. Once she'd found Kay and Ysabel, Gwen would have to visit the king and see if he would keep more of Challen's resources in this country. The king might be part of the royal Fip family, but he was part Challen too. He had to follow the Four's desires, not just the God of War's.

The top floor of the building had four doors, all closed. "Which one was it again?" Gwen asked.

"They're on the street side," Jenna answered. "I'll wager they're close to the tree, so…" she strode to the far end and knocked on the door. A man with thick gray hair answered.

"Blessings of the Four on you." Gwen seldom used the formal greeting Avatars used with supplicants, but it seemed appropriate for an Avatar's father. "Are you Master Patrick Seltich?"

He studied them before saying, "I am."

"We are the next Ava Spring and Ava Sum. Your daughter, Kay, is the next Ava Win. It's time for her to come with us to the One Oak. Is she here?"

He let out a sharp laugh. "By All Four, I haven't seen or heard from her in four years."

"Four years!" Gwen leaned against the door frame. "Why? What happened? Is she still alive?"

"We don't know." He shrugged. "We always thought maybe she'd gone to the One Oak, since she'd just come into her magic. But she never sent word back to us, and there's been no mention of her anywhere." Now he met Gwen's gaze beseechingly. "Are you sure she's not there?"

"I was there myself last moon, and she wasn't there. Sophia, the current Ava Fall, was trying to find out where Kay was herself."

Kay's father seemed to age ten years in a heartbeat. "We always thought the Four looked after their Season Avatars. If she never arrived..." He opened the door wider. "Do you want to come in? There's fish soup on the stove."

A couple of children peeked from behind their father. They looked too thin to share what must be a meager meal. "We can come in, but we won't stay for dinner," Gwen said.

The relief in the children's eyes told Gwen her instincts were right. She wished she'd brought more chals with her so she could leave some behind. Maybe she could arrange for the One Oak to send them a stipend.

The Seltich family might not have much, but they kept their home neat and clean. The curtains, mismatched seat cushions, and tablecloth were all expertly mended. Over in the corner stood a small shrine to the Four, with a vase of dried violets, an oak leaf, an acorn, and a bare branch. Jenna wandered over and touched the items. "Are the oak pieces from the tree out front?"

Master Seltich nodded. "Yes. Kay collected them. We still keep them in hope that she'll return."

Jenna carefully set everything back as she'd found it. "How did she disappear?"

"Did anything unusual happen beforehand?" Gwen added.

Master Seltich scratched his head. "I remember it stormed that night. Kay stayed by the window until bedtime, watching the wind and rain. We had to tell her to go to bed. In the morning, the window was open, and she was gone. We think she opened it sometime during the night, once the rest of us were asleep, and crept out to watch the storm. But she never came back in, and no one's seen her since."

"Why'd she go out the window?" Jenna asked.

"They lock the front door at night."

Gwen crossed over to the window and tried to open it. The frame creaked, and she strained to raise the window a few inches. How had Kay managed to open it without waking anyone? "Jenna noticed the tree out front was missing a branch. Did it extend to the window?"

"Not quite. But she might have tried to reach it anyway." Master Seltich took a deep breath. "We think...we think she fell, or jumped. Fell is more likely. That branch did come down in the storm, a lightning strike. But the next morning, there was no sign of her in the street. She didn't take anything with her, not a piece of clothing, not a quarter-chal. Was she hurt? Did someone find her? We don't know."

It didn't make sense. If Kay had fallen, she would have been injured. She didn't have healing magic, so how could she have gotten up and walked away? Maybe someone had helped her. Or maybe her weather magic had somehow saved her. Even so, why leave her family in the middle of a stormy night without any of her possessions?

"How was she acting that day? Anything unusual?"

"No. She'd been apprenticed to be a seamstress by the same shop keeper who employed her mother, so they were together at the draper's shop all day. Kay didn't say much, but then she's always been a quiet girl." He shook his head. "Her mother went over that day in her mind a thousand times. Kay didn't quarrel with anyone, she didn't see any young men, nothing. Whatever made her leave that night—if she left on her own—must have been something that happened during the storm."

Jenna's face reflected the confusion Gwen felt. "Did the storm cause any unusual damage that night?"

"It blew down a lot of tree branches in our area, and water came in through the window, but not much else."

Gwen wondered if Dorian would remember a storm from four years ago. "What was the exact date?"

"It was in summer. The fourteenth day of Corn Moon."

Since Midpoint was between Wistica and Tradetown, perhaps they could detour to the One Oak to question Dorian. Any small clue would help.

Gwen pulled her sketchpad and colored pencils from her reticule. "Could you describe Kay, please? I might be able to create a rough sketch of her."

It took several attempts, but by the time she was done, Gwen had a portrait that Master Seltich said was a respectable likeness of his daughter. According to him, Kay preferred her hair short so it wouldn't be in her eyes. It was straight, black, and chin-length; sometimes she wore a bow in it to pull her hair back. Her eyes were blue-gray and her complexion pale. Her face was narrow and small; she was shorter than Gwen. Gwen wondered how much Kay had changed in four years. Perhaps even this wouldn't be enough to find her.

Gwen offered Kay's siblings the coins from her purse, wishing she had more chals with her. Before she could speak, Kay's father said, "Avas, if you do find out what happened to Kay, we'd like to know." His voice dropped. "Even if it's not good."

"We'll pray to the Four that she's safe and sound somewhere."

They took their leave. As they descended the stairs, a drunk man leered at them and tried to grab Gwen's reticule. Jenna thwacked him with the cane. With a yell, he tried to wrest it from her. Gwen raised her hands, about to send him to sleep before she remembered her curse. "May Fall send spiders to weave your mouth shut," she said instead.

The man fled, swearing all the while. Gwen shook her head, amazed someone would behave that way no matter how drunk he was. She hoped all men weren't so crude. Otherwise she might pledge herself to be one of Fall's virgins no matter what her family wanted.

They made it safely to the hired carriage after that. When they were on the way, Gwen asked, "What do you think happened to Kay?"

"Something drove her off."

"But she didn't take anything with her," Gwen said.

"She must not have had the chance to grab anything."

"Then how did she get out of the window and down to the street without hurting herself? She would have been too wounded to go anywhere on her own."

Jenna shook her head. "Not necessarily. Weather magic's powerful."

The knot in Gwen's stomach loosened. "Even if she is still alive, why flee and not tell her family?"

"Maybe she was fleeing from them." A dark look settled over Jenna's expression.

"They didn't seem fearsome to me." Gwen wondered what could have driven Kay to such a desperate measure. "The most important question now is, where is she?"

"I wish the Four would tell us. I don't know how we'll figure it out otherwise." Jenna met Gwen's gaze. "Unless They put Kron here to help us."

"I'm still not sure I trust him, Jenna. He's linked to the shards." She shook her cursed hand furiously. "And he said nothing, nothing, about how to free me from this."

"Then you must ask him next time." Jenna sounded as calm about the matter as if she was discussing which bolt of cloth she would buy for her next dress. Gwen repressed the urge to scream at her. Jenna wouldn't be so accepting of the situation if her magic had been twisted.

"I don't think we'll stay in Wistica much longer," Gwen said once she could speak normally. "After we've met the king, we should travel to Tradetown and search for Ysabel. If our path takes us near the One Oak, we should ask the other Avatars for advice on finding Kay. Either way, we shouldn't see Kron for a while."

She wondered briefly if he would find his own way to Tradetown to search for his former wife. Perhaps they should put all other business aside and seek out Ysabel. Better to offend a temporal king than risk losing another Avatar.

CHAPTER FIFTEEN

The Ball

Gwen rose early to make travel arrangements to Tradetown with the help of Marten. The butler sent a manservant to purchase their steamboat and locomotive tickets and assigned a maid to handle the packing.

Meanwhile, Gwen and Jenna were due to appear before the king and his Court that evening, and the preparations started after lunch, with full baths for everyone. Then came perfuming, careful shaping and buffing of nails, arranging hair into intricate braids piled high on Gwen's head and held in place with jeweled pins, and finally dressing her in her Court gown with all the accessories. By the time the maids pronounced Gwen ready, it was early evening. All the cook served was cheese and bread, which did nothing to tame Gwen's magically-induced appetite. She hoped the king wouldn't keep them waiting for hours before receiving them. If she didn't have additional nourishment in the meantime, she might gnaw his hand off.

She was eating more cheese when Jenna appeared. Clad in white with green trimming, she seemed half a head taller than normal with her hair styled up. She descended the stairs slowly. Gwen had time to notice how her hands had been smoothed with an herbal lotion, gifting

Jenna with the scent of forests. She didn't handle her gown as gracefully as someone who'd worn such clothes from childhood would have, but no one would have identified her as the farm girl from Bull Rock that Gwen had met less than a moon ago.

Gwen wanted to comment on the transformation, but while she was still trying to figure out how to phrase it without giving offense, Jenna said. "You have food? Thank the Four! I swear that army of maids didn't want to feed me."

"Same here."

Jenna reached for the plate Gwen held in her other hand, but Gwen snatched it away. "There's more to being a lady than dresses. What about your manners?"

Jenna batted her eyelashes and pitched her voice higher than normal. "Oh please, kind Ava, may I have a piece of bread before I perish from hunger?"

Gwen couldn't help grinning as she held out the plate of food.

"Will we really meet the king himself tonight?" Jenna asked.

"Undoubtedly. I'm sure he'll be interested in the next set of Season Lords, since we're so important to Challen's welfare."

Jenna chewed her bread thoroughly before asking, "And we'll see lots of other nobles and royals too?"

Something in her tone made Gwen narrow her eyes. "I'm sure half of the country will be there." Why did she ask? She couldn't know many nobles, could she? Then she remembered there was another noble she might meet there, someone she hadn't heard from in what seemed like ages. "Including my intended."

"You don't sound thrilled for the reunion."

Gwen passed the rest of the food to Jenna. "There's been no word from him. He should know I'd be here instead of at my father's residence. Why hasn't he visited?"

"It's not as if you'd have been here, Gwen. You've spent the entire time tracking down Ysabel and Kay. I've barely gotten to see anything of the city. If you care for him so much—" Jenna's voice reached strident tones—"Why haven't you spared an hour for him?"

"I can't go to him." Gwen crumpled part of her skirt in her hands. Aghast at the creases in the silk, she tried to smooth them out, avoiding Jenna's intense gaze. "I failed him before leaving. I couldn't cure him of the snow sickness." She shuddered. "Or other sicknesses."

"Other sicknesses? Did you curse him?"

"I don't think so. But he did act most unlike a gentleman before we parted."

"If you mean he showed you he's attracted to you, what's so bad about that?" Jenna leaned forward, the scent of her perfume heavy in the air. "Unless you can't stand him, that is."

Gwen shrugged. "He could be annoying when we were growing up together, but he's not … bad. He's just…he has his hunting, and I have my learning and healing. We'll come together to make heirs and manage our estates, but otherwise we'll probably lead separate lives."

"It doesn't have to be like that, Gwen." Jenna reached for her, shrinking back before their bare skin could make contact. "Find someone else. I don't want to spend the rest of our lives together watching you be less than you could have been with a better partner."

"How was it like with you and your husband?" Gwen asked. "Was he the best partner for you?"

A rueful expression crossed Jenna's face. Before she could answer, Aunt Gabri descended the staircase. If she still seemed frail, her plum-colored dress and matching fan compensated for her pale complexion. "We should get going," she said, "I've had word that William will be there, Gwendolyn, so Jenna will have her pick of the bachelors." She curled her lip, as if thinking they might not want to pick a farm-raised widow with an infant. "I wish we'd have more time for dancing and deportment lessons."

Aunt Gabri found the strength to lecture Jenna on proper Court etiquette for the entire trip to the palace, making Gwen nervous about her own manners when she wasn't worrying about William. He should be long recovered from the snow sickness by now. Whether their relationship had recovered was another story.

As they pulled up to the palace, all three of them stared out of the window. The road was full of carriages boasting matched horses in their finest harnesses. The carriage rolled to a stop as they joined the procession leading into the palace. Once they made it past the gate, they discovered the one estate where spring had definitely arrived. The lawns were bright green, the apple trees in blossom, and the birds in full song. Jenna sniffed. "They forced those blooms with heat. In another half-moon, it'll all be dead again."

Gwen hoped it wouldn't be due to Chaos Season returning.

Guards in midnight blue and silver blocked the entrance. Some of them checked names against a guest list; others performed a ceremonial inspection to make certain no one was carrying weapons. When a female guard learned who they were, she ushered Gwen and Jenna to a side entrance. A pair of guards joined them. "Please follow me, Avas," said the taller guard.

"Where are you taking us?" Gwen asked.

"Directly to the king. He wishes to talk to you first before you go in front of the assembly."

The guards led them down a narrow corridor, then deposited them into a meeting room with a long table dominating the center. Cushion-covered chairs surrounded it, and plates of cold meat, bread, and cheese covered the tapestry acting as a tablecloth. The other decorations in this room were plain, as if actual work took place here.

The king sat at the head of the table, studying a report. The simple circlet of gold he wore matched his spectacles but contrasted with the silver hair at his temples. He set his report aside and nodded to them. "Welcome, Avas." His deep voice echoed from the walls. "Please, have a seat and something to eat. I know your magic requires constant feeding."

Gwen dipped into her deepest curtsey; after a heartbeat, Jenna copied her, staring at the king as if she meant to compare him with his official portrait. Unsure what the proper protocol was, Gwen chose a seat near the other end of the table. Jenna sat next to her, quieter than Gwen had ever seen her before.

"I'll keep this short," the king said, "since we have more pleasant matters to attend to. When you finish finding the rest of your quartet of Avatars, I expect all of you to return to Wistica and pledge your allegiance to me, publicly."

There was nothing unusual about his request. It had become standard after the Fips conquered the country. Still, Gwen fought to keep her expression composed. This man before her looked like a genial late-middle-aged man, but he was a descendant of the conquerors, and his brother was the current Avatar of War. No matter how many generations this branch of Fips had lived in Challen, they honored their family's god above the Four. The royal family were the only people in the country who outranked Avatars. She had to be careful in dealing with him.

"We remember giving such allegiance in our previous lives, Your Majesty." Gwen said. "We are loyal to Challen and will give it again."

"Of course. And when do you expect you'll find the other two Avatars?" He glanced back and forth between them. "You're missing Fall and Winter, correct?"

"Yes, Your Majesty. We will be leaving Wistica soon to travel to the other end of Challen, where the Ava Fall's family lives."

"Good, good." The king glanced at Jenna. "You're even lovelier than my brother reported, young Ava. Is your giant rose bush still blooming?"

She started, and she blushed until she resembled a rose herself. "N-no, Your Majesty."

"A pity. Well, I'm sure you'll have your hands full dealing with Chaos Season soon. No time for roses then. In the meantime—" he stood, so Gwen and Jenna were obliged to copy him—"let us have a night of joy and dancing first, hum?"

As they fell into a procession, with the king and his guards in front, Gwen next, and Jenna with additional guards in the rear, Gwen wondered at the king's words. Had the king's brother met Jenna before? How was that possible? And why would the Avatar of War meet with the Avatar of Summer? If only she dared link with Jenna and ask her about it.

The procession ended on a balcony overlooking the ballroom. Beneath them stood hundreds of people, all dressed in colorful clothes. Although Gwen could make out individual's faces, there were so many people she couldn't pick out her father or Aunt Gabri—or even William.

A herald stepped forward and blared a few notes from a trumpet. He had to repeat the fanfare before the crowd quieted down. "King James voy ro Fip the Third, sovereign of the blessed country of Challen, along with Lady Gwendolyn lo Havil, Ava Spring presumptive, and Dame Jenna t'Reve, Ava Sum presumptive!"

The gentlemen and ladies below swept into bows and curtseys. King James stepped forward. "Greetings, good nobles. I've called you before me today to apprise you about the Chaos Season and the Season Avatars who diligently protect us from it. It is my sorrow to report that Lady Margaret gran Granell, the Ava Spring, was summoned to the God of Winter last moon in a riding accident. Let us wish her a good sleep and a gentle rebirth."

Everyone, from the king to his servants, bowed their heads.

The king continued, "Fortunately, the Four did not leave us without protection. Already two of the next four Season Avatars have come forward. The other two will soon be found." He glanced at Gwen sharply, sending a command under his optimistic words.

A man shouted, "What about Chaos Season? When will you tame that—for good?"

"My apple orchard blossomed too early, and then frost came. When will you fix it?"

"Where's the Ava Fall? I need her to look at my prize stallion...."

Hadn't she heard requests—commands, even—like these a thousand times in other lives? People never changed. Gwen kept a polite smile on her face. "Once we are all together, it will be easier for us to help you." She pitched her voice to carry to the crowd below. "Please, be patient."

The king led them down a wide staircase to the ballroom and nodded at a middle-aged man who resembled him enough to be his brother. His red blazer hung heavy with medals and other decorations. *The Avatar of War.* Jenna let out a soft gasp, but Gwen didn't have a chance to check on her. Her father and William pushed through the crowd to stand next to the Avatar. The scowl on William's face told her he hadn't come to ask her for a dance.

CHAPTER SIXTEEN

The Avatar of War

"Daughter, I'm pleased to see you looking so well." Despite his formal words, Gwen's father's eyes gleamed. "I wish you'd come to our house in Wistica instead of the Avatars', though I suppose you have the right to that one too."

Gwen curtseyed to him, then took a deep breath and faced her intended. "William, I'm glad to see you looking so well."

"Are you?" He took a step forward. His eyes bore no warmth for her. "Then why did you take off and leave me half-healed?"

"Didn't you get my letter? Maybe it's still somewhere on the road." She glanced around, wishing Aunt Gabri was close enough to testify on her behalf. Jenna and the War Avatar stared at each other, their polite smiles strained. Jenna would be a less credible witness than Aunt Gabri in William's eyes anyway. "Please, let's find someplace less public to talk," Gwen added. If she had to explain the shard's curse to him, she didn't want to start rumors that would lessen people's trust in the Avatars.

William crossed his arms. "Just tell me when you'll be able to return home for the wedding."

"I don't know. We're leaving for Tradetown tomorrow to find the Ava Fall. It will take us a little longer to find the Ava Win." Gwen prudently left off that she didn't even know where to start looking for Kay.

"Tradetown! That's practically to Selath."

"It won't take that long on the steam locomotive."

"I'd still prefer it if you came home and finalized the marriage first." He forced a smile. "I mean, my dear, that would be one less thing for you to worry about. I'm sure a few days of connubial bliss would be pleasant for both of us."

Gwen's cheeks heated with embarrassment. How could he speak of such things in a public setting? Besides, the last thing she wanted to risk with her magic not working properly was a pregnancy. Had he forgotten her own mother had died trying to give birth to Gwen's still-born brother?

"This isn't the place to talk of such things!" She backed toward the staircase. Jenna had left her alone to dance with a count's son. Her steps were slightly out of time, but she held her head high as if she didn't care who stared at her. One of those watching from the side was the Avatar of War. He turned and nodded his head at her.

"Lady Ava, would you let me steal you away from your intended for a dance?" he asked.

In other circumstances, she would have turned him down, even if he was a royal. She didn't care how many lifetimes it had been since the Annexation; she would never forget the wounded and dying she had treated after the battle. Yes, she was annoyed with William, but the Avatar of War was far more dangerous.

"Challen and Fip have not been at war in centuries," he said as if sensing her thoughts.

She reminded herself this Avatar of War wasn't the same one who had conquered her country. "As you wish, Your Highness." She curt-seyed again. "Or may I call you Avi?"

"Avi will do. Come." He stepped past William to take her hand and sweep her onto the dance floor. His cologne smelled like spices and reminded her of Jenna. Something else about his touch reminded her of Jenna too, but she couldn't place it.

The musicians started a song from a popular opera, and the Avi brought her to the closest set of dancers that needed another pair. To Gwen's disappointment, Jenna wasn't in their set.

The Avi bowed to her, the first formal movement of the dance. "Have you known your intended for long?"

"We're neighbors. We grew up next to each other."

The next movement required all of the ladies to proceed clockwise around the set, walking around each gentleman. When Gwen returned to the Avi, they joined hands and paraded in a circle with the rest of the dancers. He asked in a low voice, "Is this alliance for the sake of your estate, or because you two are truly fond of each other?"

Startled, she looked at him.

"I can see you two weren't too pleased with each other just now," he said, "And I would like to remind you that there are plenty of others, more powerful and wealthier, who would be happy to ally themselves with you. Excuse me."

The men marched to the center of the quadrille and back, then crossed over to the ladies opposite. Gwen kept a smile in place as she followed the dance steps automatically. What was the Avi implying? Did he think she should break her engagement to William? Her wedding date was later this spring. Even postponing it—which she had to—would lead to talk.

That shouldn't matter. I'm the Ava Spring. I'll be too busy with the other Avatars to worry about gossip.

The Avi returned. "The other Avatars in your set are all female this time, correct?" he asked.

Gwen wondered if the king had told him directly. "Yes, Avi."

"A pity for you." Now he stared at her with deep, dark eyes. He had aged well. "Magic should align with magic, don't you agree?"

By All Four Gods and Goddesses, was he proposing to her? The idea was so preposterous Gwen had to choke down a laugh. "Not all magic works well together," she said. "I'm afraid our magics clash, Avi."

The dance ended. Gwen turned to the closest nobleman and smiled at him, silently urging him to be her next partner. Even if he proposed to her, he couldn't disturb her as much as William or the Avi.

* * *

"And you honestly turned him down?" Jenna asked on the way home. Her voice was too loud, but Aunt Gabri didn't stir in her sleep. "Gwen, that's the king's brother! If you aim any higher for a husband, you'll have to marry the king himself!"

"He wouldn't be able to manage the lo Havil estate personally. He'd have to hire a steward, and they're not as trustworthy as family—"

"Are you listening to yourself? There's more to marriage than business. What about breeding?" Jenna pulled pins from her hair, letting it fall out of its elaborate bun. "Or getting pleasure out of breeding? Older men make better lovers."

"Jenna t'Reve, are you trying to send my aunt to the God of Winter with such talk? I'll never forgive you if you do."

That silenced Jenna more effectively than Gwen had expected. She didn't speak again until they turned onto the right street. As Gwen stared into the darkness, straining to see if Kron was haunting their gate, Jenna said, "Does that mean you're not interested in him?"

Gwen started. "Ah, who, the Avi of War? Of course not." She sniffed. "He's probably only interested in me because of my healing magic."

"That can't be true. You're young and pretty." Jenna gave Gwen a calculating look. "Both of us are."

Why was she stating that? Was she jealous? "I'm still betrothed to William," she snapped. He'd calmed down enough by the final dance to agree to postpone the wedding for another moon. However, his grip on her had been so hard, so possessive, that she'd come very close to giving him a rash. Perhaps she should have and ended this frozen engagement.

Aunt Gabri roused when the carriage stopped. Gwen assisted her aunt with stepping down from the carriage and climbing the stairs to the main entrance. Fatigue sat on her shoulders, making her long for bed. But wailing from the nursery snapped her awake. She left Aunt Gabri with a sleepy maid and raced for the nursery, removing her gloves as Jenna caught up to her.

"I think he's sick," Jenna said as she scooped up her son. "He feels warm."

Instinctively, Gwen turned to the cradle in front of the fireplace. "Let me check."

"By All Four, Gwen, be careful!" Jenna reached past her as if she didn't want a cursed Ava Spring healing her child.

"I won't touch him with the hand that has the shard."

"But still—"

Gwen extended a fingertip and placed it on Robbie's forehead. Perhaps if she limited the contact, she'd be less likely to transmit a curse instead of healing. The child felt warm, but not deathly feverish. His ears were filled with painful liquid. Maybe she could take care of it if she was careful. Gwen cautiously eased her way in deeper to drain the infection. She halted as Robbie reminded her of someone she'd recently touched.

The Avatar of War.

CHAPTER SEVENTEEN

Suspicions

"Gwen! What are you doing?" Jenna grabbed Robbie, snapping the link between them. Still intent on Robbie's illness, Gwen reeled as she struggled to bring her mind away from the child's body and back to her surroundings. The nursery spun around her. She staggered backward, nearly falling over a wooden rocking horse. Gwen focused on the hardwood floor beneath her, the silk gown rustling and gaping from a ripped seam, as she returned to herself.

"By All Four, don't break my link like that, Jenna," she snapped.

"Sorry." Cradling Robbie in one arm, Jenna extended her other hand. The kidskin gloves she wore prevented the two of them from linking. Gwen hauled herself up and glared at her sister Avatar.

"He's not your husband's child," she said. "He's the Avatar of War's child."

Jenna released her and stared back. The dim candlelight from the sconces made her eyes look dark brown or black, not green.

"You could tell that, even with the shard interfering?" she asked.

"It blocks my healing abilities, but I can still use other aspects of my magic." Gwen shook her head. "Never mind that. How did it happen?"

"How do you think it happened?"

Gwen winced. "How did you two meet in the first place? At least please tell me it was before you were married, not after."

Jenna's stiff posture relaxed. "Yes, it was before. Lex came to see the giant rose bush you ignored." She emphasized "you" as if she was still upset about that—though Gwen didn't know why.

Jenna shifted the neckline of her dress so Robbie could nurse. "One thing led to another, and, well, I never heard back from Lex. He told me tonight he never got the letter I sent. I guess it's a good thing Thomas was interested in me. Things would have been harder for me in Bull Rock otherwise."

Robbie's cries died out, but Gwen knew his ear still bothered him. She itched between healing him—or at least trying to—and getting more answers out of Jenna. Maybe there was a way she could do both. "If you link with me, it might be easier for me to heal your son."

Jenna hesitated. "What if you make him sicker and I lose my plant magic?"

"Do you think the Four would let that happen?" Of course, They had let Kron and his frozen shards into Challen…

"I don't know any more. The Four have changed the rules on us this lifetime." She looked down at her son. "Did you find out what's ailing him? Maybe I can treat it with plants."

"He has an ear infection."

Jenna's expression relaxed. "I don't need my magic for that. Simple onion juice helps."

She'd trust an onion over me. It was a good thing Jenna refused to link, as she'd never know how much that hurt. "In that case, I'll let you treat him." Gwen pulled a few pins out of her hair. "Thank the Four we don't have to get up at dawn to start our next trip. I could sleep until noon. Good night, Jenna."

As she hurried away to her bedroom, she wondered when she could press Jenna for more details about the Avatar of War. Did he know she'd borne his child? Was Robbie in line for the crown, or worse, a future Avatar of War? If he knew about Robbie, would he pursue Jenna and leave her alone? She sighed as a maid eased her heavy gown off of her shoulders. The only good thing about the situation with Jenna and the War Avatar was that it made her upcoming marriage to William suddenly more acceptable. William might be difficult, but at least he wasn't Challen's enemy. Maybe she should encourage Jenna to find someone else. No Season Avatar should associate with another god's Avatar.

* * *

Gwen woke up fuzzy-headed the next morning, making the idea of traveling even more onerous than usual. She lingered in the breakfast room over a cup of chocolate and the newspaper. The royal ball was one of the most important stories of the day. Gwen skimmed over the list of attendees and lengthy descriptions of their outfits, searching for the inevitable gossip about herself and Jenna. To her relief, the reporter noted her dance with the Avatar of War but didn't mention his proposal. Even Jenna was portrayed sympathetically, as a pretty young widow. Gwen turned the page—

And stared at the next story: "Rare Pre-Annexation Water Clock Stolen from University."

"Kron's water clock has disappeared," she announced as soon as Jenna appeared.

She blinked. "What?"

"It's gone. It vanished from its case overnight. The same case Kron told us only he and a few other people could open."

Jenna edged toward the chocolate. Bags under her eyes suggested she needed several cups to wake up. "Maybe he took it with him," she said.

"He left Wistica yesterday morning on a westbound locomotive. The water clock was still in place last night when a watchman made his rounds."

Jenna shrugged. "Then someone else must have broken in and taken it. It's probably worth a lot of chals to a private collector."

"Who would dare steal something that's been in the paper?" Gwen asked. "You couldn't show it off without getting arrested by the watch. I still think Kron must have taken it."

"Then why would he give it to the University in the first place? You're fretting over nothing, Gwen." Jenna's voice developed an edge. "Why, you haven't even asked how Robbie is this morning."

Maybe I should ask the onion. But to keep the peace, she asked, "How's Robbie doing?"

"Better. But I think it's going to take a few days before he completely recovers." Jenna turned toward the buffet and piled her plate high with sausage and toast. "Maybe we should postpone our trip until then."

"You know how important it is to find Ysabel and Kay."

Jenna edged toward the serving dish filled with bacon. "But are we doing the right thing by going to Ysabel first? She's not likely to leave her family. Maybe it's more important to find Kay."

Gwen sighed. "There must be some vital clue we're overlooking. I feel like a failure, not finding her on our own."

"And if there's one thing an Ava Spring can't stand, it's failure." Jenna's tone sounded more sympathetic than rude. Gwen raised an eyebrow in surprise and was rewarded by a grin from Jenna. "Some things about you never change from life to life."

"Jenna, if we fail, we let the whole country down."

"So, we don't fail. We think. But not on an empty stomach." Jenna sat down next to Gwen. "If you were Kay, running away from something with nothing of your own, what would you do? Where would you go?"

It was hard for Gwen to imagine herself in such a situation, but Avatars of all classes had resources they could rely on. "I'd trade my healing talent for what I needed—if it was working. Kay hasn't been doing that, though. Dorian would have told me if she'd been interfering with the weather."

"She's got other skills, though, doesn't she? Wasn't she a seamstress like her mother?"

"You think maybe she's working as a seamstress? There are lots of places she could find work here in Wistica."

"Then why hasn't anyone seen her?" Jenna asked.

"Maybe she's in another quarter of town. No, wait." Gwen raised a finger. "I'll swear by the Four she ran as far away from here as possible to somewhere no one would know her."

Jenna snorted loudly enough to wake Aunt Gabri. "Well, it would have to be another town, then. A big one, where people are too busy to be nosy. And where there are lots of places for a young seamstress to work."

Gwen pushed her empty plate away. "Someplace near where cloth is made. Sophia and Charles would know where sheep are pastured. Then we could limit our search to towns close by."

"We should also ask the Avi Win about the storm on the night Kay disappeared. There's got to be a clue he can give us."

Gwen nodded, even though she doubted Dorian would be helpful. At least traveling to the One Oak would bring them close to Aunt Gabri's house. Maybe she could persuade her aunt to go home and rest. She also needed to talk to Sophia, Charles, and Dorian about Kron to see what they thought of him—and to warn them.

* * *

In the late afternoon, Gwen, Jenna, Aunt Gabri, Robbie, and his new wet nurse Callie boarded a steamboat headed upriver. This time, their quarters were the best on the ship, as fewer passengers were traveling with them.

While Jenna fed Robbie, Gwen attempted to treat her aunt. Even if she couldn't cure the heart condition, maybe she could make Aunt

Gabri more comfortable. Gwen put her afflicted hand behind her back to keep it as far away from her patient as possible. Then she touched Aunt Gabri with her good hand and studied her from the inside out. Her blood vessels were coated with some waxy substance that made them too narrow. Gwen wanted to remove the coating, but as she studied it, memories returned of how dangerous it could be if she wasn't careful enough. A chunk of it could completely block a blood vessel, and that could be fatal. She didn't want to attempt it as long as her magic was affected by the shard. For now, all she did was carefully compress the coating to widen the blood vessels. Then she eased her way back to herself.

Aunt Gabri's eyes fluttered open. After a few heartbeats, she asked, "Am I dying, niece?"

"Not yet, Aunt Gabri. It's not good for you to get yourself worked up." Gwen squeezed her hand. "Maybe you should go home so you can rest. We can escort you back."

"What about you? Are you going to go back home and marry William?"

"I'm not sure he wants to marry an Avatar, Aunt. And that's what I am."

She sniffed. "Someone needs to talk some sense into both of you. I'd like to go to your wedding before I visit the God of Winter."

Gwen's heart beat faster. "Then you must take care of yourself while I find Ysabel and Kay. I don't want to marry until the four of us are together and my magic is working normally again."

"You don't need magic to be a wife or mother, Gwendolyn."

Gwen retreated to the other side of the cabin and busied herself with preparing tea for all of them. The other women's stares felt like pressure on her back.

"I don't blame Gwen for wanting magic to ease her labor pains," Jenna said as she shifted Robbie to her other breast. "It took me nearly a full day from the time my water broke until Robbie came out."

"Thank the Four both of you are healthy." Gwen poured carefully, trying to avoid spilling the hot water as the boat rocked back and forth.

"Did you know someone who had issues with childbirth?" Jenna asked.

There was no getting away from it. "My mother bled to death giving birth to my brother. He didn't live either."

"And you were too young to use your magic?"

"I was six." Part of the pot handle snapped off in her grip. "Old enough to remember past lives as a healer, too young to do anything."

"That was cruel of the Four," Jenna said.

"You shouldn't say such things." Aunt Gabri propped herself up to glare at Jenna. "What would people say if they heard an Avatar speak like that?"

Jenna tossed her braid back. "Who knows the Four better than the Avatars? I serve Them, but that doesn't mean I have to agree with everything They do."

As Gwen arranged cups on a tray, she said, "I like to think the Four do what They do for a reason. Maybe They thought I'd be a better healer if I saw someone die when I was young." If it made her reluctant to marry, that shouldn't matter, should it?

"Does that mean I need to see someone starve so I make the plants grow?" Jenna frowned as she looked down at her child. "If so, I'll complain to Summer Himself!"

Aunt Gabri fanned herself. "Gwendolyn, thank you for your offer, but I think I should come along with you and … the Summer Avatar."

"By All Four, Aunt, if we can take care of Challen, we can take care of ourselves." Gwen gritted her teeth so she wouldn't slam the tea things down on the table. If Aunt Gabri was forcing herself to continue traveling when she was ill, she must think Jenna was an unsuitable chaperone. How could she persuade her aunt not to risk her health when Jenna inadvertently kept showing that she wasn't brought up like a noble? It wasn't her fault, but Aunt Gabri would never accept that.

"I still think you need a…steadying hand with you."

"And I need to change." Jenna rose, carrying her son with her. "Gwen, could you help me with the buttons, please?"

Gwen trailed Jenna into the cabin and wondered what her aunt thought about her playing maid to a farm girl. Although there was a wet spot on Jenna's dress, she made no move to take it off.

"She shouldn't be coming with us, should she?" she whispered, looking Gwen straight in the eyes. "Can't you make her go home?"

Gwen sighed. "She won't as long as she thinks I don't have a proper chaperone."

Jenna's face turned red, and her nostrils flared. "And I'm not?"

"You are younger than me…"

"By a whole three moons. That's not it, is it? She doesn't think I'm respectable."

Gwen had no tactful response to that. Instead, she forced a smile. "Maybe she wants to talk me into marrying William. Or the Avatar of War." She threw up her hands. "I don't know anymore."

Jenna leaned toward her, extending her hand as if she meant to touch Gwen's cheek and link. At the last heartbeat, her hand veered toward Gwen's shoulder, safely touching her dress. Her eyes burned with something Gwen wasn't sure how to decipher.

"Pick someone who makes you happy, Gwen," she whispered. "I can't stand the thought of linking with you, feeling your misery, for an entire lifetime. Who would you pick, if you were free?"

The answer came surprisingly swiftly. "Neither of them." That was as freeing as the idea Jenna did intend to link with her…someday.

Jenna nodded. "Then don't take one. You'll find someone more … suitable, I'm sure."

"But what about the wedding to William? I should break it off? Cause scandal? Give my aunt a heart attack?"

"You can save her, I know you can. And I'll use willow bark tea too."

Gwen scowled. "Willow bark tea won't save my reputation."

"Gwen, you're an Avatar, Spring's chosen Avatar! That's enough to make a thousand reputations!"

"Even if I can't use Spring's magic?" she asked bitterly. "I have to heal that and find Ysabel and Kay before I can even think of myself." The answer suddenly became clear. "I can't do anything about William or the War Avatar until our quartet is united. So if we don't find Ysabel and Kay soon, I may have to postpone my wedding anyway."

Jenna's eyes grew large enough to swim in. "Your aunt will have another fit."

"I know." If only she could make this boat fly. "Maybe we could travel faster without my aunt. It would be better for her, too."

"Then I must pretend to be reformed." Jenna put a vacant smile on her face, as if other people did her thinking for her. "Will this work?"

Gwen bit back a giggle. Somehow, Jenna seemed to have a knack for making her feel better, or at least feel that she didn't have to be serious every single heartbeat. "I'm glad the Four put us in the same quartet."

Jenna gave her a startled look, then turned away to inspect herself in the mirror. "So am I. Can you help me change? If I'm to appear respectable, I should wear a clean dress."

Gwen complied, but Jenna maneuvered the fabric so their skin never touched—and their link never formed. Jenna had to be hiding something else that she didn't want exposed in the link. The secret made Gwen's hand itch. If it was about their shared past, she needed to know too. Hopefully she would find out what it was before they found the two missing Avatars. Managing one Avatar was difficult enough without adding others to the mix.

CHAPTER EIGHTEEN

A Missing Shard

Jenna used her best manners for the rest of the trip back to Midpoint, but Aunt Gabri refused to leave them on their own. "I must sacrifice my comfort for the sake of the country," she said with a heavy sigh. "I only hope the hired coach won't be too rough."

Despite her earlier promise, Jenna rolled her eyes. But she was silent as they drove down the bumpy road back to the One Oak. The snow had melted, leaving mud and potholes in the road. Jenna stared at the giant oaks with a half-frown on her face. "Can you tell if you planted any of those trees in your earlier lives?" Gwen asked.

"Maybe. I can't bond with any of them again." She sighed. "I just wish...."

"What?"

"Nothing." Only when they drove into the courtyard of the One Oak did Jenna react. When the carriage stopped, she grabbed Robbie from the nursemaid and stepped out, showing him various features of the building.

The butler welcomed them in. When Jenna and Robbie entered, he raised an eyebrow. "This is Jenna t'Reve, the next Ava Sum," Gwen told him.

He nodded. "Excellent, Ava. Where is the rest of your quartet?"

"We know where one is, and I think Dorian can help us pinpoint the other one." Gwen looked around. "Where is he?"

"If you'll wait for him in the common parlor—"

"I'd rather use the Ava Spring's private parlor."

"As you wish, Ava. It is your right." The butler's voice betrayed no emotion. "Do you remember the way?"

She nodded and took the path to the Ava Spring's quarter of the house. Maybe the setting would remind Dorian of his duty to Challen. The rest of the group followed her.

"So, this is where the absent Ava Spring lived?" Jenna asked. She turned around. "It's still her place, isn't it? No one's touched her personal things."

It was true. Margaret's private parlor was immaculate. Little touches—a stack of letters here, an abandoned scarf draped over the mantel—made it appear as though she was expected to return at any moment. Gwen lowered herself into the chair closest to the fireplace, feeling more like a usurper than someone reclaiming her rightful position. Margaret would understand—at least Gwen thought she would, even though they'd never met.

Charles crept into the parlor, smiled, and took a seat close to the door. Dorian, still in full white, and Sophia entered within heartbeats of each other, with Sophia following Dorian as if she was pushing him into the parlor. Gwen wasn't surprised when Dorian glowered at her. "You're sitting in Margaret's favorite chair."

"She had good taste." Gwen glanced around and realized there were no refreshments. "Shall I ring for chocolate?"

"How long are you staying here? Aren't you supposed to be finding the rest of your quartet?"

"Dorian! Where are your manners?" Sophia sounded shocked. "You were born in a manor, not a farm!"

Jenna's face darkened.

Gwen kept her voice level. "We're trying to figure out where the Ava Win is. She disappeared four years ago during a storm in Wistica. Do you remember it, Dorian?"

He laughed. "Do you think even I can track every drop of rain that falls? Don't you have anything more specific?"

"It was on the fourteenth of Cornmoon," Jenna said. "Does that help?"

When Dorian didn't respond for a few heartbeats, Charles said, "What about your journals?"

With a sigh, Dorian strode over to the bell pull and yanked it. When the butler arrived, he instructed him to fetch a particular journal from his study. The butler bowed and withdrew. Even though no one had asked for refreshments, a maid appeared with a tray of chocolate and cheese sandwiches. Apparently the servants were well accustomed to the appetites of Season Avatars.

The butler returned as Gwen was finishing her second sandwich. "Here's the book you requested, Avi."

As Dorian flipped through his journal, Sophia sidled next to him and peered over his shoulder. He shot her an angry glare. "What, do you think I'll lie or something?"

"Why can't I see too?"

"Because you're not the Avi Win." He edged away from her. Gwen and Jenna exchanged glances. Gwen hoped this was just a minor quarrel, not the symptom of a bigger problem within the group of current Season Avatars.

Dorian flipped a page and read out loud: "The Fourteen of Cornmoon. No traces of Chaos Season in the air. Winds and light rain by the Selathen border; sun over most of the rest of Challen."

"That's it? What about the storm in Wistica?" Gwen asked.

Dorian raised an eyebrow. "Are you sure that was the right day?"

"It was in the middle of the night."

"Ah. That might be part of the next day's report, then. Let me see. Yes: 'A hard storm in Wistica overnight, with contrary winds."

Sophia continued reading: "I thought I felt them slipping out of my control, as if someone else was controlling them. Could it be the next generation's Season Avatar already? I expected another decade yet, maybe even two. When I pushed back, there was nothing."

No one spoke for several heartbeats. Gwen sighed. Dorian's testimony corroborated what Kay's father had told them, but it didn't tell them where she had gone.

"There's still the sewing angle," Jenna said. She smiled warmly enough at Charles to make his cheeks turn pink and Sophia frown. "Gwen thinks Kay might be employed as a seamstress."

"Then she could be anywhere—"

"Charles, where are the most textiles like cotton grown?" Gwen asked. "Are there any large centers dedicated to sewing? Sophia, what about wool? Where are Challen's sheep?"

"Close to the Selathen border. The biggest town is Rainbow River."

"Near Tradetown?" Perhaps the Four had put Kay and Ysabel close together. It was time They did something helpful.

"More in the north. Tradetown is in the south."

"It would still be worth looking for Kay there," Jenna said.

"We'll change our tickets when we return to Midpoint." Gwen took a deep breath. "There's something else we need to ask you about. Do any of you remember someone named Kron Evenhanded? He has magic that works on objects, and he claims to have worked with all of us in our very first lives as Avatars."

"Our very first lives?" Sophia raised her eyebrows. Outside the window, a crow cawed. "How many years ago was that?"

"Too many to remember," Charles replied.

Dorian crossed his arms. "That doesn't sound like the Four's magic. And if such magic existed so long ago, why haven't we encountered it since? Doesn't this person reincarnate with his magic?"

"That's the thing. He hasn't reincarnated. He claims to have traveled forward in time in that pre-Annexation water clock. And he brought an enemy of the Four with him."

The older three Avatars stared at Gwen silently as she repeated Kron's story. Jenna occasionally interrupted to add details.

"Kron claims he wants to help us, but he admits the shards that cursed me and killed Margaret came from that water clock," Gwen finished. "Now that the water clock itself is missing, we could all be in danger, especially Ysabel and Kay."

Dorian scowled. "If he's responsible for Margaret sleeping too soon, I'll freeze him so cold he'll never thaw."

"But...but this can't be right. A Fall Avatar born with a male twin?" Sophia asked. "I can't imagine the Goddess ever allowing that."

"She has the right to change Her mind, dear," Charles said.

"If that's the case, maybe this Kron is wrong about Ysabel being the Avatar," Dorian said. "Maybe it's her brother. Or maybe they share the magic."

Sophia couldn't have looked more scandalized if Jenna had stripped naked and attempted to seduce both Charles and Dorian at the same time. Gwen suppressed the urge to rub her eyes at the image.

"We'll find out the truth when we arrive at Tradetown," she said. "In the meantime, be wary if Kron comes here. And watch out for more shards. What did you do to the one that killed Margaret and her horse?"

Sophia pursed her lips. "I didn't want to touch it."

"So...you left it in the carcass? What did you do with that?"

"We buried it for fertilizer," Charles replied.

Gwen and Jenna looked at each other before Gwen said, "We'd better trap it before it hurts anyone—or poisons the land."

Charles offered to help Jenna, and Sophia and Dorian insisted on watching, despite Gwen's warnings. Charles chose the stoutest wooden vessel he could find, and the others followed him out of the mansion and into the forest of oaks. A stable boy accompanied them with a shovel. The ground was dry enough for easy walking, so it didn't take long for them to come to the right spot. With a sinking feeling, Gwen pointed at a narrow hole, too narrow to be an animal's burrow, off to the side.

Sophia's voice was grim as she said, "Dig there, Henry."

It didn't take the youth long to reach the carcass. The stench wasn't as bad as Gwen had expected. Sophia crouched down on one side of the hole, while her husband stood by with the basket.

"I can't sense anything foreign inside the carcass," Sophia said. "Of course, my magic works better with live animals. Let me try something else."

She closed her eyes, and heartbeats later, insects and other creatures swarmed over the carcass. Gwen swallowed her disgust, grateful her aunt had chosen to wait inside. A few moments later, nothing was left but bone. The pottery shard wasn't there.

"Kron couldn't have known about this shard," Jenna said as they walked back to the One Oak. "And I'm sure someone would have seen him if he'd come here."

"Then he must have used magic to make it come to him. But why?" Gwen shook her head, frustrated. "Why does he claim to be on our side while sending these shards against us? What is he trying to do, eliminate us so he's the only Avatar in Challen? I can't believe the Four would let him do that."

"Well, you'd better hurry and find the other Avatars from your year, then," Sophia said.

"And if we don't hurry back to Midpoint, we'll miss our locomotive."

"Locomotive?" Jenna asked. "By All Four, what's that?"

"A new type of transportation, like a carriage pulled by tireless horses. The Selathens created it." Gwen halted in front of the One Oak. "Sophia, Charles, please have our carriage made ready and my aunt escorted out here. We'll leave at once."

CHAPTER NINETEEN

Rainbow River

By evening they were back in Midpoint. Instead of stopping at the hotel where Gwen had lunched with her aunt, they drove to the other side of the city. Here, on the outskirts, stood a long wooden building in front of a platform. Behind the platform was something Gwen had never seen before. It looked a little like a carriage, if a carriage had been built out of iron; stretched out; and had several funnels, bumps, and other parts Gwen couldn't identify welded on top. Smoke belched out of one of the funnels.

"Is that the locomotive?" Aunt Gabri stared at it. "Is it safe?"

Callie, Robbie's nursemaid, clutched him so tightly he cried in protest. When the train's whistle sounded, he launched his own fit. Gwen hoped they would be able to bring him on without too much trouble.

A Selathen man—Gwen guessed his origins by his brown skin and beard—approached them. He wore a dark blue suit with gold piping, as did several other men working on the platform. "Help you, Damas?"

Gwen didn't bother correcting him. "Can we ride this train to Rainbow River?"

He nodded and pointed at the building, where several people stood in front of a window.

"Is that where we buy tickets?"

The man stared at her, a glint of scorn in his eyes. "You have no chaperone?"

Gwen gestured at her aunt, who'd persuaded the carriage driver to help her open her trunk so she could wrap herself in another scarf.

"I meant a male chaperone," the Selathen said.

Jenna glanced at Aunt Gabri before saying, "I thought we needed a chaperone to protect us from men, in case we fancied a tryst with someone we're not supposed to tryst with."

Couldn't she maintain some seriousness for more than a day? "Jenna!"

The man backed away, but not before calling over his shoulder, "And that's why women should have a man to look after them!"

"Humpf!" Jenna said. "Can't you do something to his manhood, Gwen? He shouldn't be allowed to insult us like that."

"You promised to behave in front of my aunt. Remember?" Gwen whispered. She raised her voice to include the rest of their party. "We're going to have to ignore distasteful comments like that. Selathen culture is much more...male-centered than Challen. I imagine we'll meet more Selathens as we approach the border."

"Maybe I won't bother flirting with them after all," Jenna muttered.

Partly to annoy the ticket seller, who asked Gwen which man was accompanying her on this trip, and partly because they were Season Avatars and deserved some privileges, Gwen purchased first-class tickets for everyone. The price was well worth it. As they passed the second-class coach, Gwen could see it was crowded, filled mostly with men. The scent of their cigars nauseated her. By comparison, the first-class coach behind the engine was only one-third full. Padded seats made sitting endurable after so long in the carriage. Patterns of wood in various shades of brown and gilded trim invited her to admire the workmanship. A youth came on board selling pre-made sandwiches and wicker boxes. Gwen assumed the boxes contained complete meals, but the boy opened one to reveal a kerosene burner, a couple of ceramic mugs painted with a picture of the locomotive, and a pot to prepare chocolate. Even the water, dried chocolate, and spices were included. Charmed, she purchased one.

"Now this is how we should travel." Jenna leaned back against the seat. "Can it get any better than this?"

The engine blew its whistle repeatedly; Robbie started crying. Steam hissed, and smoke billowed past the windows. Yet the locomotive didn't move. Gwen and Jenna exchanged glances. Finally, with a lurch, the locomotive and the coaches hitched forward a bit, then a little more, until the pace steadied at a speed faster than any horse could sustain. Before Gwen realized it, they had left Midpoint far behind.

Jenna winked at Gwen. "You know, Gwen, we could go anywhere we wanted to, and no one would be able to stop us."

"Go somewhere? You mean besides Rainbow River and Tradetown?" Gwen furrowed her forehead. "Why would we do that?"

"For adventure! To see Challen! Because we can!" Jenna flung her arms wide.

"Have you forgotten the minor thing called Chaos Season? You know, the magical weather storm we're supposed to tame for the benefit of our country?"

As if summoned, rain pounded on the windows. The locomotive didn't change speed.

"Shouldn't they slow down?" Jenna asked.

"The locomotive doesn't need to slow down," a Challen man wearing a locomotive uniform told her, a touch of pride in his voice. He swayed back and forth with the train as he stood in the aisle, but he didn't lose his balance. "It can maintain this speed in any weather, day or night."

"Won't it run into another locomotive?" Gwen asked.

"The other ones on this track are spaced far enough apart to make sure that won't happen."

Jenna gave the man a considering look. Although he was only a couple of years older than them, his mustache gave him an authority his youthful face lacked. Handsome enough to interest Jenna, Gwen supposed, but still not noble enough to impress Aunt Gabri.

Jenna glanced at Aunt Gabri, who held another novel in front of her face, before asking, "And how do you know so much about locomotives?"

"I'm the night driver for the *Steel Stallion*," he replied. "In two hours, I'll take over and make sure you and the rest of our passengers arrive safely in Rainbow River." His smile broadened. "I have a night off, so I get to visit my girl before returning to Wistica."

"Do you know Rainbow River well?" Gwen asked. Maybe he could help them track down Kay, or at least the best area to find her.

"I can recommend the best hotel, restaurant, and clothing store. Otherwise, the areas I know best are probably of no use to you ladies."

"A pity," Gwen said.

Before she could ask him further questions, he tipped his cap to them. "I should go check in, ladies. A pleasure to speak with you." He leaned a little closer to them. "And if the Selathens are less than respectful to you, tell the officials you know me. I'm Jon Frist."

He walked up the middle of the car without grabbing a seat for balance, then opened the door and passed into the next car.

"Frist," Gwen said thoughtfully. "Related to Frost, a Winter name. And he has a winter aura."

"You think he could be an ally?" Jenna asked. "Maybe sent by the Four to help us find Kay?"

"I hope so," Gwen said. "The Four know we could use all the help They can give us."

* * *

One thing that the locomotive lacked, even in the first class coach, was a sense of privacy. There was no provision for sleeping quarters, let alone separate ones for the ladies. Apparently the Selathens expected their passengers to sleep in their seats. Gwen loosened her stays and slipped off her shoes, but those were the only concessions she made for sleeping while fully dressed. Luckily, there was something soothing about the locomotive's motion that made it easy to fall asleep, even if Gwen's sleep wasn't restful.

She stood helpless in a field of snow, near a blinding crystal house protected by monstrous hybrids of humans and animals. A woman hovered in the air, relentlessly draining all of Gwen's magic despite eleven—eleven?—other Avatars supporting her with their own energy. One by one, the Avatars fell, without even a remnant of an aura left to tell her who was who...

Gwen fed magic into Kay as she battled a group of other Avatars, matching weather with weather. Bizarrely enough, Kron led both sides, egging the Avatars on to mutual destruction.

Gwen linked with Jenna, Ysabel, and Kay, but instead of pooling their magic, the curse still within her turned their magic into something destructive. It rippled out from them to burn all of Challen down to ash, ash as white as snow....

She jolted awake. A sconce at the front of the carriage illuminated the way to the necessities. The rest of the car was dark. The carriage still rocked back and forth. Gwen wondered if Jon was driving now. It was reassuring to think someone friendly was up when the rest of her party slept, innocent of her fears.

This lifetime was going to be different. The difficulty Gwen had had so far finding Ysabel and Kay was only a beginning. New types of magic and new magicians would destabilize the country. How could Gwen help the rest of her quartet deal with these challenges when her own magic was still cursed? She would lead everyone into the disaster she dreamed of. Maybe Challen would be better off if she did something unprecedented and refused to become an Avatar. But Gwen knew it was too late for that. The third quartet of Avatars rested with the God of Winter. Even if Spring sent their spirits back to Challen tonight, it would be another generation before they could replace her.

Gwen tried again to remove the shard in her palm, with the same result. By All Four, maybe she should have asked, even begged, for Kron to take care of it while they were in Wistica. But he'd already caused problems for the Four already, if her dreams were true. Could she trust him? Were there any other alternatives?

Spring, can You send me a sign? What should I do?

Gwen meditated the rest of the night while her companions slept. By the time the sunrise caught up with them, she was more refreshed than she ought to be after a sleepless night. However, she was no closer to an answer.

* * *

Jenna was the only one in their party who enjoyed staring at the fields of crops they passed during the day. Gwen finished reading a romance to her aunt, then wheedled a deck of cards from another passenger and persuaded the other three women in her party to play a few rounds while Robbie napped. It was a relief when the official from the locomotive announced they were approaching Rainbow River.

After they disembarked at a tiny station and collected their luggage, Gwen glanced around, trying to figure out their next move. It was late afternoon, about an hour or so before sunset. This town was a little bigger than Lake Verdan. The main street boasted several general stores and taverns; boarding houses and single-family homes surrounded the main street. Several long, low buildings clustered around the river that gave the town its name. No carriages were available for hire, so she paid a few boys to carry their luggage and direct them to the hotel Jon had recommended.

"This is the best hotel in town?" Aunt Gabri grimaced at the room she and Gwen were sharing. The walls were stained, and the drapes and bed linens worn. "I knew I should have gone back home while I had the chance!"

Gwen wished she had too, but she put on a smile for her aunt's sake. "Well, the sooner we find Kay, the sooner we can leave. Jenna and I will walk around for a while and stretch our legs."

Aunt Gabri narrowed her eyes. "It's close to dark, Gwendolyn."

"The textile factories will close soon. Perhaps I can spot Kay's aura when she leaves her job. Will you have dinner downstairs, or should I ask them to send up a tray?"

"A tray please, dear. I didn't sleep well last night."

Gwen nodded and hurried to the room Jenna shared with Robbie and the nursemaid. Perhaps they could find some willow bark extract before the general stores closed. Jenna agreed, and concealing their silk dresses under wool cloaks, they left the hotel.

The night was chillier than it should be in Rainmoon, perhaps because they weren't far from the Western Mountains. Gwen wondered if it was snowing on her family's estate. A few wagons drove by, and street vendors hawked everything from cooked potatoes to bottles of beer. Gwen bought skewers of meat drenched in a spicy sauce, rolls to ease the bite of the spices, and some of the weak beer. It wasn't the type of food she would have eaten at home, but hunger made her less demanding than she would have been in other circumstances. As she and Jenna stood near a bridge and ate, a lamplighter came by. While he worked, low-pitched bells chimed loudly enough to be heard by the entire town.

"What is that?" Gwen asked, putting her hands over her ears.

"It must be a signal," Jenna said. "Look across the river."

People in patched cloaks and thread-worn shawls streamed out of the buildings, heading toward them. As workers crossed the bridge, Gwen scanned them for a bright blue aura. A crowd of this size guaranteed there would be plenty of winter-born mixed with the other seasons, but she couldn't see an aura strong enough to be a Season Avatar's.

They waited until all of the workers had gone home or into taverns or restaurants before slowly making their way back to the hotel. Gwen clutched her cloak tightly around herself. Maybe it had been too optimistic to think they'd find Kay their first night here. Gwen couldn't have scanned the entire crowd; she might have missed Kay's aura. They couldn't waste too much time in this city; though. If they didn't find Kay in the next day or two, they would have to move on.

Jenna stopped at an apothecary. "Did you want willow bark extract for your aunt?"

Gwen nodded. At least she could accomplish something today.

Jenna approached the clerk and demanded to sniff his extracts before purchasing a bottle. While they haggled, Gwen studied the other medicines on display. Had Kay ever come here for healing? Would the clerk remember her? She pulled her sketchbook out of her reticule and approached the counter.

"Excuse me, but have you seen anyone who looks like this?" she asked, displaying the drawing she'd made of Kay.

The clerk shrugged. "There are hundreds of workers in this town, Dama. I can't keep track of them all."

"And do they all work across the river?"

"Most do, but there are smaller workshops on the other side of town." He returned his attention to Jenna. "Have you decided, Dama?"

She flashed a seductive smile. "I'll take a full bottle, well-wrapped, and a dropper."

"Certainly, Dama. No charge for the dropper."

Jenna's smile deepened as if she were gloating. For once, her flirting didn't bother Gwen. If they hadn't seen all of the workers in this town yet, then there was still a chance they could find Kay here. She vowed they'd find a way to check all the workshops in Rainbow River if necessary.

* * *

The next morning, Aunt Gabri declared herself unwilling to traipse around after Gwen and Jenna. "That's fine," Gwen said as she passed more oatmeal to her aunt. "We can visit the workhouses while you shop or take some air by the river."

"You really intend to visit factories?" Aunt Gabri's fleshy chin wobbled. "That doesn't sound suitable. Maybe you should print a notice in the paper and insist she meet you here."

"We're not sure she is here, Aunt Gabri," Gwen said. "If she wanted to meet other Avatars, she could have gone to the One Oak first. There must be some reason why she didn't."

"I still don't approve, Gwendolyn."

"I still have to do it."

Aunt Gabri scowled at her bowl. "Then if you simply must do it, find a carriage. I need a place to wait while you visit those dreadful places."

Tension left Gwen's shoulders. "Thank you, Aunt Gabri."

Jenna looked up from the oatmeal she was trying to spoon into Robbie while the nursemaid watched with an awkward smile on her face. "Yes, thank you, Lady lo Havil," Jenna said.

Aunt Gabri's perpetual frown eased.

The hotel had to send someone to a nearby stable to arrange for their carriage, so it was mid-morning before they drove off. "What do you think Kay will be like, once we find her?" Jenna asked.

"She's quiet, isn't she? I seem to remember that much." Gwen wondered when she would be able to safely link with Jenna or Kay. Sometimes Avatars presented themselves one way on the surface but felt different within the link.

They clattered over the bridge and approached the factory area. Half-a-dozen long, low buildings, all looking very much alike, confronted them. Gwen directed the driver to take them to the farthest one first. They could work their way back toward the bridge, then drive to the other side of town and search for the small workshops the clerk had told them about.

Only one door was visible, and when Gwen tried it, it was locked. Her raps didn't seem to penetrate the thick wood. Jenna headed over to a window. "Gwen, I see weavers!" she called. "Can you read auras through a window?"

"I can, but I can't be sure I'll see everyone in the building. What if I miss Kay because she's stuck in a corner?"

The door jerked open, and a huge man scowled at Gwen. "Lady, we don't sell directly from the factory. Our store is on the corner of the main street. Why don't you and your companion go there and stop distracting my workers?"

Gwen drew herself to her full height. If ever she needed the full authority of an Avatar, now was the time. "We're here to inspect your workers." Inspiration struck. "As the next Spring Avatar, I want to make sure they're healthy."

He snorted. "Of course you're the Spring Avatar, and I'm the king of Challen."

"You're summerborn, and you suffer from gout." She sniffed. "You should water your beer down and eat less kidney pie."

He stared at her doubtfully for a few heartbeats before asking, "Could you make the pain stop? It keeps me up half the night."

Gwen rubbed the ridge in her palm covering the shard. The curse would interfere with her normal healing magic, but what if she could pass the curse into the gout? Cursing the gout would eliminate it, and maybe then it would be safe for her to heal people normally. She had to risk it sometime, and this seemed like a good opportunity. "Let me in to see your workforce—they don't even need to stop working—and then I'll take care of your gout."

With a shrug, he opened the door to let her and Jenna inside. The hallway was dark at first, but then it opened up onto a brightly lit area. Lanterns hung down from the ceiling, suspended well above the flammable fabric. Threads in a multitude of colors stretched across weaving frames. Maybe this was the rainbow river this town was named for.

"The best place to supervise everyone is from the catwalk," the supervisor said. He gestured toward a narrow flight of stairs. Gwen lifted her skirts just enough to make climbing steps easier without displaying herself.

Once on the narrow catwalk, Gwen leaned over the railing and focused on the workers below. Even with a couple hundred people competing for her attention, it was still easy to make out people's auras. But none of them was the one she was looking for.

"Is this everyone?" Jenna asked.

"Yes, Lady."

Gwen straightened. "Then where are the seamstresses?"

"The seamstresses?"

"That's what Kay was, so that's the type of job she would seek."

The factory supervisor shifted his weight. "We don't employ seamstresses."

"Does anyone in this town?"

"Only Dama s'Ivena. She makes infant and children's clothing."

Gwen smiled. "Then we have to visit her. Where is her factory?"

"Her workshop is on the corner of Main and Red, with the mannequins in the window." The supervisor's eyes narrowed. "Are you still going to cure my gout, or was that just a ruse?"

"No. But let's not do it here." If something went wrong, Gwen didn't want either of them tumbling over the side.

"Are you sure this is a good idea?" Jenna whispered to Gwen as they descended.

"If I can't get rid of the shard on my own, I have to figure out a way to perform my duties anyway." She quickly explained her idea, then caught Jenna's gaze. "Will you link with me in case I need your help to override the curse?"

Jenna hesitated before replying. "Maybe you should try it without me first and signal if you need my help."

Gwen swallowed, concealing her disappointment.

The supervisor's office was so tiny the roll top desk and chair occupied most of the space. Gwen looked away as he took off his boot and sock, then propped his foot on the chair. His foot reeked strongly enough for her to block her sense of smell. She laid her cursed hand over his toe and willed the curse to break up the crystal that was causing the pain. The foreign magic refused to obey her. Considering the magic didn't belong to her, she shouldn't be surprised. But maybe if she combined it with her own....

Gwen forced her magic to flow through the shard, wincing as it picked up the taint. For a moment, she wondered if it was wise to use this magic on another person. *I'm not using it on him, just what's ailing him*, she reminded herself. She injected it into the crystal, pleased when it shattered. She pursued the pieces, hunting them down and breaking them up until they were harmless.

She released the man and asked him, "How does it feel?"

He wriggled his hairy toes. "Much better," he said with a smile. "Do you want a bolt of cloth? I'll send one to the One Oak."

"I don't have time to pick one now." Giddiness at her success made her want to dance in the street. "Something with blue and yellow would be lovely, thanks."

"Blue and yellow?" Jenna asked as they left.

Gwen wiped her hands on her dress. Even Jenna's lack of support couldn't dampen her spirits. "In honor of Winter and Spring. We're so close to finding Kay, can't you feel it?"

Aunt Gabri looked up from her book. "How many more of these factories do you have to investigate, Gwendolyn?"

"None." She turned to the driver. "Take us to Main and Red, please."

"What about lunch?" Jenna asked.

"Not when we're so close to finding Kay." Perhaps they could all have lunch together. Would Kay be glad to be found, or would she run from her sister Avatars too?

As the supervisor had promised, a shop with several mannequins in the window stood at the correct address. The dresses they displayed featured puffed sleeves, which had gone out of fashion before winter. The workmanship was comparable to any dress made in Wistica, though.

Aunt Gabri raised her head. "I wonder if they have gloves. I could use a few new pairs."

"Come with us and check."

Gwen didn't wait for the coachman to assist them out of the carriage. She jumped out, ignoring her aunt's disapproving look, and hurried into the shop. More mannequins posed with fans, parasols, or reticules, and sketches of more designs covered the walls. But no seamstresses were in sight.

A middle-aged woman with a measuring cord draped over her shoulders appeared from the back of the shop. "May I help you, Lady? Are you new in town? I don't think I've seen you before. We're the finest dressmakers in this part of Challen—"

"Very good. Do you have seamstresses on the premises?"

The woman gestured toward a screened-off corner. "I can take your measurements right here, Lady."

"I don't need measurements. I need to see your seamstresses. Now."

"By All Four, why?"

Gwen raised her head proudly. "I'm on the Four's business."

The woman clasped her hands. "You're from the One Oak? You wish to order something for the Ava Fall?"

"No, the Ava Win." At the woman's puzzled look, Gwen added, "She might be one of the seamstresses here."

The woman paled. Before she could speak, the doorbell jangled. Jenna escorted Aunt Gabri into the shop. "How adorable!" Jenna squealed and knelt next to the figure of a small boy dressed like a lord. "Something like this would be precious on Robbie!"

"The gloves, where are the gloves?" Aunt Gabri demanded.

The shopkeeper pulled a long box from a shelf. Jenna caught Gwen's gaze and nodded. Maybe she meant to distract the shopkeeper so Gwen could slip back behind the counter. She wouldn't normally do that, but she didn't think the shopkeeper would lead Kay out like another piece of merchandise. Hoping she wouldn't cause a scene, Gwen waited until the woman had her back to her before moving, pressing her skirt to her side to stop it from rustling.

She squeezed through a narrow hall made even tighter by piles of fabric and thread. She ended up in a large room, where six young women stitched together scraps of cloths and lace. Several more women around another table cut the cloth to the right size and passed it to the seamstresses. One of the seamstresses had the bright blue aura Gwen had been seeking for so long. Her face was thinner than the one Gwen had painted, but the coloring matched the features Kay's father had described.

At last, Gwen had found Kay. Now all she had to do was talk to her without frightening her.

CHAPTER TWENTY

Kay

Kay didn't look up from the sleeve she was stitching together. She held it close to her face, as if she had trouble seeing in the gray light. Gwen wondered how long she had been sewing to have vision problems when she hadn't even turned eighteen yet.

"Hello, Kay," she said softly. "I've been looking for you a long time."

Kay started, then winced as she missed a stitch. She corrected her mistake before meeting Gwen's gaze. "Looking for me? By All Four, who are you?"

"Lady Gwendolyn lo Havil, Ava Spring. Your sister Avatar."

Kay stared at Gwen for another few heartbeats. Her face grew even paler, something Gwen hadn't thought was possible. "No. No. I love Winter, but I'm not ready to visit Him so soon." She dropped her work and dashed to a back door so quickly Gwen didn't have time to react.

"Don't let her get away!" Gwen said.

The shopkeeper emerged from the hall and crossed her arms. "Why did you scare off one of my best workers?"

"She's not a seamstress, she's the next Ava Win!"

At that, everyone stopped what they were doing and stared at Gwen in astonishment. "Is this a joke, Lady? Kay, the Ava Win? She doesn't even like going out in the rain!"

Something was very wrong if the Ava Win couldn't tolerate rough weather, but Gwen didn't have time to ask Kay's co-workers for more information. She had to catch her before she disappeared.

Gwen ran for the back exit as the shopkeeper said, "I demand an explanation!"

"Ask the Ava Sum up front."

"The Ava Spring and the Ava Sum?" More seamstresses stopped working to stare at Gwen. Some dropped their work and reached for her. "Please, Ava, my eyes..." "Ava, my fingers..." "My back...."

Who would have thought a seamstresses' job would be so unhealthy? Muttering, "Sorry, not now," Gwen ran after Kay. She'd lost precious heartbeats, and Kay's thinner dress and fewer petticoats wouldn't weigh her down as much as Gwen's clothing would.

Gwen drew on her magic to give herself strength, speed, and stamina. Ladies weren't supposed to run, but she moved faster than she'd ever done under her own power. She didn't care who saw her ankles as she held her dress out of the way.

She exited onto an alley overflowing with trash. Gwen muted her sense of smell, but she could still detect the stench of rotten food—and worse. Where was Kay? Something blurred at the end of the alley, and Gwen instinctively ran after it. Green shot up before the other person like a fence being slammed into place. Gwen skidded to a stop a few feet away, but the weeds wrapped themselves around the other person. Instead of struggling, Kay hung limply in place. "I deserve your punishment, Summer," she whispered.

By All Four, why would she think that? "It's all right, Kay," Gwen said as she approached. "We're not here to hurt you. Jenna, let her go."

Footsteps sounded behind her as Jenna came forward. "You sure, Gwen? What if she runs from us again?"

Kay turned her head. "Who are you?"

"That's Jenna t'Reve, the next Ava Sum."

"So, where's the next Ava Fall?"

"We still have to go to her. I'm not sure who's been harder to find, you or her."

The weeds withered and released Kay. She turned to stare at them. "Why? Did she run away from her duty too?"

"Why did you run away?" Jenna asked. "Your family has no idea where you are, or if you're even still alive."

Kay looked straight at Gwen. Her pale blue eyes looked big in her small face, and the color contrasted shockingly with her black hair. "The only reason I'm still alive is because I hid and stopped using my weather magic."

"What?" The weeds curled up at Jenna's cry.

"Why do you say that?" Gwen asked.

Kay hugged herself. "The very first time I tried to use my magic, I almost got killed. Since then, whenever I dream, I hear a voice telling me I'm going to die before I tame the Chaos Season."

Jenna shook her head. "The Four wouldn't let that happen, especially since the other Ava Spring went to visit Winter. We need you to tame Chaos Season."

Gwen rubbed the shard in her palm and wondered if Kay had been cursed too. Her first dream had occurred years ago, before Kron had arrived in this time with the water clock. Something else had to be going on here.

Kay hung her head. "I know I should trust the Four—I do trust the Four—but the dream always seems so real I wake up chilled."

Gwen and Jenna glanced at each other. An Ava Win could control the temperature around herself. Even when she slept, she ought to be comfortable.

As the leader, Gwen felt it her responsibility to ask the difficult question. "How much have you practiced your magic?"

"I haven't used it since that night."

By the Four, what use was an Ava Win who wouldn't use magic? About as much as an Ava Spring with tainted magic, Gwen told herself. If she'd found a way to work around the shard, Kay would have to figure out how she could do the same. Still, her words came out harsher than she intended. "Then how do you expect to tame Chaos Season? The weather part is the hardest."

"I go over weather patterns in my head," Kay said defensively. "I don't dare use magic. Magic will kill me."

She trembled so much Gwen removed her own shawl and offered it to her, being careful not to touch Kay as she held it out. Kay didn't comment on their failure to link. She wrapped herself in the saffron shawl, looking as lost as a child.

She's really afraid. I don't think I've seen her like this in any of our previous lives. She's going to have to get past that before she can use her magic. A pity Gwen's own magic worked on the body, not the mind. However, maybe the link would help—if it was safe to use it.

"Come with us back to the One Oak," Gwen said. "Remember, I have healing magic. I promise by All Four Gods and Goddesses I won't let you die."

Hope crept into Kay's expression. "Do you mean it? Is that possible? I thought you couldn't bring back the dead."

"I can't, but as long as we're together, neither accident nor illness will threaten you." Gwen clenched her fist. "And maybe with the link, we can figure out why you're having such strange dreams."

Jenna shot Gwen a warning look, as if she needed reminding about the risks of linking to other Avatars and spreading her curse to them. Even Kay seemed dubious. "Does the link count as magic?"

"I don't think so. It's within us, and it has nothing to do with weather."

"It might be safer if you just tell us what your dreams are like," Jenna said.

Now it was Gwen's turn to glare at her sister Avatar. Kay frowned. "Are both of you supposed to be women?"

"By All Four, what does that mean?" Jenna made Kay look even smaller than she already was.

"It's just…I remember you two were always opposite. And you marry more often than not."

Jenna's expression became bitter for a heartbeat, then she swept her hand as if clearing away the rest of the weeds. "Not this lifetime we won't. Now, your dreams?"

Kay looked away. "They're always the same. There's a fog so dense I could wrap myself in it. There's a voice, old, female, whispering to me like dry bones skittering over my back. The words aren't in our language, or anything I recognize, but I know what they sound like by heart." She wrapped herself in another layer of shawl. "And, no, I won't say them out loud. She might hear me."

"If you don't understand her words, how do you know you'll die if you use magic?" Gwen asked.

"I see pictures. Snow, rain, hail, me in the center. Dead."

Jenna chewed on a loose strand of hair. "You're sure you're dead, not just linked to the weather system?"

"By All Four, Winter is Death too! You think I wouldn't know? I haven't even told you the worst part." Kay glanced around as if making sure no one else was listening to them. "I feel something preventing me going to the God of Winter. I see she wants to…she wants to…steal my soul so I can't visit the God of Winter and be re-born."

In unison, Gwen and Jenna traced the sign of the Four over their hearts. Kay's words were impossible; everyone in Challen returned to the Four upon death. Even violent criminals faced the God of Winter before He froze their souls. An Avatar's soul would be much more precious to the Four. Gwen forced herself to keep her voice composed. "No one can separate you from your chosen God. That voice is lying to you, Kay."

Some color finally rose in her face. "You think so?"

Gwen and Jenna nodded simultaneously.

"But it seems so real. I'm wearing the same pale blue dress in all of them...." The air around them crisped with chill. When Jenna opened her mouth, Gwen raised a finger to stop her. Kay had to make this decision on her own.

Finally, Kay raised her pointed chin. "The Four must be stronger than any single voice. Let me get my extra clothes and my sewing kit." She frowned. "And write a letter to Jon."

"Jon?" Gwen asked.

"My betrothed. He drives a Selathen locomotive. He just left on another trip, and he won't be back for days. He has to know why I'm leaving." Her face turned pale again. "I hope he forgives me."

Gwen urged her back to the carriage, wondering if Aunt Gabri had found new gloves. She softened her voice to speak to Kay. "Does he know you're an Avatar?"

"No. I kept it secret from everyone." Kay mouthed the words, "Just in case."

* * *

Retrieving Aunt Gabri from the shop proved to be a challenge. The store owner didn't want to pay Kay the wages she was owed. Worse, she insisted the interruption had cost her the rest of the day's work from all her seamstresses and demanded compensation from the One Oak. While Gwen and the shop owner argued, Aunt Gabri blithely selected so many accessories she could have been preparing her own trousseau. Gwen finally settled everything by agreeing to pay twice what the items were worth. At least she found a couple of nice pairs of gloves for herself as well.

By the time they were done, late afternoon had brought a chill to the air. Out-of-season snowflakes drifted down onto the streets. Gwen eyed them warily, then looked at Kay. She walked as stiffly as if someone had sewed a steel rod into the back of her dress. "You're not causing this, are you?"

Kay shook her head. "It's Chaos Season." She hung back as they approached the carriage, and both Gwen and Jenna had to urge her to get in.

"How deep is it going to get?" Jenna asked as the carriage started off.

"Enough to cover your shoes, but not much more than that."

"How long will it stay?" Gwen asked. "Will we have problems traveling to Tradetown? And where do you live?"

Kay pointed to a side street. "Down two more blocks, then first building on the left. And you should go To Tradetown by locomotive. It does a better job of clearing the snow off the rails than anyone does for the road."

"Please tell me we won't leave until tomorrow at least," Aunt Gabri said. "I need a decent night's sleep before boarding that leviathan again."

Gwen had picked up a schedule at the station. She searched her reticule for the schedule while the carriage took them to a boarding house. It needed new shutters and a new coat of paint, but unlike the other buildings, there was no garbage piled outside.

Kay squirmed. "I won't be long."

Gwen wondered if she planned to barricade herself in her room and refuse to come out. "We can come with you."

"Gwendolyn! Surely that's not necessary!" Aunt Gabri said.

"I can explain the situation to your landlady if there's a problem with the rent."

Neither Kay nor Aunt Gabri could argue with that. Gwen glanced at Jenna, silently inviting her to come along, but she tilted her head at Aunt Gabri. Maybe she intended to watch her and make sure she didn't get worse. That should have been Gwen's job. However, Gwen thought Kay needed her more right now.

Kay's cheeks turned red as she led Gwen inside a dimly lit hallway and up a narrow flight of stairs smelling of vinegar and cabbage. "I'm sure this isn't what you're used to," she said. "You were born to a noble family, right? I always thought the Four sent us to lives that would help us prepare to be Avatars."

"They always put us in different classes, don't They? Places where we can learn skills that will help us."

Kay's flush darkened. "I know I haven't practiced my magic as much as I should have. I swear by the Four I'll do my best to be ready when we're needed."

"Unfortunately, the other Ava Spring has gone to the God of Winter. We're needed now."

Kay's face paled. She stopped outside a door and fumbled for a key before opening it. The room itself was tiny, with only a narrow bed, a stand for a wash basin, and a scratched wardrobe. However, the bedspread was unwrinkled, and Kay's brush and comb were lined up neatly next to the wash basin.

"It won't take me long to pack, Lady lo Havil." Kay pulled a valise from the bottom of the wardrobe and stacked an extra change of clothes inside.

"We're sister Avas. Call me Gwen." She wondered if she should offer to help. She'd gained some experience in packing during her recent travels. Her folding skills, however, weren't up to Kay's. Maybe she could help in another way.

She said, "It's a touch cold in here. Could you warm up this room?"

"My room?"

"Yes, just this room. No one else will be able to sense it since it's inside, right?"

"The woman in my dreams." Kay spoke slowly, as if she'd returned to her dream. "She'll know. If she can send me dreams in that bed, she'll know if I warm up the air."

"You have to do it sometime, Kay, and soon." Gwen gentled her voice as if she was singing a child a lullaby. "Might as well start small."

Kay stared at her for a few more heartbeats before saying, "All right. I'll try."

Gwen tried not to show how relieved she was. "Wonderful. Do you want me to link with you?"

Kay shook her head. "It's best if I try to do this on my own. I have to be able to support my quarter during Chaos Season."

She took a deep breath, touched the hot air duct near the bed, and closed her eyes. Gwen wondered what she was trying to do; that wasn't how the Wins normally worked. Kay pulled away and turned back to the room. She raised her hands high above her head. The air in the room began to stir; the heavy curtains swung back and forth, a doily flapped, and stray hairs that had escaped from Gwen's bun tickled her skin. Kay frowned, and everything stilled again. She lowered her arms and pressed her hands together. This time, Gwen could feel perspiration bead on her forehead. The room grew even warmer, as if it was now Heatmoon.

"That's enough!" Gwen said.

Kay abruptly released the heat. The temperature plummeted. She staggered, then collapsed, her head missing the wardrobe by inches.

Gwen knelt next to her, touching her with her good hand. Her reserves were low. She needed to eat and sleep more. Gwen carefully fed her some energy, then roused her.

"You did it," Gwen said. Kay's spirit needed tending as much as her body.

"I did, didn't I?" Her smile was brief. "It was harder than it should have been. I've failed the Four. I shouldn't have bottled up my magic for so long."

"You did what you thought was best. Let's get you packed up and back to the hotel. After you eat, we'll try again."

Kay grimaced. "Again?"

Gwen glanced out the window. Snow came down even harder than before. "We're not leaving today, so we may as well start making up for lost practice time."

CHAPTER TWENTY-ONE

Tradetown

Kay's wardrobe was so worn, despite her mending, that the three women braved the snow and visited the largest store in Rainbow River before returning to the hotel. They purchased a trunk for Kay along with two new dresses, a pair of boots, and some other essentials. The clothes weren't as fine as an Avatar deserved, but after Kay changed into her gray wool traveling dress, she held her head a little higher. Then she examined the sleeves as if she was thinking of altering them.

In the middle of the night, Kay woke Gwen up with her moaning. While Jenna and Aunt Gabri snored, Gwen crossed over to Kay's bed to listen. "Save me, Winter," Kay pleaded. Gwen's hand hovered over her forehead. Should she link and try to enter Kay's dream? Regretfully, Gwen forced her hand down. She wasn't sure it would do more good than harm, especially if whoever was sending Kay the bad dreams became aware of her.

In the morning, the snow had piled up deeper than Kay had predicted. Jenna scowled as she looked out the window. "This is bad. I'll have to work extra hard to bring the plants where they ought to be this time of year."

Kay didn't respond, but she rubbed her hands together. Gwen didn't push her. Her color looked a little better than yesterday, but the dark shadows under her eyes hadn't disappeared. She wasn't ready to tackle a major weather system on her own yet, and linking still seemed dangerous.

"Let me see what I can do once we go outside," Kay said. "I may not be able to melt everything, but maybe I can keep the locomotive tracks clear."

When they arrived at the station, the ticket seller not only recognized Kay, but gave the whole party reduced fares and promised to deliver a sealed letter to Jon for her. She walked up and down the platform, staring at the engine while the crew attached a snow plow to the front, until it was time for them to board. But once they were underway, she sat at the front of their car near a window. Smoke from the locomotive seemed to seep inside as Kay stared at the landscape. Water beaded on top of the snow before it melted. Still, this train proceeded more slowly than the first one had, and they didn't reach Tradetown until sunset.

The Tradetown station was big enough to boast multiple tracks and an indoor seating area. Passengers and officials dashed back and forth. It took Gwen a few moments to realize almost all of them were men. Gwen's party was going to attract attention simply by being female. Would that help them find Ysabel, or delay them?

As they waited for a porter to collect their luggage, Jenna took Robbie away from the nursemaid and stood next to Gwen. "So, Lady Ava Spring, are we just going to march up to Ysabel's house and ask her to join us?"

"Of course not," Gwen replied. "I'd rather ask around about her family first."

Jenna scrubbed a bit of dried food off of Robbie's mouth. "It's the men around here who would give us trouble, right? We just have to wait until her father leaves the house and then call on her."

"Finally you're acting as if you have manners," Aunt Gabri muttered. Her eyes gleamed. "But how do you intend to introduce yourselves? You can't just march there and announce you're Season Avatars. Who are these people? How will you arrange an introduction? You can't have any mutual acquaintances in this part of Challen, can you?"

Gwen shook her head. Her aunt was right; it might be suspicious if they called on strangers, but she didn't know how they could avoid it. "We could say we wanted to make the acquaintance of another Challen woman."

"But who is she?" Aunt Gabri asked. "Who's her family?"

Gwen fished the note with the information out of her reticule. "Ysabel s'Ivena Lathatilltin. Her parents are Mattie s'Ivena Lathatilltin and Haltin Lathatilltin."

"What?" Aunt Gabri clutched her own reticule even tighter. "Mattie? Mattie s'Ivena? Are you sure you wrote that name down correctly, Gwendolyn?"

"I'm certain," She looked at her aunt with hope. "Do you know her?"

"Know her? We were roommates at the University! She studied music and was good enough to play concerts in Wistica. By All Four, this town is the last place I would have expected to find her, especially married."

"Why?" Jenna asked. "Unless it's…"

Her voice trailed off as a group of passengers flocked toward the next departing locomotive. Perhaps one of every eight people in the group was a woman. The women dressed in sober colors of brown and black, with the occasional dark blue for variety. Plain bonnets covered their hair, and they didn't look around or greet each other. Instead, they followed two or three steps behind the men, focusing their gaze on the ground.

Aunt Gabri shook her head as she watched them. She drew the group into a secluded corner. "I can't imagine Mattie dressed like that.

She always preferred bright colors." She lowered her voice. "And she was a Fallswoman too."

Fallswomen chose to forsake marriage and children. Sometimes they were noblewomen, sometimes they were artists or shop owners who wanted to devote all their attention to their own pursuits. It didn't matter what the woman's birthseason was as long as she chose to devote herself to Fall. Gwen had even heard of Avatars from other seasons who were considered Fallswomen. She'd never heard of one leaving the life to get married.

"What Fallswoman deserts the Goddess for a man?" Kay asked.

"Fall sent Her Avatar to be born to Mattie," Gwen pointed out. "She must have had a reason for that." Maybe they would figure out what it was once they called on the Lathatilltins.

Aunt Gabri sighed. "Let's find a hotel—By All Four, a better one this time—and I'll send her my calling card and a note."

They had to wait several minutes before a carriage stopped for them, and the driver looked their group over as if they didn't meet his approval. However, the hotel he drove them to was nicer than the one in Rainbow River. A young woman with bared shoulders played a pianoforte in the lobby as they checked in. The clerk wore an unusual timepiece: a jet black case with six silver marks spaced evenly around the edge. As Gwen studied it, he turned red and slipped it into his pocket.

"We serve an excellent supper in the ladies' restaurant," he said.

"Ladies' restaurant?" Gwen asked.

"A cozy room where ladies may relax with chocolate and light refreshments. I'm sure it would suit your party admirably."

"Just light refreshments, though? Not a full meal?" Gwen couldn't keep the disappointment out of her voice.

"It's a private room just for ladies, so they don't serve men's portions."

As Gwen wondered how to explain she could out-eat a farmer at harvest time, a familiar voice behind her said, "At last, you're here. What took you so long?"

Gwen turned. Kron Evenhanded stood behind them. He'd altered his clothes slightly to blend in with the Selathen locals. The scent of violets clung to him. He inspected their party with open interest, finishing with Kay. "I think you were Caye, correct?" The beginning was softer, and the ending more drawn out, but the name was otherwise identical to Kay's current one. She stepped back in surprise, clenching her fist as if she meant to hurl lightning at him.

"How do you know my name, sir?" she asked.

He raised an eyebrow. "That's your current name too? The Four like to keep things consistent, I see."

The hotel clerk scowled for a moment, then put on a pleasant expression as Kron turned to him and said, "The ladies will be joining me in the main dining room."

"As you wish, sir."

Gwen wasn't sure whether to be annoyed men received better treatment in this town or grateful Kron had given them a chance to obtain a filling meal. At least here was her chance to question him about the shards. He led them into a dining area that smelled of roast beef and cigars and requested a table in the corner, away from other diners.

"I am right, am I not?" he said once the waiter poured their wine and left. "You have three of your quartet now. Only Bella remains."

"Ysabel," Gwen corrected. "Sir Evenhanded, I must ask you—"

"Yes, Ysabel. In my heart, she'll always be Bella. Have you seen her yet?"

"We haven't even seen our rooms." Aunt Gabri swallowed half her glass of wine. "Are you staying here, Sir Evenhanded? Are the rooms suitable for women of quality?"

"They're fine."

"Sir Evenhanded, what have you done with the water clock? And the shard from the One Oak?"

Kron's mouth hardened. "I read about the water clock in the paper. By All Four Gods and Goddesses, I didn't take it. Perhaps Salth or Sal-thaath did."

Jenna sat up straighter, grinning. Gwen wondered how much she would crow about being right—if Kron wasn't lying, that is.

"I tried searching for more shards, but their location kept shifting west. I thought I traced some here, actually, but they disappeared. Perhaps Salth and Sal-thaath transported them over the Challen border. I can't fathom why, however. Their magic doesn't rely on artifacts."

Kay frowned. "Shards? Artifacts? What do they have to do with magic?"

"I'll tell her," Jenna said. She handed Robbie back to the nursemaid, drew her chair closer to Kay, and whispered. Kay's eyes widened.

Gwen waited until the waiter served them soup before asking Kron, "Do you think we Avatars are safe now, or will shards attack us again?"

He stared at her. "I thought the Four protected you while you were in Challen."

Does that mean the Four let *Margaret die and me be cursed?* Gwen decided to change the subject. "When did you arrive in Tradetown?"

"Just yesterday. I've been by Bella's—I mean, Ysabel's—house, but the maid wouldn't let me in. Then I visited her father's shop, but it was closed. Strange. He has many black-and-silver watches in his window, and they seem quite popular in this town."

"We'll call on the Lathatilltins tomorrow." Gwen sipped the peppery soup. "My aunt knows Ysabel's mother, so we should have no problem being admitted."

"May I come with you?" Kron asked.

Part of Gwen still distrusted him, despite his help. Besides, he wasn't an Avatar, and their business was more important than his.

"If I understand this correctly, the Four make sure the four of you are reborn together, life after life. Is that what happens?" Kron leaned forward, bringing with him the smell of violets again. "I'm sure you're anxious to meet Ysabel again, but it's been far longer for me since I saw her last."

Jenna gave him an odd look. "Why do you smell like violets?"

"Oh, I almost forgot." With a sheepish smile, he pulled a flower out of his coat pocket. "This was on my pillow this morning when I woke up."

Kay stared at it as if wondering how it got there. Gwen wanted to ask that question herself. But before she could, Jenna asked, "Could I see it?"

Kron passed it over to her. The plant was complete except for the roots, but when Jenna turned the flower upside down, the bottom of the stem was smooth, with no sign of having been picked. The leaves were still fresh and strong, and when Jenna tugged one, it didn't come off.

Awe spread across her face. "This isn't a natural plant. I swear I can feel Summer Himself created it."

Then what was Kron doing with it? Why did the Four grant him so much favor and ignore the Avatars who had faithfully served them for centuries? Maybe Gwen and her sister Avatars were no longer worthy of the Four. What with Gwen's shard, Jenna's child, and Kay's lack of practice, Gwen could understand if the Four wanted to replace them with another Avatar. But not when they were so close to completing their set....

"I don't know why They would send me a flower." He sounded bemused. "Maybe I'm supposed to give it to Ysabel."

"This isn't a fall flower," Jenna said, "it's a spring one. So maybe Gwen...."

She passed it to Gwen. Like a living bracelet, the flower wrapped itself around her wrist above the shard. A pleasant warmth spread from the flower down to her hand. Once the warmth reached the embedded shard, it flared. For a heartbeat, Gwen's hand felt as if it was on fire on the inside. Before she could use her own magic to counteract it, the pain died. Her hand felt stiff for a moment, then eased as she flexed her fingers. The shard shifted within her. Hoping that perhaps she could remove it now, Gwen pressed on it. She still couldn't open her skin to let it out.

"Are you all right?" Jenna leaned forward, eyes darker than her normal green. "You looked like you were about to faint for a moment."

"I don't faint." Her voice came out waspish.

"Of course not. That's what made it worrisome."

"Did it do something?" Kron watched her as if he was more curious than concerned.

"You don't know what it did?" she asked. "And yet you gave it to me?"

"Jenna said the God of Summer created it," Kay said. "Have the Four ever given us anything like this? If so, I don't remember it. They had a reason to make the flower and send it to you through him. They could have given it to you directly if They chose."

Gwen stared down at her hand. Maybe this wasn't another curse, but something to counter the shard. She'd have to test it at the first opportunity. She ought to thank all Four Gods and Goddesses for Their unprecedented gift. The Four must want her to work with Kron, even if he wasn't an Avatar—or she wasn't sure if she could trust him.

She turned to her aunt. "Aunt Gabri, when you send your note to Dame s'Ivena Lathatilltin, please include Kron Evenhanded in our party."

She hoped the former Fallswoman was prepared for the arrival of three Avatars, an unknown magician, and a nursemaid with an infant.

CHAPTER TWENTY-TWO

The Former Fallswoman

Jenna decided the next morning that Robbie should stay behind with his nursemaid, so it was only a party of five to call on the Lathatilltin family the next day. Dame s'Ivena Lathatilltin must have been eager to meet them, for her messenger came back within the hour inviting them to lunch. That should have been a good sign that their mission would proceed smoothly, but Gwen couldn't shake the feeling that things would go wrong.

"By All Four, Gwen," Jenna said as the carriage took them all to Amity Street, "Stop scowling. You'll frighten Ysabel off as soon as we meet her."

"I wonder who else will be there." Gwen forced herself to stop twisting her gloves. "Do you think her father will be there?"

"We can handle him," Jenna said, holding her head high.

The streets were crowded enough for Gwen to worry about making it to the house on time. As before, far more men than women were out. They sold food and newspapers on street corners, gestured wildly as they walked in groups to restaurants, and gathered around a speaker standing on a park bench. His words penetrated the carriage: "The time is coming for us to return to our ancient homeland! Soon, we won't have to pay tribute to any god! We will be able to pursue knowledge without any cursed magic interfering!"

"Magic is only another tool!" a black-and-gray garbed man called out. "Handle it properly, and we can turn it to our side!"

"And I say we will never be truly free until magic and gods are gone!"

Kay gasped and made the sign of the Four over her heart.

The carriage turned, and the shouts receded in the distance. No one, not even Aunt Gabri, spoke for a few minutes. Gwen twisted her violet bracelet, seeking comfort. Why would anyone want to deny the Four, Who'd devoted centuries to the welfare of Challen? Why would anyone say magic was more bad than good? And how would these people react if she openly proclaimed herself an Avatar?

"Maybe this is why Mattie lied about Ysabel's birthday," she said quietly.

"Ysabel was born years ago," Aunt Gabri said. "Have these people been complaining about magic for that long? And why would anyone resent magic when it makes our lives better? Well, except for Chaos Season." She curled up inside her shawl, looking even older than she really was. "Chaos Season could make anyone hate magic."

"If these are the people whose ancestors originally lived to the west of the mountains, then they have reason to hate magic," Kron said. "Salth drained all the life from their land. They were lucky to escape." He stared into the distance, his mouth pressed into an unhappy line as if reliving bad memories.

Gwen listened for more complaints against the Four, but the streets quieted as they entered a residential area. The houses here were brick and stone, with geometrical patterns making each one unique. No servants or visitors walked about. All the windows were covered with drapes so no one could see in or out. Gwen wondered what, if any, animals were around to give Ysabel a chance to practice her magic.

"Why would the Four send Ysabel to grow up here?" Jenna asked.

"So she could understand these people," Kron replied.

Gwen leaned forward. "And how do you know that?"

"Spring told me." The carriage halted. "Ah, this must be the place." Kron beamed. "Soon, Dearest, soon we'll be reunited." He bounded out of the carriage before Gwen could ask him when—and how—he'd spoken with her Goddess.

Something black-and-white ran around the corner of the house toward the front door, then halted and turned to look at them. It was a small cat, but its gaze felt out of proportion to its size. Maybe it was Ysabel's anilink. If she'd bonded with an animal that could enhance her magic, that was a good sign. At least she'd managed to practice some magic despite the Selathens' hatred of it. As Gwen walked up the stone path to the porch, she noticed more details about the cat. Its hair stood on end, and its eyes gave off an eerie glow even in the noon light. It might be picking up on distress from Ysabel. What was bothering her? Would she object to taking up her Avatar duties as Kay had done?

Gwen lost track of the cat when the maid let them in. She took their wraps and directed them to a dining room. Gwen studied a portrait above the fireplace. It was of a youth with dark brown hair and a light brown complexion. He had a strong chin and heavy eyebrows, but what captured Gwen's attention was the slight smirk on his face. Whoever had painted this picture must have known the subject well. She wondered what the young man was like in the flesh.

"He looks like he'd be a good kisser," Jenna whispered.

"Really? You can tell from his portrait?"

"Just look at those lips."

For a moment, Gwen imagined doing more than looking. Then she reminded herself she was here to meet Ysabel, not potential husbands. As if her family would consider the son of a Selathen merchant good enough for her. Once the Avatars were reunited, Gwen would have to decide for herself what she wanted in a husband.

The maid removed a place setting from the table, leaving six. There were already five in the party, so they would have only one hostess. Would it be Ysabel or her mother?

Gwen's hopes were dashed when a portly middle-aged woman with a strong resemblance to the youth entered the room. She wore a plain navy blue dress with no adornment, but she'd twisted a flamboyantly embroidered scarlet scarf over her hair. Her complexion was an unhealthy color, but her green eyes lit up when she saw Aunt Gabri. "Gabri, I don't believe it! Here, after all this time!" She opened her arms to embrace her.

Aunt Gabri hugged her friend with visible restraint. "Mattie! How wonderful to see you again! I never expected you to end up here in Tradetown, married to a Selathen."

"Neither did I." A wry smile twisted her lips. "The Goddess had other plans for me." She examined Gwen, Jenna, and Kay, then raised her eyebrows as she studied Kron. He paid her no attention as he watched the door. "We have so much to catch up on. But first introduce me to your companions."

"This is my niece, Gwendolyn. She's going to be—"

Dame s'Ivena Lathatilltin held a finger to her lips. "Married soon, perhaps?"

"She should have been married by now. This headstrong girl thinks she has more important things to do."

Gwen flushed before she could stop herself. She hoped her aunt had a good reason for embarrassing her like this.

"And Gwendolyn has companions her own age, I see." The dame gestured for them to sit at the table, taking the head place. "Such a shame Ysabel's not here to meet you. I'm sure it would have pleased her very much."

"We'd love nothing more than an introduction to her," Gwen said. "Where is she? Will she be back soon?"

"I don't know." The lines around her eyes and mouth deepened. "Her father insisted she put on her best dress and leave before sunrise with him. He said he had someone he wanted her to meet. He hinted at a possible marriage.”

“What?” Kron’s attention returned to the group. “Spring Herself said Ysabel was free!”

Ysabel’s mother put her finger over her lips. “It’s…unseemly to speak of the Four in Tradetown. One never knows who might overhear you.”

“I can fix that,” Kron said grimly.

“One moment first.” Ysabel’s mother pulled the bell cord by her chair. A moment later, a housemaid appeared. “Zilla, go ahead and lay out lunch on the side board, then hurry to the butcher and order a leg of lamb for dinner.”

“But Dame, that’s on the other side of town!”

“We can serve ourselves while you’re out. Perhaps you can stop by the grocer and pick up more ground chocolate too.”

The maid brought in broth, a couple of meat pies, bread, cheese, and a tray of tarts, then hurried off.

“Are you worried about any other eavesdroppers?” Kron asked.

“The cook is sympathetic to the Four, but the butler is my husband’s man.”

“Humm.” Kron took an empty wine glass and struck it four times with a silver spoon. The chime resounded in the room, then ebbed to a constant note sounding in the background. “That should stop anyone from overhearing us.”

“By All Four, what did you do?” Dame s’Ivena Lathatilltin’s eyes narrowed. “That’s not the Four’s magic. You’re not an Avatar, are you?”

“I’m an ally of the Four. And the Avatars, of course. I know Ysabel…well, I knew her a very long time ago.” Kron’s face turned red, and he gulped down a glass of wine. “Now, what’s this about her father marrying her off before I even have a chance to see her again?”

"Please, eat." Ysabel's mother gestured to the side board but made no move to help herself. Jenna rose to fill her plate; after a few heartbeats, Kay copied her. For once, Gwen had no appetite.

She leaned forward. "Is Ysabel really the Fall Avatar? If so, why did you register her birth with the wrong date?"

"And with a male twin?" Jenna added.

"Her brother was born the day before the fall equinox, right before midnight," the dame replied. "Ysabel was born as soon as the midnight gongs ended. It seemed safer to give her her brother's birthday so her father wouldn't suspect."

"Well, he must have figured it out," Gwen said. "Why would her father marry her off now? Who is her betrothed?"

Ysabel's mother twisted a napkin. "I'm not sure there is a betrothed."

Jenna turned toward the table. "What?"

"You're not familiar with this part of Challen, are you?"

"We're Avatars—" Gwen began.

Ysabel's mother held up her hand. "You don't know the Selathens. Their numbers are greater this close to the border, so they're bolder with their beliefs—or lack of belief."

"What do you mean?" Gwen asked.

"They originally came from Selath, the Dead Land."

Kron sat up straight. "Is that what they call it these days? I suppose Salth would be flattered, if she cared about what ordinary people think."

"Salth?" All color drained from Ysabel's mother's face. "How do you know their goddess's name? Are you one of them?"

"One of who?"

"Salth worshippers." She grimaced. "Some Selathens reject all magic and gods, preferring to use reason and technology. They say it's because magic makes the Dead Land dead. But even if nothing can live there for long, there's still plenty of gold, gems, and other valuable materials in the land, and other Selathens have found a way to live long enough to get them."

A sick feeling in Gwen's stomach made her glad she hadn't eaten. "What's that?"

"They offer a young life to the goddess of the land."

Jenna's plate crashed to the floor, sending cheese, bits of meat, and pie crust flying. "Robbie!" She dashed for the door, but halted as Dame s'Ivena Lathatilltin continued,

"By the Four Who asked me to spy on these frozen people, I think they've got Ysabel."

CHAPTER TWENTY-THREE

Traveling with Kron

"What?" Nausea rose in Gwen's throat. Finding Ysabel had been hard enough; she'd thought all she'd have to do here was announce they were Avatars and collect Ysabel, overriding her parents if they refused to let her go. The last thing she'd expected was a rescue mission. Hopefully the violet bracelet would let her use her magic to its fullest despite the shard. They were going to need her healing and linking abilities to get Ysabel back.

"My husband is ostensibly a watch merchant, but he trades in gold and precious metals too. He sends teams of men to the Dead Land to get them. They give chals to poor mothers with too many children." Ysabel's mother took a deep breath. "The children never come back."

Anger raced through Gwen's veins. She schooled herself to keep her emotions from showing. Kay's eyes appeared a darker blue, and her short hair drifted up as if she'd conjured up a breeze inside the room.

"Why hasn't anyone done anything about this sooner?" Gwen asked. "And what makes you think they took Ysabel this time?"

"The men in this town don't allow women their fair share of power, and the women are too cowed to take it." Ysabel's mother suddenly seemed ten years older. "I've tried talking to them. A few of the younger ones are interested in worshipping the Four, but most of them feel that the Four don't care about Selathens."

"What about Ysabel?" Kron asked.

"Did you notice how quiet the street was?" Ysabel's mother continued. "Normally we have songbirds serenading us from before dawn to sunset. Fall must be watching over us, otherwise someone would have surely suspected Ysabel's the next Fall Avatar by now."

"Maybe they just followed her to wherever she is now," Jenna said, more doubt than confidence in her tone.

"Some are always here. She must be in trouble if the animals are hiding too."

"If Ysabel's in trouble, she could summon animals to aid her," Jenna said.

"Not if they take her into Selath. There will be nothing there to summon."

Gwen wondered if the Four would prevent Ysabel from being brought out of the country. She couldn't remember if an Avatar had ever left Challen before. Why would they leave the country of their gods and goddesses? And what would happen if they had to?

"Do you have any idea exactly where they might be taking her?" Kron pushed his empty plate away. "If they left at dawn, they have several hours of travel time on us, and I don't know this country well enough to portal in it."

Some fire returned to Ysabel's mother's eyes. "My honored husband thinks all I do is order the servants about and play the pianoforte. He doesn't know how handy I can be with a hairpin."

Aunt Gabri gasped. "By All Four, Mattie, you didn't—"

"I did. Every time he went on a business trip, I broke into his office and copied his records. His team's excursions into the Dead Land always take the same route and cross the Chikasi River right at the border between Challen and Selath. Does that help?"

Kron looked thoughtful. "Do they travel by river or over land?"

"Over land. And there's no locomotive track leading there, so they have to ride."

Kron closed his eyes for a moment. "I came up the river by steamboat. It was much easier than our last trip. I could portal us to the last dock, and then we could try to find someone who will lend us a boat." He opened his eyes and studied the door. "Dame, are you absolutely sure no one else will come into this room?"

"They shouldn't."

"Good. Then I hope you won't mind if I borrow a doorway."

Kron rose and studied the doorframe for a few moments, then traced a single unbroken line around the entire entrance, including the floor. The line glowed, and the view of the hallway transformed into a dock. The Chikasi River lapped at the rowboat tied to the end.

"By All Four," everyone, including Gwen, gasped in unison.

"What kind of magic is that?" Gwen added.

"My own. Come." He strode through the doorway as if it was still normal.

Gwen and the others exchanged glances. Aunt Gabri said, "Well, I don't trust it. At least when you get into a carriage, you know what to expect. I'll stay here and exchange gossip with Mattie."

"What about Robbie?" Jenna asked. "He's got to be safer here than chasing baby killers, but how will I get back to him?"

"Through another portal. Come." Kron turned and frowned. "The longer you delay, the more time the Selathens have to hurt Ysabel."

Jenna, still looking at Gwen, raised her eyebrows as if to say, "You're the leader, you go first."

Biting back a sigh, Gwen clenched her violet bracelet for the Four's protection as she stood up and advanced to the doorway. Before she could pass through, the cat bolted out from under the dining table and to Kron.

Well, if a cat can do it, so can I. Gwen forced herself to keep her eyes open as she walked through. One heartbeat, she was breathing in stale, heated air; the next, the breeze attempted to coax a few hairs free of her chignon. She wished she'd thought to fetch her shawl before crossing over, as the air was cooler near the river. The dock creaked under her feet. Somewhere close by, a rotting fish had washed up on the shore. Gwen lingered for a moment, thrilled that she had traveled somewhere else so quickly, before Jenna joined her. Kay came last, glancing around warily as if she expected the Selathens to be there.

"By All Four Gods and Goddesses," she said, "I've never seen magic like this before."

"Actually, you did in your very first life as an Avatar." Kron looked up and down the dock. "At least this time we can use a smaller boat, so we can sail farther upriver. Kay, can you manage currents now, or still only winds?"

Dismay showed in Kay's wide eyes for a heartbeat. "Winds, maybe." In a lower voice, she added, "But this close to the border, she'll know I'm using magic."

"We're all in this together," Gwen reminded her. "If we lose Ysabel, our four-fold magic won't work."

"We can't lose Kay either," Jenna said.

"I know, I know." Gwen's stomach growled; maybe she should have eaten when she had the chance. She hurried over to Kron. "Do they have a steamboat in a small enough size for us?"

"A steamboat? If not, I suppose I can make one. It should be easier this time around. First I have to find a regular boat." Continuing his monologue, Kron wandered down to the end of the dock, where a shed guarded a few boats smaller than the one William had once taken Gwen for a ride in. Gwen followed him at a distance, with Jenna and Kay tagging along as if they weren't sure if they should be there.

"Are we sure this is the best way to find Ysabel?" Kay asked.

Gwen regarded her bracelet. "The Four must think so."

"That may be, but he's still…odd."

"I suppose the world was quite different eight hundred years ago," Jenna said. "Do you suppose we seem strange to him?"

"Keep your voice down, or we'll seem rude."

If Kron had overheard them, he didn't mention it when they caught up to him. He clambered into each boat while an elderly man watched him inspect them. "By All Four," he said, "don't tell me these ladies want a boat too. They're not suitable for such delicate creatures."

Jenna let out a choked laugh before a glare from Gwen silenced her.

"We'll take the middle one," Kron told the man. "How much?"

"How far are you planning to take her?" he countered.

"We're not sure, so we want to buy it outright."

"Seventy-five chals then."

"Will you take fifty?"

The man raised his bushy eyebrows. "My price is final. If you don't have it…"

"Oh, we can manage it." Gwen felt for her reticule, then realized she'd forgotten to fetch that from Ysabel's house too. Biting back an oath, she pulled a topaz ring off her finger. "This should cover it and more."

The man's jaw dropped. "Lady, this could buy all my boats."

For a moment, Gwen wondered if it would be a good idea to take a second boat so they would have more room. But Kron said, "Then can you throw in a paddlewheel too?"

"For a boat this size?"

Kron sighed. "What do you have on hand?"

The men went inside the shack, so Gwen inspected the boat. Four people might squeeze into the seats if they didn't mind squashing each other. There was no canopy or shelter to block out the weather—which could be useful or miserable depending on what they encountered and how much skill Kay had. Gwen had only been on a boat this size a few times, so she didn't know what else she should look for. Otherwise, it seemed sturdy enough to her.

"Is Kron really going to put a steamboat paddlewheel on this boat?" Jenna asked. "Because the boat is smaller than the paddlewheel."

Gwen shrugged. "I hope he'll think of something." This boat had no sail, so their only other option was to row. "Is there anything we should bring with us?"

"Too bad we didn't think to bring food," Jenna said. "Is there any way we can go back and get some?"

Gwen checked behind her, but the door leading back to the Lathatilltin's house wasn't visible. "I guess we're on our own."

Kron returned with a variety of wooden pieces, cloths, and some metal gears. The old man approached Gwen and insisted on pressing a double handful of small coins on her. Maybe they could stop somewhere and buy some food. While she distributed the chals to Jenna and Kay, Kron knelt in the back of the boat and assembled his strange items. When he was finished, it looked like a toy version of a steamboat paddlewheel.

Jenna raised both eyebrows. "That's going to take us upriver?" she whispered. "I hope he has enough cloth for a sail. We'll need Kay's weather magic after all."

"No, you won't," Kron said. "I just hope this will be faster than their transport. Step aboard the *Avatar II* so we can give chase."

One by one, they climbed into the boat with his assistance. The cat jumped in and found a spot up front. Jenna and Kay took the forward seat; Gwen sat in back next to Kron. With a mild twinge of guilt, Gwen was grateful her aunt wasn't here to object. She shifted to the edge to avoid touching him. He fussed with his contraption, muttering to himself in his ancient tongue. How long would it take him to get it working?

Kron leaned on part of the boat, and it surged forward. Gwen bit back a shriek and held on. Jenna and Kay bounced around so much she worried they would fall out. Kron moved his hand several times. Each time he touched the hull, the boat jerked in a different direction.

Finally he nodded and pressed the center of the boat. It leapt forward, faster than a galloping horse. Gwen fervently prayed they didn't encounter anyone else on the river. He'd never be able to sail around them at this speed.

The country zipped by them so quickly Gwen found it hard to pick out details. They passed a few people, who watched them with astonished faces. Geese swimming on the river took off in a hurry as the boat bore down on them. At first they rode by a few small towns about the size of Bull Rock. As the country grew more barren, all that was left were stretches of pine trees. Then they disappeared too, and the air grew cooler, as if they'd left spring behind too. The boat veered unexpected from side to side, but they didn't crash.

Finally, Kron eased off on the speed and steered them to a sandy patch on the bank. Gwen paused to catch her breath before climbing out. Her legs wobbled as if she'd run the entire distance.

"Thank the Four we're alive." Kay made the sign of the Four before Gwen and Jenna helped her over the side of the boat. "Where are we?"

Kron looked at a wooden device in his hand. It resembled a compass, but it lacked markings. A single garnet glowed in one corner, opposite the arrow. "Still not as close to Ysabel as we need to be. But she's that way." He pointed to a grassy area that extended as far as Gwen could see.

"Is it far?" she asked.

"I'm not used to how you measure distance in this time. I think it's less than the distance from one end of Wistica to the other, though."

That seemed like a long way to walk, especially when Gwen's shoes were more like slippers than boots. She raised her skirt to ankle-height, placed Ysabel's anilink on her shoulder, and followed Kron. Jenna and Kay trooped after her.

At first, no trails, not even an animal's, were visible in the knee-high grass. Gwen wondered if they should ask Jenna to lead the way, as she could part the grass without damaging it. Gwen glanced back to ask her, only to find Jenna had trailed behind, sweeping her hand behind her to restore the damaged grass. Soon, however, the grass grew shorter and more yellow-looking. Then it gave way to a moss that tore out of the ground when they stepped on it. Gwen slipped a few times, smearing her dress with soil and green streaks.

"Maybe we should hold hands so we can help each other," Kay suggested.

"That would trigger the link," Jenna said. "We should hook our arms together instead."

Hurt that Jenna still didn't want to link with her, Gwen halted. "Jenna Dorshay t'Reve, do you doubt the Four?" She held up her hand and shook the violet bracelet. "This has to protect the three of you when we link. We should test the link before we need it."

"Right this heartbeat?"

"We don't know what we're facing," Gwen said. "What if we need to link our magic to rescue Ysabel? We can't afford to fail."

Before Jenna could respond, Kron strode back to them. He wasn't having difficulties keeping his footing, Gwen noted with irritation.

"There's a trail up ahead," he said. "I believe the Selathans use it to cross into Selath. Ysabel must be close by, but I can't detect Salth or Sal-thaath. The Four wouldn't allow them inside Challen. If we have to cross into Selath, we might lose the Four's protection."

"Can we even cross the border?" Gwen asked. "I didn't think that was possible."

"The Four don't seem to want us to travel much," Jenna muttered. "I've probably seen more of Challen in the past moon than I did in my previous life."

"If you three were once Galia, Janno, and Caye, then you sailed with Bella and me the first time we tried to defeat Salth," Kron replied. "We crossed over into Selath then. I wish you remembered more of it." He shook his head. "Back then, I provided you with artifacts to protect you from Salth and Selath's time magic. I made some new ones using current timepieces. You'd better put them on before we get closer to the border."

He pulled three black-and-silver watches from his coat pocket. At first, they looked identical to the ones they'd seen in Tradetown, the ones that indicated the wearer bore allegiance to Salth. When Gwen examined it, she noticed the hands had been removed from the timepiece, and the face of it had been scratched. A circle of gold wrapped around the edge.

"Do we need to do anything with these?" she asked.

"All you have to do is wear them," Kron replied.

"There's no chain."

"Sorry. It's a man's style. Apparently women in Tradetown don't have to keep track of time. Do you want me to put it on a chain or adjust the links to fit you?"

"I'd better have mine on a chain," Gwen said. "I wouldn't want it to interfere with the Four's bracelet."

Kron grabbed the watch by the band and massaged it with his fingertips. The links narrowed, lengthened, and resolved into loops of silver. Soon the chain was long enough to go over Gwen's neck. When Jenna and Kay held out their watches, he created necklaces for them to wear too.

"How come you're not wearing a watch?" Jenna asked.

"My clothing is enchanted to ward off magic, and I have a few extra artifacts that should surprise Salth and Sal-thaath." He held up a gem. "I've been using this to hide our magical signatures so we can sneak up on them."

Gwen still found it hard to believe his artifacts could do everything he claimed. "What about the Selathens? Will it work on them too?"

"I could create something that would block them from seeing and hearing us," Kron replied. "But it would take time and use up my materials, plus it would only work as long as we're together. I don't want to leave my wife in their hands any longer than necessary."

"We can handle the Selathens," Jenna said, stretching herself to her full height and glancing from side to side as if searching for a weapon.

Gwen nodded. Now that the shard in her hand was neutralized, she could send the Selathens to sleep with a single touch. Her hand itched. The shard quivered inside as if it had come to life. What was wrong with it? It should be powerless now. By All Four, why hadn't Spring given Kron a way to take it out?

"Then you three take care of them," Kron said, "and I'll rescue Ysabel."

We should do that. We've known her for lifetimes. How long did you two have together? Gwen bit down her jealousy and nodded. Maybe they'd get a chance to help Ysabel directly. If so, she would take it.

As Kron had promised, a packed trail appeared in the moss. Gwen was grateful she didn't have to worry about slipping. However, although the Western Mountains were still a long way off, the ground became hillier, much steeper than the gentle slopes near the lo Havil estate and Lake Verdan. Jenna kept up with no issue, but Kay lagged behind. Gwen halted frequently, both to recover her breath and to let Kay catch up.

"What am I supposed to use for a weapon?" Jenna asked. "I haven't seen so much as a twig since we got off the boat."

"Can't you force-grow something?" Gwen asked.

"From what? I don't carry acorns in my reticule."

"Maybe you should." Gwen gestured at Kron, who hadn't taken any rest stops and was now far ahead of them. "He carries a lot of supplies with him. I wonder where he puts them all."

Kay straightened. "I wonder how close we are to the border. Will we be able to tell if we cross it? Will the Four still protect us?"

Shouts sounded from up ahead. Gwen gathered her skirts. "Hurry! Kron needs us!"

She had to draw on her magic to run the entire distance as quickly as she could. Legs burning, she pushed herself up a hill, then staggered as she stopped herself. Below, Kron confronted two Selathen men, each holding a pistol trained on him.

By All Four...does he know what those are or how dangerous they are? A shot to the head or heart could kill him faster than she could heal him.

The cat bounded off of her shoulders and sprinted back the way she'd come. A pebble under Gwen's feet slipped and rolled down the hill. One of the men glanced up. With no cover available, Gwen dropped to the ground. Her bright yellow dress would stand out against the dirt, but she wasn't going to make it easy for the man to shoot her from a distance. He had to come to her.

The man shouted something she didn't understand. She curled up to protect herself. Acting frightened wasn't difficult to do. But even as she put on a scared expression, she gathered her magic into her uncursed hand, ready to use it on him.

The second man continued shouting in Selathen. Kron replied in Challen, "Where is Ysabel?"

The man switched to Challen. "You and the girl come with us."

"Where's my wife?" Kron countered. "Let her go, and I won't hurt you."

"Fine words indeed from someone not holding a pistol," the second man said. "Holth, get the girl. The Goddess will be especially pleased with our offerings this trip. They may be a little older than normal, especially the man, but the extra lives will be valuable."

Gwen shivered. Ysabel's mother had been right; these men did intend to sacrifice Ysabel—and her too. The God of Winter would freeze these Selathen's souls and stop them from reincarnating once they died. She could send their souls to Him, but Avatars weren't supposed to kill anyone, even Selathens. Hopefully the Goddess of Spring would forgive Gwen if she made him suffer, however.

The sound of more rocks rolling away alerted her to the approach of Holth. "Come on, girl," he said in broken Challen. "You come with me. You please me, you live."

She wanted to retort that he didn't please her, but she pressed her mouth together, willing him to come closer.

"Come, girl. Or die here." He cocked his pistol. At this range, he'd be unlikely to miss.

She let out a whimper. "My ankle, I think I sprained my ankle. Help me up, good sir."

With a mutter, he extended his free hand, still keeping the pistol aimed at her forehead. Gwen grabbed his hand and sent enough magic into him to make his nerves dance on their own. He convulsed, his fingers gripping her so hard she had trouble breaking away. He wobbled for a couple of heartbeats before crashing down, still gripping the pistol. How long would it take for him to recover? Biting back a curse, Gwen reached over and put him to sleep, forcing him into unconsciousness for several hours. It still seemed wise to disarm him.

She jerked on the pistol, and something stung her arm. She had to look twice before she could believe her sleeve was ripped. Even worse, there was blood on her dress. Her maid would be upset when she saw the damage. Pain made her realize what had happened. The other man had shot her. Fortunately, it hadn't struck anything critical. She brushed her violet bracelet against the wound. The Goddess's gift combined with her own healing magic to heal her. Within heartbeats, her wound healed from the inside out, knitting muscle and flesh together. All that was left was her torn dress and a thin white line that disappeared as Gwen watched.

"Avatar!" the Selathen screamed. "An enemy Avatar!"

A man poked his head out of the ground and pulled himself out, followed by another one. Both of them bore more pistols.

"Gwen," Kron asked, "Are those weapons that they carry?"

Was this his first encounter with pistols? "Yes!" How could she send them to sleep? She'd never get close enough to touch them.

"Throw that other one down to me," he said.

"Hands up!" one of the new men ordered. "No magic tricks, or I shoot you in the heart."

"How powerful are these weapons?" Kron asked.

For answer, the man who'd spoken aimed for a rock at the top of the hill. Before a heartbeat passed, his bullet chipped the stone.

"The next one I put in you," he added.

"Impressive." Kron sounded as calm as if he was leading a tour of the University's treasures. He even took a few steps toward the men, who kept their pistols trained on him. "Technology truly has advanced much since my time. I'd love to examine one of those."

"The only thing you're going to examine is the bullet!"

While everyone else was focused on Kron, Gwen slowly sank to the ground so she would be less of a target. Maybe she could crawl up to the Selathens without them catching her. If only there was tall grass or rocks she could hide behind. Where were Jenna and Kay? She could use their help.

"Oh, I don't think so." Kron spread his hands wide. Something sparkled in the air. "Are you sure those weapons are reliable?"

With a growl, one of the men aimed straight at Kron's chest and pulled the trigger. Gwen gasped. She wouldn't make it to him in time. But only a click sounded, not a shot. Kron remained standing. The men tried their pistols a few more times before dropping them and charging toward Kron. Gwen pushed herself to her feet and ran toward the battle, gaining speed at every step from the rush downhill.

Kron contorted so that every blow landed on his torso; Gwen winced in sympathy. He curled his fist around something Gwen couldn't see, then struck each of his attackers. They staggered back as if they'd been struck by a god. The taller man recovered first. He dodged Kron's next blow, then grabbed his arm and twisted it behind Kron's back. As Kron went down on his knees, Gwen caught up to them. The man shifted his grip so he held Kron in a single hand and swatted at her with his free one. A mistake. All she had to do was grab his hand and send sleep into him. He crashed so quickly she had to jump out of the way. By then, the other attacker had recovered. He held back out of Gwen's reach, waving his pistol as if he meant to club both of them with it. Kron beckoned him. The pistol tugged the Selathen forward, but he clung to it with both hands and dug his heels in. While the Selathen fought his own weapon, Gwen touched him and sent him to sleep too.

She and Kron stared at each other for a couple of heartbeats. "Good job, Galia—I mean, Gwen," he said. "Have you done such things before?"

"Only when my former betrothed was sick." She was glad Aunt Gabri was a long way away, back in Tradetown. She wasn't sure what was worse: touching the flesh of strange men, or ruining her dress. "What do we do now?"

"How long will they sleep?" He raised his eyebrow. "They are sleeping, aren't they?"

"Of course. I wouldn't kill them." She remembered what Ysabel's mother had told her about the infants sold by their own families, and her fists clenched. Maybe she shouldn't be merciful…but the Four had reserved justice for Themselves, not for Their Avatars. She kicked the closest man in a sensitive spot anyway. "I hope Winter freezes them so they never reincarnate. What do we do now?" And where were Jenna and Kay? They still hadn't appeared. Should Gwen and Kron wait for them or search for Ysabel?

A glowing circle caught her eye. The man at her feet stirred, opening his eyes while coming to his feet. The pistol flew back to his hand, and he flailed as if he was seeking his balance. No, falling in reverse. Even with magic, how could that be possible?

While she watched, he swung his pistol at her head. Gwen tried to dodge. For an instant, she felt frozen in place, but not from cold. Then Kron's defaced watch grew warm, freeing her. Even so, her reflexes were too slow. The Selathen caught her on her temple. A flash of pain, of seeing the ground coming up toward her, then no more.

CHAPTER TWENTY-FOUR

Spring Meets Time

Gwen woke up to an ache streaming down her skull. Blood had trickled down her cheek and dried, crusting off when she grimaced. She banished the pain, making it easier to think. She could smell dirt and damp air even more strongly than when she'd been on the hill. Under her was something soft.

"A double-rich find," a high-pitched voice said. "First a Fall Avatar, then a Spring one comes into my hands. Mother will be happy with so much magic. Maybe she can even strike at the Foul Four through you."

Gwen opened her eyes. The light was so dim here—wherever she was—that it took her a few heartbeats to adjust her vision. All she could see was dirt. Even the walls and ceiling were rough. Light shone in through a single hole with a ladder poking through it.

She had to be underground, in the same place where the Selathens had been hiding. Where were they? And if they were here, what about Kron, Jenna, and Kay? For that matter, what about Ysabel? She had to be here too. Gwen strained her neck, searching for her. At last she saw her in another corner. All that was visible of her was a light-colored dress and her glowing scarlet aura. She was spread out on a stone slab, wrists bound together with rope. Gwen couldn't tell if her ankles were similarly tied. If Ysabel were awake, she could summon rodents to chew her bonds away. But she lay so still she might have been drugged. Gwen hoped it was only that, not something worse. This wasn't how Gwen had imagined their meeting would be like.

She tried to sit up, but her limbs were numb. Maybe she'd been drugged. She searched her body for signs of a sedative without finding a trace of one. Her heart beat normally, and her head felt clear.

"I've put your arms and legs out of time. I would have done the rest of you too, but then you'd never know what had happened. That wouldn't be fun." The speaker giggled.

Who was talking? Gwen couldn't see anyone. With great effort, she tilted her head down. A small boy pulled at the violet bracelet on her wrist, scowling as it didn't come off. Something about his expression was sharper, less innocent, than any other child Gwen had encountered. Despite his cold fingers on her skin, he didn't seem real. Could she be hallucinating without realizing it?

"Where's Kron?" she asked.

"Mother's men hit him too hard. He's not awake yet. I want him to watch you and his Fall Avatar die before I send him to Mother and make him fix the crystal house. Even with time magic, I can't break the wards on his clothes. He's clever, but we're stronger than him. We will break him, and break you Avatars, and then your Four."

Gwen shivered.

The child yanked on her hand, pulling it closer to the light. He came into better view as well. His coloring was ordinary, light brown skin with darker brown hair and eyes. She couldn't identify him as Challen, Selathen, or Fip; his facial features didn't match any of those countries. His clothing was also rough, a homespun tunic and leggings. Pieces of pottery had been stuck to his tunic. Gwen let out a sharp breath. The pottery matched the piece she'd first found and the shard still in her hand.

"Kron makes better magic than he knows," the child said. "Magic still clings to the pieces of the water clock he and I used to travel to this time. At first, I wanted to use the shards to attack all the Avatars, but then I realized they could shield me from your Foolish Four. I had to summon the shards back to me and recreate the one Kron destroyed. There's only one piece I haven't recovered, and that's the one in your hand."

Gwen finally realized what made the boy seem unreal. He had no aura. How was that possible? What was he?

"Give me that shard," the boy demanded.

"And give you something you can use against the Four?"

"You don't have to serve them anymore, you know. They're too nice to take your magic away even if you betray them. You are pretty powerful—for a mere human."

This child had to be Sal-thaath, Kron's ancient enemy. If he opposed the Four too, Gwen had to fight him.

"You don't want that shard anyway," Sal-thaath said, "It hampers your own magic. Just let me have it, and you can go back to whatever it is you Avatars do."

"I thought you were planning to sacrifice me," Gwen said. "If I give you the shard, will you let me and Ysabel go?"

"You, maybe. But not Ysabel. Kron needs to see her suffer."

If she had been tempted by the boy's offer, that would have made her change her mind. "You'll have to carve it out of me first."

Gwen gritted her teeth and hardened the flesh of her palm, expecting him to cut the shard out of her. It wasn't that easy. He touched her skin, pushing a foreign magic into it. It reeked of death and decay, ancient enemies of spring. Her skin shriveled and dried out. Gwen pumped healing into her hand, restoring it to its natural state. Sal-thaath continued his attack. She lost track of how many times she had to undo his magic. The shard felt warmer than the surrounding tissue, as if it was absorbing the boy's magic. Gwen hoped it wouldn't burn her from the inside out.

Her world shrank to a few square thumb-lengths of tissue less than a quarter-thumb-length deep. No matter how much magic she forced into her hand, the child's power was greater. With no food to draw on for extra energy, Gwen reached into her own tissue for reserves. Her awareness was limited to her core, so she had to be careful not to draw too much from a vital organ. At best, she could only buy herself a few moments before this child would claim the shard. How much damage would he be able to do with it? Would he continue to attack the other Avatars? Who would be able to stop him?

Gwen couldn't do it alone. She needed the support of her sister Avatars right here and now, to give her the strength she needed to defeat this evil child. Jenna and Kay had to be close by. But how could she summon them when they'd never linked before?

"Jenna! Kay!" she called. Her voice was too feeble to escape this hole. "Ysabel! Ysabel s'Ivena Lathatilltin, wake up! The Four need you! I need you!"

If only she and Ysabel were close enough to touch and activate their link. But they were at opposite ends of the tunnel, and the only way Gwen could reach Ysabel would be by growing her arm out to four times its normal length. Even under ideal conditions, Gwen's magic couldn't do that. But if Ysabel was awake and could summon animals to bridge the gap….Gwen bit back her exasperation. If Ysabel was awake and able to use her power, they wouldn't be in this predicament.

There had to be something Gwen could do. Could she use Spring's bracelet to extend her link? She curled her fingers, but she couldn't bend them far enough to reach her wrist. She couldn't shake her arm to slide the bracelet closer to her fingers. Perhaps this was the wrong idea anyway. If she lost the bracelet, the boy might be able to take the shard from her hand. Even with it, she was losing flesh and blood.

Flesh and blood—if touching skin would trigger the link, what about blood? If she could shoot a few drops of her blood onto Ysabel or even Kron, she might be able to help them.

Gwen turned her attention inward, speeding up her heartbeat. The shard twisted inside of her, attacking muscles and nerves as it tried to push through her skin and rejoin the other pottery pieces. Every move hurt more than anything else Gwen had experienced. For once, she had to leave the damage unhealed. She let one tiny part of her skin rot away, exposing the point of the shard—and a pool of her blood. The boy's eyes brightened with excitement. Before he could pry the shard out of the opening, Gwen pushed with all of her magic. Blood spattered, then arced in a fountain, stretching farther and farther until it reached Ysabel. Several drops anointed her forehead.

YSABEL! Gwen didn't speak, not wanting to alert Sal-thaath. *Ysabel, wake up! By All Four, wake up!*

Something flickered in her mind. It vanished when she tried to focus on it. Gwen splashed more blood on Ysabel, picturing it destroying the drug. She felt it sink into Ysabel and spread throughout her body. Ysabel stirred. Confusion filled Gwen's thoughts, but she knew it wasn't her own.

Ysabel? Can you hear me? I'm Gwen, your sister Ava Spring. We're in trouble, and we need your animal magic if we're going to survive.

What? How are you talking to me inside my head? Is this real?

By the Four, it is.

Pain brought Gwen out of the link. Sal-thaath had extended the wound in her hand and was trying to pry the shard out with his fingernails. She contorted the muscles in her hand to pull the shard back inside her. Then she regenerated the skin over her wound—or tried to. Her skin refused to grow. Worse, the wound spread, sweeping across her entire hand. Sal-thaath laughed gleefully and prodded her again—then jumped back as a clod of dirt landed on his head, followed by a shower of worms. The paralysis holding her limbs lifted. Gwen seized the opportunity to direct energy into her hand. A new layer of delicate skin bloomed over the shard, sealing it in place.

"Worms? Is that all you can do?" The worms covering Sal-thaath shriveled and died. He shook himself, sending pieces flying. Gwen didn't flinch when they landed on her.

A wave of beetles, ants, and other bugs came next. Some of them crawled over Gwen, tickling her. She trembled as she reminded herself they weren't going to hurt her. The insects launched themselves at Sal-thaath's eyes, flew in his ears, and stung him everywhere. Each one that touched him died instantly, but they kept coming. Gwen wondered where they came from, especially this close to the dead land. Maybe there was more life underground than Salth and Sal-thaath realized, or maybe the Four had sent the insects to help Their Avatars.

Gwen tested her legs to see if she could stand. If she could make her way to Ysabel and touch her, they could link and multiply her magic. She'd drained herself so much she couldn't get up. Maybe she could persuade Ysabel to come to her—if she was well enough to move and could spare some attention from her animal magic. How could she do that without alerting Sal-thaath?

Something black-and-white jumped down into their cavern. Ysabel's cat, the one Gwen had carried here. He ran over to his mistress and head-butted her. The insect army faltered for an instant, then surged even faster toward Sal-thaath.

"Ugh! By All Four, what is this?" a welcome voice asked.

Jenna descended into the cavern, followed at a distance by Kay. Hope and fear warred within Gwen. If they were able to link, they might be able to defeat Sal-thaath—as long as he didn't turn his time magic on them first.

Sal-thaath flung his hands out, and the flood of insects halted. "Don't come any closer, or I'll age you all into crones!"

As one, Jenna and Kay displayed the watch artifacts Kron had made for them. Gwen checked for her own. Joy at being able to move her arm again faded when she discovered her artifact was missing. One of the Selathens must have taken it while she was unconscious. Without it, she was vulnerable. So was Ysabel, unless one of the other Avatars had an extra one to lend her.

Gwen flexed her still-sore hand. This child's time magic obviously was stronger than her own healing magic, but was it stronger than the shard he sought? If she tried to put him to sleep, or even send the curse into him, what would happen?

Before she could worry about the consequences, she grabbed him with her wounded hand. The skin was still tender, and she gritted her teeth at the pain. Hoping she didn't injure herself again or give him the shard he wanted, she sent the magic stored in the shard into him, willing it to damage him as much as it had her. She detected no heartbeat, no breathing, no digestion. Only magic animated this child-corpse. No wonder he lacked an aura. Whatever had killed him was long past healing, even if she had wanted to help him. Gwen's only option was to give him the same decay he'd given her. Doing that went against all her instincts as an Ava Spring. She reminded herself he deserved it for his blasphemy against the Four.

Under her touch, the boy's skin became soft and brown. She grimaced at the odor of decomposition but forced herself to hold on to him. Sal-thaath turned to glare at her. Power surged back at her. For a heartbeat, their power matched perfectly. Then it slipped—in his favor. Gwen steeled herself, resolving to fight him as long as her strength held out.

The scent of roses clashed with the scent of decay. A firm hand clamped down on her wrist, followed by a smaller one with callused fingertips. Jenna. Kay. Their strength, their essences flowed into her. Then a fourth, still hesitant but just as determined. Ysabel. The Avatars of Spring, Summer, Fall, and Winter united at last.

With a fierce cry, Gwen gathered her sister Avatars' energies and thrust them at Sal-thaath. He jerked out of her grip. "You Avatars have grown more powerful since the last time we met. But you're still not as powerful as me." He sneered. "Especially since there's only four of you, not twelve."

Twelve? When was the last time all twelve Avatars had been active at once? That didn't matter. They had another ally. With the link,

Gwen was able to extend her magic and help others at a distance. She searched for Kron and found him in another tunnel, just starting to waken. She sent him healing magic to speed the process. Then she tried to link with him. *Kron, can you hear me? We're over here. So is Sal-thaath—and Ysabel.*

He didn't react, not even to the last two names. The link must not extend to him. They would have to find another way to contact him. In the meantime, how could the four of them use their magic against Sal-thaath?

A foreign magic battered against the link, trying to break it. Jenna and Kay—and through them, Ysabel—maintained a firm grip on Gwen. Sal-thaath's face turned red as he threw time magic at them. Kron's artifacts provided partial protection, but there were only two of them for the four Avatars. The boy's attacks came faster and faster— or were they slowing down? They needed Kron's magic to counteract Sal-thaath's.

Ysabel, tell your cat to fetch Kron. He's here. Gwen pictured the tunnel where Kron was.

Who's Kron? Ysabel asked.

Gwen replied, *Someone who can help us* at the same time as Jenna said, *Someone who says he was married to you in one of your previous lives. Isn't that romantic?*

I hope he's older than this child—and nicer.

The cat bolted off. To distract Sal-thaath, Gwen told the others, *Let's try to surround him.* Maybe encircling him would make their magic more effective.

Kay released her hold on Gwen to take Jenna's free hand. Ysabel grabbed Kay's other hand. They weren't in seasonal order, but Gwen hoped that wouldn't matter. The important thing was to complete the circle. Sal-thaath stepped in front of Ysabel and held up his hand. Ysabel slowed as though she was made of thick syrup. Gwen pooled magic from Jenna and Kay and passed it to Ysabel, but it didn't help.

Sal-thaath poured more magic on Ysabel until she froze in mid-step. He reached for her—

Quick! Someone do something! Gwen shouted through the link.

Jenna shook her head. *I have no seeds or sunlight.*

Kay, lightning?

Kay's panic shot through Gwen. Sal-thaath bore a strong resemblance to the woman from Kay's nightmares. Kay couldn't perform magic when she was so distraught.

Gwen called the magic back to herself. Maybe if she could make Sal-thaath's head rot off, that would stop him. She wasn't sure what else would at this point.

As she reached for the boy, Ysabel's cat bounded back down the corridor. Behind him ran Kron, brandishing a watch in his hand as if he meant to bash Sal-thaath's head in with it himself.

With an angry hiss, Sal-thaath disappeared. He didn't escape from the circle or use a portal like the one Kron had conjured; he simply vanished as if the air had swallowed him.

Gwen dropped the link and sank to her knees. Now that the danger was gone, exhaustion weighed her down despite the exultation dancing in her blood. The link with her sister Avatars had restored some of her strength, but she needed a good meal and rest.

"Your hand is still scarred," Jenna said. "Do you need more strength to heal it?"

Gwen studied her palm. White lines criss-crossed each other so often they were hard to count. "They were caused by magic, so I can't heal them completely." She flexed her fingers, stretching knotted muscles and tendons. Maybe they would improve over time. "Thank the Four I can still use my hand."

"Bella? Ysabel?" Kron halted in front of the Ava Fall and stared at her. "Is it really you?"

"Who are you?" she countered.

"I'm Kron. Kron Evenhanded. We were married in your first life as an Avatar."

Jenna and Kay turned to face the couple, away from Gwen. Gwen sighed as she watched too. William would never have pursued her over such a distance, and the Avatar of War only sought her for her magic. Would she ever find a man who cared about Gwen first and her magic or property second?

Jenna turned to wink at Gwen. "You did it, Gwen. By All Four, we're together again, thanks to you." She beckoned Kay and Ysabel closer. "Four cheers for our Ava Spring!"

"Hurrah, huzzah!" The three other Avatars twirled in unison. "Tra-la-la and sis-boom-bah! Hail Gwendolyn, First of the Spring Avatars!"

Gwen smiled at them. Ysabel's cat rubbed its head against her, and she stroked it, taking comfort in the animal's warmth. She'd managed to find Jenna, Ysabel, and Kay, and the three of them had defended Challen from an enemy. With practice, they would learn to tame Chaos Season. Then, perhaps, Gwen could find someone who could partner her as well as her sister Avatars did, someone who would accept her even if she wasn't perfect.

Spring might be almost over, but her season as an Avatar was just starting.

Afterword

Thank you for reading my book; I hope you enjoyed it. Please consider leaving a review on the website where you bought this or on Goodreads to help other readers discover this book. It also helps me promote my work so I can eventually fulfill my dream of writing science fiction and fantasy full-time and getting more stories out faster.

I would like to thank my beta readers for their input in helping me improve this story. They are Bert Hammerstad, Elizabeth Hull, Lauren Jankowski, and Kristin Smith. Maria Zannini of Book Cover Diva designed the cover, and the template for the interior book design (for both the paper and eBook versions) came from Book Design Templates. As always, special thanks go to my husband, Eugene, and my son, Alex, for their love and patience as I spent many hours at the keyboard writing, editing, and formatting this book.

I'm currently working on the first draft of *Chaos Season,* the third book in this series. It may be ready by the end of 2015, but I can't guarantee that. I'm also preparing a short story collection called *Young Seasons,* which will feature Gwen, Jenna, Ysabel, and Kay as children and young teens. If you'd like to know when my next work will be available, you can watch my website, blog, or Facebook page for announcements. Or you can also subscribe to my newsletter (link is on my blog). I hate spam as much as anyone else, so I'll only send it out for announcements of new work and sales. Eventually, I plan to offer bonus stories to subscribers as well.

Best,

Sandra

The Season Avatars

(Names in parentheses are from the Avatars' first lives as shown in *Seasons' Beginnings*.)

Group 1 (Future Avatars)

Gwen (Galia)—Spring

Jenna (Janno)—Summer

Ysabel (Bella)—Fall

Kay (Caye)—Winter

Group 2 (Current Avatars)

Margaret (Magstrom)—Spring (deceased)

Charles (Carver)—Summer

Sophia (Sylva)—Fall

Dorian (Domina)—Winter

Group 3 (This group is currently between lives. The names listed below are from *Seasons' Beginnings*.)

Tylan—Spring

Flilya—Summer

Hala—Fall

Ocul—Winter

Other Works By the Author

Science Fiction: Catalyst Chronicles Series

Lyon's Legacy (novella)
The Mommy Clone (short story)
Twinned Universes (novel)
Seasonal Stories from the *Sagan* (short story collection)

Fantasy: Short Stories

The Book of Beasts
Letters to Psyche
Silver Rain

Poetry

Life at Seventeen Syllables a Day: A Journal in Haiku

Fantasy: Season Avatars Series

Seasons' Beginnings
Scattered Seasons
Chaos Season (expected late 2015/early 2016)

About the Author

Sandra Ulbrich Almazan started reading at the age of three and only stops when absolutely required to. Although she hasn't been writing quite that long, she did compose a very simple play in German during middle school. Her science fiction novella *Move Over Ms. L.* (an early version of *Lyon's Legacy*) earned an Honorable Mention in the 2001 UPC Science Fiction Awards, and her short story "A Reptile at the Reunion" was published in the anthology *Firestorm of Dragons*. Other published works by Sandra include *Twinned Universes* and the fantasy *Season Avatars* series. She is a founding member of Broad Universe, which promotes science fiction, fantasy, and horror written by women. Her undergraduate degree is in molecular biology/English, and she has a Master of Technical and Scientific Communication degree. She currently works for an enzyme company; she's also been a technical writer and a part-time copyeditor for a local newspaper. Some of her other accomplishments are losing on *Jeopardy!* and taking a stuffed orca to three continents. She lives in the Chicago area with her husband, Eugene; and son, Alex. In her rare moments of free time, she enjoys crocheting, listening to classic rock (particularly the Beatles), and watching improv comedy.

Sandra can be found online at the following links:

website (www.sandraulbrichalmazan.com)
blog (www.ulbrichalmazan.blogspot.com)
Twitter (@ulbrichalmazan)
Facebook
(https://www.facebook.com/SandraUlbrichAlmazanSffAuthor)
Goodreads
(http://www.goodreads.com/author/show/5282664.Sandra_Ulbrich_Al mazan).

www.ingramcontent.com/pod-product-compliance
Lightning Source LLC
Chambersburg PA
CBHW070003120726

47909CB00003B/793